three good things

WENDY FRANCIS

Simon & Schuster Paperbacks

New York   London   Toronto   Sydney   New Delhi

Simon & Schuster Paperbacks
A Division of Simon & Schuster, Inc.
1230 Avenue of the Americas
New York, NY 10020

First Simon & Schuster trade paperback edition January 2013

SIMON & SCHUSTER PAPERBACKS and colophon are
registered trademarks of Simon & Schuster, Inc.

For information about special discounts for bulk purchases,
please contact Simon & Schuster Special Sales at 1-866-506-1949
or business@simonandschuster.com.

The Simon & Schuster Speakers Bureau can bring authors
to your live event. For more information or to book an event contact
the Simon & Schuster Speakers Bureau at 1-866-248-3049
or visit our website at www.simonspeakers.com.

Designed by Esther Paradelo

Manufactured in the United States of America

1   3   5   7   9   10   8   6   4   2

Library of Congress Cataloging-in-Publication Data
Francis, Wendy.
Three good things / Wendy Francis.—First Simon & Schuster
trade paperback edition. pages   cm
1. Sisters—Fiction. 2. Divorced women—Fiction.
3. New mothers—Fiction. 4. Coffeehouses—Fiction. I. Title.
PS3606.R36535T48   2013
813'.6—dc23   2011048000

ISBN 978-1-4516-6634-2
ISBN 978-1-4516-6641-0 (ebook)

For Nicholas

Kringle (krĭng'gŭl): A butter-layered pastry, introduced to the States in the late 1800s by immigrant Danish bakers. In Denmark, the *kringle* is traditionally pretzel shaped. In America, it is typically oval shaped, with a fruit or nut filling.

—*The Book of Kringle*

Spring

1

"[The] very process of mixing, rolling, and folding layer
upon layer for each *kringle* makes for a yoga of its own kind."
—*The Book of Kringle*

Ellen McClarety was thinking about serendipity, more particularly about serendipitous encounters, on her way into the shop this morning. The snow fell in heavy, leafy flakes, their distinct edges outlined against the car's windshield before evaporating on the glass. A blanket of black stretched on either side of her. It was a darkness she'd grown accustomed to with her three a.m. risings for work, but this morning, the dark had a softness to it. No wind cutting through her parka to her clavicle, just enormous flakes drifting down from the sky. The weatherman had predicted up to a foot of snow, all of this in April, but that was Wisconsin weather. Just when a person thought she was well on her way to spring, the gods of winter doled out a blizzard.

She was looking forward to a day's swift business. More people dropped by the bakery during a storm, the plowers who'd been out all night and those hoping for early news on the cagey weather. *Plenty of serendipitous encounters to be had,* a thought that made her smile as she drove along slowly, wiping condensation from the windshield with the back of her hand. She would need to make extra coffee this morning, extra dark.

As she turned down Curtis Road, she could see that a thin topcoat already skimmed the fields, like a wide expanse of flour. A light shone from the Curtis barn, where they were well into the early-morning milking, and she could just glimpse a handful of black-and-white Holsteins gathered outside, looking bewildered by the snow. Cows were dense animals; she knew that much from her grandfather, a farmer. They would stand in a snowstorm and freeze to death if you didn't move them to shelter. God's saddest creatures, her grandfather had called them.

"Look into their eyes," he once said. "Have you ever seen a more mournful face than that?"

And Ellen, only twelve at the time, had to admit they did look pretty depressed. But who could blame them? They were destined for the milk machine or the butcher block. No wonder they never demonstrated much enthusiasm.

But her granddad also helped her appreciate their beauty. He bought only Black Angus cows, the stocky, sturdy bovines that typically sold for meat, and whose dark, silky coats she loved to run her hands over. It was her first lesson that in nature, as in so many things in life, there was both inexplicable beauty and sadness.

She turned down the main street into town, the pavement growing slick beneath the wheels. At the third light, she turned right and pulled into the back lot. White funnels spiraled in the air as she exhaled, braced herself for the freeze beyond the door. Gingerly she let herself out and walked around the corner to the storefront, where bright green stems poking up from her window boxes greeted her. Daffodils under snow in April! It didn't seem right. Inside she stomped the snow from her boots, flicked on the lights—and inhaled: the scent of yesterday's kringle, raspberry and pecan, lingered blissfully in the air.

"Good morning, store," she called out. Such words were her mantra before beginning each day. She believed the greeting, like a yogic blessing, whisked away any demons that might be lurking in the shop's corners. She found an old broom in the closet and used it to sweep off the front steps, then tried her best to brush the snow from the budding daffodils with her hand. She was tempted to wrap her scarf around their stems but thought better of it: She needed to get started on the kringle if she was going to be ready for the hungry masses today.

In the back room, she removed her snowy parka, her hat, her boots and shoved them all into the closet. She tied on a fresh apron, slid on her clogs, and smoothed her hair into a ponytail. After washing her hands, she went to pull out the dough that had been chilling overnight. Before leaving yesterday afternoon, she'd rolled out the dough, shaped it into squares, and then smoothed a sheet of pure Wisconsin butter over the middle of each. After that, it was a matter of folding up the sides of each square to cover the butter, then turning the dough a quarter of the way around, and rolling and folding it again. Rolling and folding, rolling and folding, it was a delicious process, her own personal meditation as she felt her arm muscles working. She could work through any worries of the day—Had she ordered enough supplies for the week? Did her sister seem overtired yesterday? Did she pay the electricity bill?—and feel refreshed, her world righted again. By the time she was finished, each square was larded with twenty to thirty layers of scrumptious butter, while her mind was emptied, momentarily free of any burdens.

Now, when she released the doughy cakes from their cool confines, she smiled to see that yesterday's hard work had paid off. They had puffed up pleasingly, each a work of art. She set the oven and began the process of feeding the chilled dough through the sheeter, an industrial, steel contraption that stretched it even further, yielding a large paper-thin swath. She knew that the dough's thinness determined whether she got a heavenly puff confection or, like a batch last week, a heavy, chewy disaster. From there, it was a rhythmic routine that she fell into easily each morning; stretch the dough across the long wooden table to yield four rows of eight narrow rectangles; add the day's filling—today it was apple and blueberry—fold the sides over, and seal with egg, until the table was lined with thirty-two loaves, each resembling a jelly roll.

Then, with a quick flick of the wrist, she knitted together the ends of each to create an oval-shaped kringle, which got tossed onto the baking board—and *voilà*! The morning's work was nearly complete. She still had a ways to go before she was as skilled as Erik, the pastry chef under whom she'd apprenticed for three summers in Racine when she was a teenager. When Erik worked, it was as if each kringle got shaped in midair, the ends magically adhering in the short trip from the table to the baking board, the finished pastry delectably flaky and light.

She set the timer for seventeen minutes and checked her watch. Five thirty. Soon her customers would be arriving.

Out front she gave the counters a fresh wipe and started brewing the coffee. She pulled the bright-blue chairs off the tables, setting them right-side-up. On the board behind the register under *Today's Drips & Tips* she wrote:

Drips: *Hazelnut; Vanilla; Almond Decaf*
Tips: *Contrary to popular opinion,* IRREGARDLESS *is not a word. However, you might say: "Regardless of this weather, we still have plenty of delicious kringle to eat."*

She didn't even need to consult her edition of Fowler's *Modern English Usage*, the well-thumbed paperback crammed between the cash register and her cookbooks. The news guy on the radio had said *irregardless* this morning, and it made her skin prickle as it did anytime she heard someone abuse the English language with such abandon. She was proud that her customers had come to expect a grammar tip from her each day, even though her sister, Lanie, chided her that it was condescending. The way Ellen saw it, she was linking the gustatory to the literary; her daily tip was her one small contribution to making the world a better place. So what if she put off a new customer every now and then?

At the front of the counter near the register, she kept a glass candy bowl that was currently filled with bits of paper. The sign on its front read: GIVE US YOUR WORST GRAMMAR; WE'LL GIVE YOU OUR BEST! She encouraged customers to contribute their sightings of egregious usage, and once every few weeks she'd sift through the folded-over papers, like tiny fortunes, and pick one for the board.

She had come a long way from the day she'd rediscovered her mother's battered copy of *The Book of Kringle*, buried in a box of her things in the attic. For some reason she'd held on to it all these years, even though her mom had passed away when Ellen was just sixteen. What she had been searching for originally in those dusty old boxes she couldn't recall, but when she thumbed through the book of Danish recipes and folk wisdom, the scent of her mother's baking came wafting off the pages. And there, at that very moment, shortly after her husband had left, the first kernel of an idea for a kringle shop was planted.

When the abandoned old pizza place went up for sale downtown shortly thereafter, Ellen knew it was a sign. *Serendipity inviting her in.* She could almost feel her mother brush up against her shoulder, giving her a little shove. "Go for it," Ellen imagined her saying. "You've always wanted to create something of your own. This, my love, could be it."

And so, without further thought, Ellen McClarety, recent divorcée, former university secretary, bought the store. She revamped the entire space, scrubbing the grease off the walls with bleach, giving the place, not to mention her soul, a full cleanse. Each swish of the sponge wiped away years of caked-on dirt and grime. *How easy*! she thought to herself at the time, to rid herself of a husband and most of her savings in one fell swoop. She installed new ovens in the back and transformed the storefront from a high glimmer, red-and-white pizza motif into a cozy café, the fake sheen of her marriage tidily tossed off for more humble beginnings.

Perhaps the divorce would be the catalyst she needed to begin the life she was meant to live. Ten long years ago, she'd been drawn to

Max like wind to a hurricane, the attraction so intense, but eventually the hurricane had hit land. She'd assumed marriage was about two people caring for each other, but Max never seemed to fully reciprocate. Whenever she'd needed him, he would perpetually come up short—or disappear. And then there had been the baby: After years of trying they'd lost their only child, just two months along, in a miscarriage. Ellen didn't know if she'd ever recover, but Max had moved on so easily, as if it were no big deal. Maybe it was part of his happy-go-lucky nature, though Ellen had come to see it as selfishness. Max, a dreamer, could always see the forest for the trees, imagining what *could be*; it just seemed that after ten years of marriage, he kept running into trees.

Ellen woke up one morning and thought, *Enough*.

Her sister, Lanie, joked that she should christen the store The Midlife Crisis, but a friend suggested The Singular Kringle—and it stuck. He designed an elegant sign for above the door, festooned with a single pretzel shape—the traditional Danish kringle form—and the store's name in swirling blue letters. Her dream made real at last.

For the first few weeks only a handful of customers dropped by, and Ellen busied herself by rereading the classics, a lending library soon blossoming in her shop. She had forgotten how funny Nick was in *The Great Gatsby*, or was it just that she'd never noticed when she first read it in college? *Pride and Prejudice* and *Little Women* were still as heartbreaking as ever, and she'd rediscovered one of her favorites, *Middlemarch*. She couldn't help but to both pity and be angry with Dorothea all over again.

But then, word of mouth traveled, and the next thing she knew, her local customers were joined by farmers from their outposts, their wives, and professors who commuted the twenty miles to the university but made their homes in Amelia, population 5,320. Suddenly, she could barely keep up.

Amazing how time flew.

A fresh cup of coffee in hand, she went out back to check the kringle and was greeted by the sweet scent of apple mingling with blueberry. She pulled the piping-hot pastries from the oven and set them on a cooling rack.

"Perfect," she announced to no one in particular.

The secret to a perfect kringle, she knew, was balance: When a person bit into a true kringle, she should taste equal parts pastry, filling, and icing. So many of the imitation kringles these days were all chewy dough, laden with frosting. But Ellen understood that no one element should overwhelm or supersede another.

When the bell on the front door jingled, she started. She'd almost forgotten she'd flipped over the OPEN sign out front; it was so easy to get lost in the wee hours in the back room while baking. Jack Singer, her punctual first customer each day, had been running the hardware store down the street since before anyone could remember. If she described a leak below her basin, he knew exactly which washer or screw she needed. She heard him stomp the snow from his boots, take a paper, and find his way to a table by the cash register.

"Good morning, sweetness," he said as she swung through the kitchen doors. "Looks like the weatherman got it right for once . . . that's quite a storm we've got brewing out there. No pun intended." He laughed at his own joke.

Ellen knew she should be offended by his endearments, but over the past year they'd grown on her, like a familiar hangnail that wouldn't go away.

"Looks that way," she said as she arranged the mugs into neat rows on the counter and poured him a cup of coffee. She knew such would be the opening line for every conversation today. "Can I get you apple or blueberry? It'll be just a few more minutes, I'm afraid."

"Blueberry sounds perfect." He unfolded his paper, then added, "Please."

After tidying up a bit more, she went back to decorate the pastries with icing. The blueberry was bursting with fat, purple fruit, and the apple looked invitingly tart. Carefully, she inched them onto the baker's board and carried them out to the display counter, where she eased them onto delicate, pretty doilies.

"Mmm. . . . If that doesn't warm my belly, nothing will." Jack winked at her as she cut him a slice. She noticed that his paper was open to the horoscopes. Lately, she'd grown tired of their platitudes, and more particularly, of their pessimism. It seemed to her that horoscopes should buoy someone first thing in the morning, not send him off in search of a life raft. Still, she couldn't help but listen when Jack started reading aloud from the "Cancer" section.

"Today's forecast: 'You may be tempted to come out of your shell, but it's best to keep your head down for a few days. Don't make any rash decisions as you're bound to regret them.'"

She laughed out loud. "Honestly, what kind of horoscope is that?" Jack shrugged. She wondered if astrologers—and she used the word loosely because, after all, what kind of training *did* you have to have to become a certified astrologer?—could be sued for dispensing bad advice. It seemed they should be.

Slowly more customers began to trickle in, looking snow-shocked, not so unlike the cows earlier this morning. They brushed the white powder from their spring jackets and shivered their way to a table, nodding a hello in her general direction. One young woman, bundled in a navy pea coat, peeked out from behind a green scarf, her eyes seemingly frozen in a permanent expression of surprise.

When Henry Moon came in, Ellen grabbed his coffee and kringle right away. A gardener who ran the town nursery, he was a bit of an odd duck, but Ellen maintained he was more sensitive than odd, a wounded soul. He'd seemed a tad off ever since his wife died in a car accident more than a year ago. Each day between seven and eight, like clockwork, he stepped into the store. His hair and clothes always looked disheveled, as if he'd lost not just a wife but also a mother, someone who'd iron his pants, tuck in his shirt.

"Henry, will my daffodils survive in this snow?" she asked him while pouring a cup.

He took a sip, rubbed his lips together. "Who was it that said: 'And then my heart with pleasure fills / And dances with the daffodils?'"

She put her hand on her hip and looked at him. "You surprise me, Henry. That's lovely. Was it Shakespeare?"

"Wordsworth, I believe. But your daffodils should be fine—and dancing in no time. They're hardy plants. They expect a little snow once in a while."

She liked how he made it sound as if flowers had interior lives, vibrant souls. As much as she loved literature, Ellen couldn't recite lyrics to save her life. She was a bit jealous, not to mention humbled.

"Well, that's good to know. Thank you."

Henry nodded, said, "You bet."

Larry and Erin came through the door just then, covered in white. Recent UW grads trying to make a living in the theater, they helped Ellen out at the store five days a week. Loyal customers, they'd come in and sold her on why she needed the help—her store was growing; the long hours were too much for one person to handle; they'd attract the younger clientele (though as far as she could see most of the young people went straight to Madison and didn't waste their time in a town like Amelia).

She had to admit, though, they had a point. Larry, with his hair down to his shoulders, was handsome in a hippie-rocker kind of way, with striking green eyes and a sense of humor that immediately set customers at ease. Erin was more refined, but quietly lovely. Most days she wore her long brown hair in a ponytail, high on the back of her head.

"Busy day today," Ellen warned as they began taking off their coats. "Better get your game face on."

"You mean you think we'll actually get some customers besides Henry and Jack?" Larry asked and tied on his apron.

Ellen slapped him on the arm.

"Better be careful what you wish for," said Henry.

"We do have other customers in the store, you know." She nodded to the undergrads and the two men in the corner, farmers in their hats and overalls huddled over steaming drinks and talking in hushed tones.

When a fresh group of customers burst into the store, Larry shouted "Morning!" and hurried to help them with their jackets. She liked that about him; he always seemed to go the extra mile. She supposed when she was younger she would have been drawn to Larry since she'd always been a sucker for that rocker-poet mystique. It made her a little sad to think that he probably considered her old enough to be his mom. Ellen liked to think of herself as hip and attractive but knew better: She was a middle-aged divorcée without so much as a sugar daddy. Indeed with nary a prospect in sight.

As she twirled such depressing facts over in her mind, she noticed Erin's eyes follow Larry, a slight smile gracing her lips. When she caught Ellen looking at her, she quickly turned away to refill the cream canisters. But Ellen was sure she had seen it: a crimson flare bursting onto the girl's cheeks. Just for a moment, but long enough.

She turned to ring up a customer's order and smiled to hear the register's old-fashioned bell echo her satisfaction. At a certain age, she had come to understand, a person made her peace with living vicariously. She'd have to tell Lanie about the new lovebirds. When the phone interrupted her thoughts, she picked it up expecting to hear her sister's voice.

"Hello, Singular Kringle," she said with a smile. She would have never guessed in a million years who would return the hello.

"Quiet!" Lanie rolled over and hit the snooze button for the second time that morning. Benjamin had woken three times last night, and the third time she'd been unable to get him back to sleep for an hour. She had tried all her tricks, rocking him, giving him an extra bottle, singing, then finally pulling him into bed with her and Rob. She loved the warm snuggle of his body close to hers, feeling his weight shift and get heavier in her arms as he finally drifted off to sleep. But it had made for a hell of a night.

Rob groaned next to her. "How can it possibly be morning already?"

It was seven thirty. Benjamin lay sound asleep between them, his belly going up and down between breaths. His round little face, slightly parted lips, and long, dark eyelashes, all the image of idyllic sleep.

"Speak for yourself," she quipped. Rob hadn't gotten up once to help.

"Someone's a little cranky." He rolled over and kissed her cheek. "If you haven't noticed, I sleep in this bed, too."

"Shh . . . you'll wake the baby."

Lanie's eyelids felt like sandpaper. The muscles in her lower back ached. How she was going to win her plea in court today was beyond her.

The radio alarm came on again, the disc jockey reminding folks to drive carefully.

"Oh, no. I forgot about the snow." They had been forecasting a spring blizzard last night, not so uncommon for this part of the country, but Lanie had hoped the meteorologists would get it wrong. "Perfect. Just perfect."

"I'll scrape the windows, get the cars warmed up." She could smell Rob's breath, slightly sour. She knew this was the closest she'd get to an apology or a thanks for the fact that she'd had only a few hours' sleep, while he'd had a blissful night.

Benjamin stirred beside her, smacked his lips. He was still the cutest baby ever, even if he was responsible for the immense sleep deprivation in their lives over the past ten months. The pediatrician had assured her that eventually he'd fall into his own nocturnal rhythms after she'd asked, with swollen eyes, if she'd ever sleep again. And it was true, most nights the baby slept soundly now, but every so often came a night when he was inconsolable.

"It's probably his teeth, huh?" Rob tried.

"That or he's trying to kill us." They were still waiting for his top front teeth to poke through. And true, it wasn't until she'd smoothed some gel onto Benjamin's gums last night that the baby had finally settled in her arms.

She pushed herself out of bed and pulled the curtain back.

At least three inches of snow coated the driveway. She groaned. "Doesn't God know it's April?"

"Yeah, and he's got an excellent sense of humor."

"Shh!" She shushed him again, then whispered, "Very funny." Lanie could feel herself being crabby, but she couldn't help it. She was too tired.

"Watch Benjamin for a minute, will you?" She sleepwalked out of the bedroom, down the hall to the bathroom. The toothpaste tube still lay on the counter from last night, the blue gel oozing out in an unappealing zigzag. She squeezed a small dab onto her toothbrush and brushed, then splashed cool water onto her face.

God, she looked awful. What was it that Ellen said? God made babies cute to distract everyone from looking at their exhausted mothers? Something like that. But Benjamin wouldn't be in court with her today. The judge wouldn't care that she'd been up half the night or that she'd more than likely have washed drool off her blouse minutes before entering the courtroom. She slathered on her trusty concealer, her one "can't-go-without" make-up trick. She always laughed at the celebrities who said they wouldn't step foot outside without curling their eyelashes or applying self-tanner. Lanie was lucky if she remembered to apply mascara. She did so this morning, though, the black liquid coming out in uneven clumps. She frowned. Already, faint lines were starting to show around her eyes and lips. Random sunspots bloomed on her fair skin.

She brushed her hair behind her ears with her fingers. Shortly after Benjamin had been born, she'd acquiesced, done what she swore she'd never do but that Rob had predicted all along: cut off her long, curly auburn locks to tame them into something resembling the "mom bob." Some days she missed the sexy feel of long hair, but mostly she was just glad not to have to bother with it. Practicality, she'd discovered, was highly underrated. She pulled silver loop earrings through her earlobes, added a touch of gloss to her lips. *Ready to go.*

No time for a shower this morning, but nothing that her favorite navy suit wouldn't fix. She was damned if she was going to lose this plea, a motion for a restraining order against a twenty-three-year-old loser who'd beaten both his ex-girlfriend and his toddler and was now making noises he'd do the same unless they moved back in with him. The woman had come to Lanie's office in tears yesterday, saying she feared that the next time he beat her he'd kill her.

It was almost impossible to believe that such things happened in the evolved city of Madison that prided itself on its bohemian, liberated culture. But they did on a daily basis. Lanie loved being able to help, but more often these days she found herself carrying her clients' stories back home, despite her promises to Rob not to. Work was like a bruise that she couldn't help pushing on again and again to see if it still hurt.

Rob, however, was an architect who worked in the laws of right angles and degrees, in the language of square footage and arcs, levels and foyers, concrete and marble. It was not a job that required much of an emotional investment, as far as she could tell. Her husband left his work on the drawing table at the office, and when he was home with her and Benjamin, they got all of him, one hundred percent. For this, she loved him dearly, but she also envied him. He had chosen a profession that built the right-angled spaces people lived and worked in; she had chosen a career that plunged her into the messy lives inside them.

She slipped into her skirt and a sheer white blouse. She'd leave the blazer off till she dropped Benjamin at day care. The baby stirred again as Rob got up to shower. His eyes opened briefly, then closed.

"Good morning, sweet boy," she whispered across the room. Her baby, now ten months, seemed to take up so much space. Once just a tiny infant whose feet she could barely find inside his sleeper, he had grown nearly into a toddler. Precious baby fat still coddled him in all the right places, but he was longer now, his head larger. Her little boy growing up. She felt a slight twinge in her chest at the thought. He was growing up every minute, while she spent the majority of his days working with other families. The irony did not escape her. She tried not to dwell on it.

Now he stretched his arms above his head like an old man. It was a move he'd practiced ever since they'd brought him home from the hospital. The first time Rob called her into the room, laughing and pointing to Benjamin, who reached his fingertips to the sky, his yawning mouth stretched into a perfect O. It had been miraculous as so many of those baby firsts were. Now he looked around, rolled over, and pushed himself to sit up. He gave her a big gummy smile.

"Well, hello there, sleepy boy. Did you have a good sleep in Mama and Dada's bed?"

She leaned over to sweep him up and give him a kiss, his body still warm with sleep.

He looked at her, then pointed to the bedroom door. "Bah," he said, his new favorite word. It was funny to her how he could go from zero to sixty in a heartbeat, ready to start the day almost as soon as he woke.

"We'll go get your bottle in a sec," she said. "First, we have to change your diaper and get you dressed."

She gave him another kiss, smoothed his hair, and carried him into the nursery. She loved the cool colors of his room. She'd decorated it with a nautical theme, at odds with their Midwestern corner, but she couldn't resist the happy blue whales that swam on the borders of a crib bumper they'd found when she was pregnant. From there an entire sea had been born. Bright tropical fish hanging from Benjamin's mobile, a table lamp covered in starfish with smiley faces, stuffed whales for snuggling, and even a diaper holder embroidered with conch shells.

The baby fussed as she changed him, something he never liked, but was happy again the moment she sat him on the floor, his fat belly sticking out over his diaper. She pulled out warm fleece pants, as tiny as a doll's clothing, and a red sweatshirt to cover his pint-sized turtleneck. She managed to get it all on him without too much fuss. She could hear Rob singing in the shower down the hall, some

Bruce Springsteen tune, and was surprised to find herself smiling. Benjamin bounced up and down on his knees, waving his arms, his signature dance.

She hoisted him onto her hip and carried him down the stairs, twenty-three hardwood steps to be exact. She and Rob had counted them when they first moved in, after they'd made love at the top, christening the old windy farmhouse as their own.

"Brr, baby," she said and drew Benjamin closer now. The chill of the night had settled into the lofty spaces of the high-ceilinged first floor. She turned the thermostat to eighty to get the heat cranking.

"Why don't we live in California again?" she asked.

The truth, she reminded herself, was that while both she and Rob had lived in California for a spell, each had returned to Wisconsin, as if a rubber band had pulled them back with a snap. Lanie had always thought that a certain sense of superiority lurked in the humbleness of Midwesterners, that they were a people who weathered the blistering cold, temperatures unimaginable to most, and so were able to endure more of life's challenges than most.

It was a mentality she'd tried to shake again and again, traveling first to Berkeley, then to a clerkship in Seattle, then to Boston, yet all roads had led back to Madison. She and Rob laughed about this peculiar fact on their first date over brats and beers on State Street: A Midwesterner spent his life trying to escape the cold winters but always ended up back home.

Though she would never admit it, she'd loved coming home. She returned in late July, fresh from a tour of the Eastern seaboard, places like Portland, Maine; Gloucester, Massachusetts; a last hurrah in New York City. She and her housemate at the time, Julia, had packed their bags, sold the rest of their belongings in a yard sale, and set out for three weeks of carefree abandon. It was a fitting farewell to a coast that had served her well. She'd been working in tax law in Boston, a job that helped pay off her loans, but she jumped at the chance to join one of Madison's top firms.

While Lanie was expected to bill a certain number of hours at

Brandt & Smith, she was in the fortunate position of being able to balance lucrative divorces with, to her mind, the more pressing family dispute and social restitution cases. When Ellen asked what compelled her to work with people whose lives were so depressing—beaten women and children, abandoned children in foster care—Lanie answered easily and with certainty: It was her calling. It was the reason she had gone to law school in the first place, to help those less fortunate. That she was able to return home to do so was only icing on the cake.

When she arrived in midsummer, three suitcases and her briefcase sitting at her feet, Ellen greeted her at the terminal, her sleeveless shirt collared with perspiration, her brown hair frizzing in the humidity. Lanie had always envied her sister her heart-shaped face, her kind eyes, and over the years Ellen had come to embody the maternal role she'd always played in Lanie's life. Her once slim figure had morphed into that of a woman who was comfortable with a few extra pounds, her formerly slender arms now round.

When their own mom passed and Lanie was just six, Ellen had become like a second mother to her. Their father, on the edge of his own despair, was helpless to guide her. So Ellen, just sixteen, moved from her own room back into her sister's. Ten years later it was Ellen who rode in the jolting car up and down the school parking lot when Lanie got her learner's permit; Ellen who pressed their mother's letter into her hands on the night of Lanie's high school graduation, saying, "Mom wanted me to hold on to this until you graduated. I've done my best to preserve it. It's a little battered around the edges, but it still has her scent."

And, indeed, when she held the envelope to her face, Lanie could detect the sweet aroma of lilacs, her mother's perfume. Later, after a celebration under a sweeping white tent in their backyard, she opened the letter in the privacy of her bedroom and cried to see the faint pink of her mom's lipstick on the edges of the inside seal. It was as if her mother were sitting there on her bed, rubbing her back again, and Lanie, still six.

She had ridden home with Ellen from the airport that July day nearly six years ago. A thunderstorm had recently passed through, and she rolled down the window to open herself to the sweet scent of sugar corn and wild grass hovering over the fields in fat droplets of humidity.

"Hmmm," she said. "That smells nice." She stretched her arm out the window, as if she could reach the dewy drops, bottle them up like the lemonade they'd sold in Mason jars when they were little girls. The stretches of country road brought her back to days of eating cherry popsicles on the front porch, so cold they'd stuck to her tongue, and of catching fireflies late into the night till the stars popped out and their mother called them in, once, twice, three times, her voice more insistent on her third trip to the door. Then she'd strip Lanie's body of her sweaty clothes and throw her into the bathtub, right after Ellen, the dirt from her sister still ringing the tub.

"There's no sense in wasting water," their mother always explained when they inquired why they shared the same water. Their mom, a farmer's daughter, possessed a farm girl's practicality when it came to husbanding resources.

Lanie smiled at her memories while they drove along, the telephone poles ticking by, Queen Anne's Lace and wild blue chicory dotting the roadside. She remembered many things about Harriet McClarety. Like the way she would bite into a tomato, whole, like an apple, or the way she'd make lemonade with fresh lemons, never concentrate, but would add so much sugar that all they could taste was the sweetness, not the tart. Lanie remembered, too, the hot summer nights they'd sit on the front porch swing, her mom patiently combing through her wet tangles while they swung back and forth, Ellen acting out tales of great kingdoms on the porch's grainy floor. Her mom would work out all the knots, one by one, as if it was the easiest thing in the world to do, and laugh her sweet laugh at her sister's antics.

On that hot summer day, her sister driving her back to her childhood town, Lanie knew she'd come home at last. It felt right. She wondered if she'd ever have her own child's tangled hair to smooth out, her own little girl or boy to whisper to, "Now just sit still; this won't hurt a lick."

Now she went to fix Benjamin's bottle. They had switched to formula once she went back to work, three short months after he was born. The whole breast-pumping thing was beyond her. She couldn't imagine toting a pump back and forth to work, having to pump behind closed doors, or even worse, in the bathroom stall at the courthouse every few hours. She knew that studies claimed breast-feeding up to a year was best for babies, but she tried to convince herself that Benjamin had gotten a full dose of antibodies in those first few months. Her pediatrician reassured her that it was okay, that the most important thing to remember was that "a happy mom meant a happy baby."

She threw the afghan around him now and watched as his lips fastened hungrily onto the bottle's nipple. She rocked him gently and clicked on the news with the remote. Up to a foot of snow, maybe more, they were predicting. Rob came down the stairs whistling, dressed in a navy jacket, khaki pants, and the yellow tie that Lanie had laid out for him the night before. He seemed happy, as if all the snow was cause for celebration. She, on the other hand, fretted over the practicalities—getting Benjamin to day care safely, making it to court on time, her clients' making it to court on time.

"I'll get the car warmed up and ready," Rob said as he slipped into his coat. "You guys will be toasty."

"Thanks," she offered.

"Benjamin, baby, when's this snow going to stop?"

He looked into her eyes, wide-eyed and knowing, but didn't offer a word. His lips puckered around the nipple, sucking away.

When Rob came back in, he seemed surprised by the strength of the storm.

"Be careful out there. It's pretty slick. I've sanded the driveway, but it looks like the plows came through a while ago."

"Okay." She nodded, half-hearing. "Thanks, honey."

She could feel him hesitating by the front door. Benjamin sat up to look.

"Do you think day care will even be open today?"

"No cancellations yet." Lanie had been watching the closings scroll across the bottom of the screen. Still just a few. There was a local joke that the schools in Wisconsin didn't close unless the snow was piled so high that you couldn't open your front door.

"Do you want me to drive you guys this morning?" She could tell from the timbre of his voice that her husband was being kind.

"No, you go. I know you've got a big day ahead of you, too. We'll be fine."

He came to give her a kiss and picked up Benjamin. "Bye, buddy. Have fun at school today. Maybe you'll go sledding, huh?"

Benjamin kicked his feet, waved bye-bye. He'd come to know that these early-morning rituals, including a kiss on the forehead, meant daddy was going to work. "It's a caffeine kind of day," Rob said on his way out the door. "See you tonight."

"See you tonight," Lanie said, but she'd already turned back to the news and was propping the baby up for a burp, wondering how on earth she was going to make it to court in time for her nine o'clock hearing.

Rob couldn't help it. As he negotiated the slippery roads on the way into the office, all he felt was relief. Relief to be going to work; relief to be leaving Benjamin's tired cries of the night behind; relief to be free of Lanie's guilt-inspiring looks. So what if he didn't get up last night to help with the baby? He certainly had done his fair share during those first few months. And both he and Lanie knew that the only thing Benjamin wanted at two in the morning was his momma. As much as Rob tried to be supportive—offering to get up in the middle of the night to fetch a bottle, rubbing Lanie's back when she fell back into bed, playing with Benjamin as soon as he got home from work—sometimes it just didn't seem like enough.

He was glad that Lanie had gone back to her firm after maternity leave. He supposed that made him a little unusual since most of his colleagues seemed to prefer that their wives stay home and raise the kids. But that was such an old-fashioned attitude, almost cavemanesque. He knew Lanie well enough to understand that she needed some kind of activity to get the wheels in her brain spinning again. She had read and reread all the baby books during the first few weeks of her maternity leave, highlighting sections, to the point where he'd taken to slipping them into the back of bookcases, hoping she'd put all that advice aside and just enjoy the mommy thing. But it was typical Lanie: wanting to get her arms around every detail she could about a case (or in this instance, their son), analyze them, and then come up with a game plan.

Of course, as they'd both come to realize quickly, there was no such thing as a game plan for a three-week-old or even a seven-month-old. Having Benjamin had taught them that all the book smarts in the world couldn't help them when it came to giving their baby the love he needed. And, once this realization sunk in, they breathed more easily, trusted themselves. They were the two people in the world who knew their little guy best—all his little quirks and baby pet peeves. It made Rob feel powerful and indispensable in a way he'd never fathomed possible. This little human being depended on him and Lanie totally and completely. *They were it.* They were whom Benjamin got in this life, take it or leave it.

God, how he hoped he didn't screw it up.

As he drove into the office, he ticked through his mental to-do checklist: Get a reservation at someplace nice for their five-year anniversary that was coming up; pick up his dry cleaning (he was out of shirts); and get the final plans for the west wing of the art institute signed off on. He was tired of waiting around for Eli's approval. Eli had only a few years on Rob at the firm, but he always seemed to weigh in at the most inopportune moment. Because he was the lead guy on the project, Eli had to sign off on every little thing. If he didn't like it, Rob might as well start over.

Rob pulled into the garage and turned into his assigned parking space, L01. It always looked to him like LOL, as if someone higher up knew what a joke his job was. As if Frank Hobbs himself, the president of their firm, were saying, "Poor Rob, all that hard work, and not much to show for it." He knew he was being paranoid, but still. LOL? Really? Did he need a parking slot that mocked him each and every day?

When he stepped out of the car, the cold stung his nose immediately. His breath came out in a white arc. He buttoned his top button and made for the elevator, hearing the *thwack* of his boots on the pavement. The mostly empty garage made it feel like a Saturday. He'd managed to push his guilt aside on the drive into work, but now it crept up on him again as he waited for the elevator. The roads *had* been pretty slick. He probably should have given Lanie and Benjamin a ride. He'd feel better if he called her to check in when he got into the office.

When he stepped off the elevator into the lobby, a wall of white swirling just beyond the window greeted him. Choppy waves cut through the lake below. What was it that T. S. Eliot said about April? "April is the cruelest month"? Or was it March? Or was it Yeats who wrote that? He'd have to ask Lanie tonight. She would know and would laugh at him for pretending to know. But it would be a good laugh, one that was familiar to them, each trying to outsmart the other. It would be nice, he thought, as he headed toward his office, if they could get some of that back, even for one night.

"Good morning, boss. Glad to see you made it in."

His assistant, Kate, was in a perpetually good mood. He found it to be an exceedingly rare quality the longer he worked in the business. Architects in general seemed to be a dour lot, always playing out worst-case scenarios. For Kate, though, the sky was unfailingly blue, even on a day like today, and while some might find her cheerfulness counterfeit, he was grateful for it. Plus, she always looked professional. He supposed that was a sexist thing to say, but again, another underrated quality as far as he could tell in the new wave of graduates coming out of the university. It was as if young women today felt they had to make a statement with their asymmetrical hairstyles, body piercings, and thrift-shop clothing. Kate, on the other hand, wore her thick black hair straight, in a neat shoulder-length cut. She wasn't pretty in the usual way, yet everything about her exuded competence, helpfulness. He wondered for a brief moment if she had a small tattoo hidden somewhere discreet, like on her hip or the small of her back, then chided himself.

It was none of his damn business.

Once when Lanie had returned from a girls' weekend with her college roommates, she'd asked Rob if she should get a tattoo. His name? A little bird? He'd laughed at the time. It seemed so unlike her. But maybe it had been her attempt to spice things up one last time before they started trying for a baby, a family?

Would she do it now, if he asked?

When he put the question to his buddies—was it typical for the passion to wane around year five—they assured him that he was experiencing the "baby blues." "We've all been there, dude," his friends commiserated with him. Things would get back to normal soon enough. "By the time Benjamin's five, at the latest," his buddy Tom joked. Rob couldn't imagine a five-year stretch of sleep deprivation and next-to-no sex. Sometimes he felt as if Lanie had forgotten he even existed, and then he felt even smaller, like a petulant child hungry for attention.

"It's natural. She's fallen in love with your son. Give her time. Once he hits the terrible twos, she'll remember what a well-mannered guy you are and how much she loves a man who doesn't throw his peas across the table." Rob tried to take what comfort he could from those words.

"Good morning to you, too," Kate tried again.

"Sorry. My mind's somewhere else." He brushed the snow from his overcoat, then rifled through the mail laid out on the ledge above her desk for his review. "Let it snow, let it snow, huh?"

"I said to Mark yesterday, it smells like snow. I bet it's going to snow." She took a sip of her coffee, leaving maroon lipstick marks on the rim. "I can always tell. So, do you want the good news or the bad news first?"

Rob sighed. "There's already both?" He glanced at his watch. It was only eight thirty.

She nodded. "Bad?"

"Okay. The bad news is that Eli doesn't like your latest tweaks to the west wing. Says it feels old-fashioned. He wants something more 'in tune with kids today,' whatever that means." She rolled her eyes.

"Shit," Rob said under his breath. Kate had lost no time in telling him what she thought of Eli a few weeks after she'd been hired. "He's a chauvinistic pig. Looks at my boobs every time he talks to me." (Rob had stared intently at Kate's face when she said this.)

"It would be one thing if he was hot, but he's just a nerdy guy." Rob had wanted to ask how it would be different, how that would make it okay. But he bit his tongue.

True, Eli was a little pathetic in the way those kids in school who never quite fit in were. He imagined Eli wearing button-down shirts in high school, no date at the prom. But Eli was also the kind of guy who was going to end up with a boatload of money, and he'd caught Hobbs's eye out of the gate. Rob agreed he was a smart architect, anal in his calculations and drawings, but he lacked what Rob liked to think of as architectural intuition. No sense for how the space would work once people were *actually in it*. Their team had been struggling to refine the plans for Madison's new art institute for weeks. Every time it seemed as if they were in the home stretch, Eli threw them a curve ball. "Let's get Walter on the phone, shall we?"

"I've already got a conference call set up for ten thirty."

Rob smiled. "Figures."

"Now for the good news: Lanie called. She says court is shutting down early today, and she'll be able to pick up Benjamin from day care this afternoon. So you're off the hook."

"Oh," Rob's heart sunk just a bit. Why hadn't she just called his cell? Then he remembered he'd forgotten to charge it last night. It was dead in his pocket.

"Not good news?" Kate asked, raising an eyebrow.

"I was looking forward to cutting out early myself today, with this crap weather."

"Well, *I'm* not stopping you." She turned back to her computer. "Don't worry. I'll cover for you, like I always do," she added, her nails clicking away at the keys.

"Your boss is such an ass. I don't know how you stand him."

"You and me both," Kate said matter-of-factly. Then, when Rob paused for a moment: "Well, are you going to do *any* work today?"

"Probably not." He grabbed his coffee and walked into his office, directly across the way. He dropped his briefcase on the cluttered desk, hung his coat on the hook behind the door, plugged in his cell. The snow outside the window was blowing hard now, almost horizontally, and when he touched his finger to the pane he pulled it quickly back from the cold. He sat down at his drawing board and retrieved the plans from the drawer. Etching upon etching detailed all the modifications they'd already made to the west wing, meant to be devoted to a children's museum. He'd see what he could do to appease Eli without redrafting it completely. As with so much in life, it was a matter of two steps forward, one step back. Eventually, he had faith that they would get there.

Then he remembered he'd meant to call Lanie, make sure she and Benjamin had made it in all right. He picked up his desk phone and started punching the numbers.

When he heard her voice, he smiled. "Hey," he began.

"Apple? Apricot? Pecan? The magic of *kringle* lurks in the first bite. What fruity, nutty filling will blossom on the tongue? Will it be almond or something more tart, perhaps rhubarb? The surprises delight each time."

—*The Book of Kringle*

"I'm eating ice cream out of the carton," Ellen announced when Lanie walked through the door. She had put out her distress call an hour ago.

"So, I see." Her sister crossed the living room and laid her jacket on the sofa. Ellen hadn't seen Lanie since the storm had hit and Madison had been buried for two days straight. Lanie looked around now, hands on her hips.

"Well, if this isn't the House of Mirth, I don't know what is."

"No need to be fresh." Ellen pulled up her feet in their fuzzy yellow slippers, leaned back against the sofa's big cushions, and cinched her robe tightly around her waist. "*You* certainly look better than you did the other day."

"Thanks. I can't remember the last time I was so tired. This baby thing can be brutal." Then she paused, as if she'd realized her misstep. Ellen and Max had never been able to have kids, despite years of trying.

"Anyway," she quickly tried to change the subject. "I thought I was here to help *you*."

"You're right." Ellen sighed. "As they say, I've come undone."

"I doubt it's that bad." She gave Ellen a squeeze and reached for the bag she'd brought, pulling out some trashy magazines. It had become a tradition when they were kids: Whenever one of them felt lousy, they'd buy up a bunch of the weekly tabloids. Reading about the various celebrity emotional car wrecks always made them feel better about their own lives.

"I assume we're talking about Max?"

Ellen nodded and sniffled.

"He called the store. Out of the blue." She blew her nose. "I told you that part already."

Lanie plopped down in the chair opposite her and nodded. "I didn't know what to think or say. Thank goodness it was a bad connection."

Lanie looked at her wide-eyed. "Right . . . and you said he mentioned something about an e-mail?"

"He sent it to my old account, one that I haven't looked at for ages. But when I checked it, there it was, sitting on the screen, daring me to open it. I printed it out."

She retrieved a piece of paper from the floor and handed it over. Lanie began to read aloud:

Dear Ellen,
    I won't beat around the bush. I miss you—a lot. I wanted to let you know where I've landed in case your feeling the same way. I've moved to Sint Maarten, land of happiness! A buddy of mine invited me to join him on a little business venture down here.
    You would love it! Part of the island is Dutch/English. The other half is French. You could practice your French, if you came to visit! I know it's been awhile since we've been in touch, but being down here gives a guy plenty of time to

reflect. Lots of sand and sun! I always felt like the divorce was a rush thing. Maybe we should have taken more time to think things over? I'd hate myself if you'd had a change of heart and didn't know how to reach me. My new e-mail address and number is at the top. Hope to here from you soon!

Fondly,

Max

"Well, that's unexpected, isn't it?" Lanie looked up from the e-mail.

"That's putting it mildly." Ellen paused. "I'd forgotten what a terrible speller he is."

"Hmm . . . it's embarrassing, especially in the age of spell-check." Lanie rolled her eyes.

"Listen to me!" Ellen threw up her hands. "I sound ridiculous, don't I?" She started to laugh, then cry. Her sister set down the paper and went to get more tissues from the bathroom. Of course Max had to write, "I miss you—a lot." He knew their private code would get her worked up. After they'd dated only a few months and felt their affections growing stronger, they'd whisper to each other, "I like you—a lot," in lieu of the more frightening confession, "I love you."

Lanie handed her the tissue box, and Ellen helped herself, blew her nose. "I'm too old for this kind of nonsense."

"First of all, you're not *old*. Okay? Forty-five is far from old. Second of all, I can't believe you're getting upset about a guy you've been divorced from for more than a year. I don't need to remind you of all the reasons why, do I?"

Ellen sniffled, raised her eyebrows expectantly.

"Like he was always coming up with big schemes to make money but could never bring home a steady paycheck? Or that he had a wandering eye whenever you two went out. Or that he was more of a roommate than a supportive husband?"

All true, Ellen knew. Initially, she had dismissed his flaws as charming, but she had come to see them for what they really were. The wandering eye, however, had always been tough to justify.

"You're right," she said, crossing her arms. "He was a good-for-nothing." She sighed. "But he was *hot*."

"Oh, come on. You're not going to play that card again, are you?" Ellen looked at her sister.

"Absolutely not. We're not going there. Don't even think about it," Lanie warned. "Sure, he might look like a young Paul Newman, but where does that get you in life, unless he's the real thing?"

"A lot of salad dressing?"

Lanie laughed. "And I haven't even mentioned the annoying overuse of exclamation points in his e-mail."

Now it was Ellen's turn to laugh. She remembered when she and her sister had made a list of pros and cons when discussing whether she should leave Max. It had quickly dissolved into an anti-love poem called "Let Me Count the Ways I *Don't* Love You." Although, come to think of it, that was a little mean. She *had* loved Max, had been smitten with him from the moment he asked her to the movies and dinner and his big blue eyes had swum with a mix of infatuation and admiration. Those eyes had won her over instantly.

Not that she hadn't had her share of boyfriends in high school and college, but Max was different. He was tall, athletic, easy to be around. Strangers warmed to him immediately; it seemed he could find something in common with anyone, the kind of guy you'd want to share a beer with. And for women, well, he'd always been magnetic. A charmer, head-turning handsome, with those striking blue eyes and chiseled cheekbones, a slight cleft in his chin. Ellen liked that all the women would look when they walked into a restaurant together.

She laughed now. "Can you imagine? Us getting back together again?"

"Whoa. Hold on there," Lanie interjected. "No one is suggesting rekindling anything. This is just Max's wishful thinking. Lonely, wishful thinking. He always was a dreamer, remember?"

Ellen blew her nose again.

"You're right. He probably had one too many mai tais before writing this. I should just throw it out and not respond?" It sounded like a question. "Even though he called to ask if I got it? Even though he sounded like he really missed me?" She had cut the conversation short when he called, begging off with the excuse of customers, her heart racing.

Lanie came over to the couch, sat down, and put an arm around her big sister.

"I know you're usually the one to give the advice, but yes. I think that would be best. You've moved on. In a positive way. There's no sense in going back to Max-land."

Ellen smiled at the mention of "Max-land," what she and Lanie used to call it when Max would come up with another one of his harebrained schemes: "He's in Max-land right now."

Lanie was right, of course. All the spring snow was making her stir-crazy. She'd lost her head, her good sense. She curled up next to her sister as they watched the end of a made-for-TV movie.

"What is this anyway?" Lanie asked.

"No idea." Ellen paused. "Something about angels."

"Heavenly."

A few pints of butter pecan ice cream later, as the credits rolled, Lanie turned and asked, "Are you going to be okay?"

"I'm fine." Ellen waved her away. "Get back to your husband and son. And here, take this with you."

She shoved the half-eaten container of ice cream, the spoon still protruding from the carton, into Lanie's hands. "That's the last thing my hips need. You know, it's so much easier to stay skinny when you're not depressed."

"You should write a book about it." Her sister thought for a second. "Something like, *Grin to Stay Thin.*"

"That will be my *next* midlife crisis." Ellen sighed.

Lanie gave her one more hug. "You're not depressed, just in shock. I'll check in on you tomorrow. Get some sleep."

Ellen walked her to the door, locking it securely behind her before heading upstairs to bed.

But the next morning Ellen woke up in a dour mood. She hadn't slept well, tossing and turning most of the night. She had tried counting backward, then forward, then visualized herself on a beach sipping piña coladas but Max popped up beside her on a beach towel with a schoolboy's grin. At three in the morning she put on her slippers and robe, went downstairs, and poured herself a tall glass of milk. She was upset with herself for letting Max get to her. That was old business, done and through. Why had one little e-mail and a phone call suddenly gotten the wheels spinning in her head? She knew better.

She went to the living room and looked out at the yard. The shadows of the birch branches danced across the lawn in the moonlight. The Lannigans' house across the street was dark, and she imagined the elderly couple sleeping soundly under their warm blankets, not a care in the world. Her milk finished, she went upstairs to call on sleep again.

But to no avail. She had gotten maybe two or three hours the entire night, hardly enough to sustain her. She'd have to make do somehow. Some days were meant just for getting through.

She'd heard on NPR about a study on happiness and the effects of smiling. Apparently, just the act of smiling could make a person happier. Something about hormones kicking in, tricking your brain into thinking you were happy when it sensed you were turning up the corners of your mouth. She had practiced grinning several times in the shower this morning, wide, teeth-baring grins, and was still waiting for the happiness quotient to kick in.

As she turned the key in the lock at the store, she felt her usual pep was missing. Gone was that initial rush with the first step onto the hardwood floor, the anticipation of the day ahead, of her customers' stories. She set her purse down on the shelf underneath the register, took off her coat, and replaced it with her apron. She whispered, "Good morning, store." Out front, she got the coffee and filters from the bottom cupboards and filled the brewers: hazelnut, vanilla, and decaf. She waited for the first drops of hazelnut to brew and caught them for herself in a cup.

In back she pulled her hair into a ponytail and washed her hands at the sink, wiping them dry. Her hands were perpetually rough, it seemed, ever since she'd opened the store. She pulled the chilled rectangles from the refrigerator and patted the dough, letting the cool sink between her fingers. Then she fed each through the machine, watching the lumps dissolve, thinking how this lump looked a bit like Max's nose, this one like his ear. Next, she folded the thin, stretchy swath over onto itself, back and forth, to better move it to the baking table. *Just like her life these days,* she thought, *back and forth, back and forth.* When she was sure she'd moved on, here was Max popping up again like a renegade lump of flour.

She uncapped the fillings for the day, raspberry and almond, and spread them evenly on top. Then she folded up the sides of each rectangle and brushed egg white onto the seal. Almond was how she was feeling; raspberry, she hoped, was a cheerier flavor that might boost her spirits. At last, thirty-two elongated rolls lay before her like horizontal hieroglyphics.

She wished they held some answers.

Max's e-mail, she felt certain, had been written after a few cocktails on the beach. He was positively drunk if he thought she was going to visit him. Perhaps she hadn't let him down hard enough when she filed for divorce citing "irreconcilable differences"?

Their split had been quick. Indeed, she'd barely seen the door hit his ass on the way out, but that's what they'd both wanted. Or so she thought. Ten years was enough time to know whether a marriage was working or not and when she'd broken the news to Max that she was pretty sure theirs wasn't, he hadn't seem surprised. Maybe a little disappointed, even sad, but not surprised. She'd interpreted this as agreement. She had done enough soul-searching before filing the papers not to want to revisit the matter again. And yet? Carefully she knitted the ends of the doughy ropes together and transferred the ovals onto the baking board before slipping them into the oven.

Back in the front, she tidied up and pulled open the blinds. The sun was beginning to peek out. Erin had wiped down the tables the night before, but now Ellen turned over the chairs, scrubbed the counter, and filled the milk and cream canisters at the help-yourself-station at the back. She restocked the napkins, spoons, and knives. Then she picked up the chalk and in yellow letters wrote:

Drips: *Hazelnut; French Vanilla; Decaf*
Tips: *Sally gave an orange to Tim and me.*
*(*Me *is the object of the preposition* to. *It should not read,*
as so often is the case, to "Tim and I," which, though it
may sound intelligent, is incorrect.)

She stood back and admired her work, then put the chalk down and brushed off her hands. She offered up a silent prayer that her customers would provide some inspiration and enlightenment today. Surely there were lessons to be learned from their lives. Ty's wife had left him, and he was still pining for her. Ellen most certainly did not want to be that kind of ex-spouse.

She then noticed a small package wrapped in brown paper sitting by the door. There was no note, only her name printed in all caps. As she pulled back the paper, fastened charmingly with masking tape, she saw the familiar bold letters of an F and an M poking through. The cover was yellowed, slightly torn in the upper-right-hand corner. She opened the book to the copyright page. Sure enough, it was.

A rare first edition of Fowler's *Modern English Usage*! The book she'd come to consider as close to a bible as she'd ever have in her lifetime. She held it up and breathed in its musty scent, then thumbed through the first pages. She took a little breath to see that there was a handwritten inscription on the title page: "To my dear Gretchen, whose words give rich meaning to each day. All my love, Anthony."

How romantic! The black ink was smudged, the "thony" in

34

Anthony blurry. *Who were they?* she wondered. *Star-crossed lovers? Fledgling poets or writers?* Her mind swum with the possibilities.

When Jack walked into the store, Ellen held up the book for him, told him about the gift she'd discovered. "Crazy way to tell someone you love them, if you ask me," Jack said. "The inscription, I mean, on a grammar book."

"Don't spoil it for me, Jack. I need a lift today. Let me just enjoy the romance of it all for a minute." Then: "I wonder who on earth would get this for me."

She thought of Lanie first. Something to cheer her up. Her sister must have snuck it into the store last night with her spare key. But even Lanie didn't have time for such thoughtfulness. Could Jack have been making light of it on purpose? Maybe he left it for her? A secret admirer all this time? She looked at him, thumbing through the sports section of his paper. It seemed unlikely. What about taciturn Henry? He had mentioned the other day how he loved all the Peterson *Field Guides to Flowers*. He seemed to relish a good reference book as much as she did.

But if it were Henry, why wouldn't he have left a note? There was no reason to hide. Then it dawned on her: Larry, of course. He appreciated a good turn of phrase as much as herself. His minor was in literature. He must have left the book when he closed up the shop yesterday afternoon. She'd have to thank him later in the day, once she'd sorted through the Max saga spinning in her head.

"Clearly someone who doesn't have much of a life." Jack chuckled. "No offense."

"Just because someone is thoughtful and appreciates a rare edition when he," she caught herself, "or *she* sees it, doesn't give you an excuse to poke fun. You can help yourself to your own coffee today," she said, enjoying the surprised look on Jack's face.

When Henry came into the store later that morning, his arms were full of books.

"What's all this?" Ellen asked.

"I was clearing out some old paperbacks, and I thought maybe your lending library could use a few new ones."

"Well, I hope they're not just dull gardening books," she teased, but she was secretly delighted as she was anytime a customer added to her library. Then her heart skipped a beat. Might Henry have left her the Fowler's after all? But no, she was reading things into his unexpected kindness.

"Nah, mostly mysteries."

"Well, thank you." She watched while he unloaded the books and then made his way to a table. Ellen went to inspect the titles, most of them of the Nelson DeMille and Tom Clancy variety.

"So does that mean that Tim and you had to share an orange? Or did you both get an orange from Sally?" Henry interrupted her thoughts.

Ellen had to stop and think for a minute.

"Oh right, the board. Don't be silly, Henry. Of course, we both get an orange." Erin cocked an ear in her direction. That *did* sound a bit rude. Good old Max. Even across southern seas he was ruining not just her night but also her day. Lanie was right; she wouldn't honor Max's foolish e-mail with a response. All that sun was going to his head. Sure, Ellen had her own doubts from time to time, wondering if they'd done the right thing, worrying she'd signed up for a life of celibacy and loneliness after divorcing him. But, on her better days, she didn't think so.

"Well, I don't think it's clear. Maybe you'd better have another look."

Why was Henry being difficult all of a sudden? Honestly, she didn't have the patience for it. She was about to brush him off, go out back and tell Erin to deal with the customers, when another thought came to her. Maybe Henry had a point.

Maybe she should rethink the oranges. After all, she hadn't written that Sally was handing out two oranges. On second glance it *was* a little unclear. She picked up the chalk, erased, and rewrote the sentence so that it read: *Sally gave one orange each to Tim and me.*

"Better?" She looked at Henry.

"Better. Now I understand what you're talking about."

And, instead of feeling slighted for being corrected on her muddy grammar, she was grateful to have someone paying attention for once. Instead of turning on her heel, as she might have a day ago, she turned to him now and asked, "Henry, would you like to have dinner at my house next Friday?"

He paused for a moment. "With you?"

"Yes, with me, you dimwit." A hush fell over the store. Ellen swore she could hear the coffee dripping in the pot behind her.

"Well, in that case, I'd be honored. Thank you."

"Good, now be quiet about Tim and Sally and their orange, won't you?"

And she turned to pour the coffee, butterflies fluttering in her stomach, wondering what on earth she had just done.

She had to admit, mommy biases aside, Benjamin was pretty cute. Adorable, really, when he stuck out his pudgy pointer finger at his stuffed elephant, the stroller, his juice cup. *How did babies know to use the pointer finger instead of, say, the thumb?* she wondered. She loved it when he babbled with his intonations, as if he were punching up specific words with meaning, recalling events from his day. He'd get excited, clap his hands together, ending with an animated "Oooh!"

"Is that so?" she'd ask. "Tell me all about it."

And he'd continue on, filling her in. One day last October, when she'd just begun to feel comfortable in her mommy shoes, she strapped him in his stroller and rolled him under the big maple tree in the front yard while she planted mums along the stone fence. He was an outdoors baby, for sure. She had been bent over, sticking in the bright purple blooms, only to look up and see his five-month-old face with a big toothless grin, tilted toward the canopy of leaves above, taking it all in.

She thought of this now as she strolled him around the neighborhood, the air crisp and inviting on a Saturday. Rob was at work again and so she was enjoying her alone time with Benjamin on this gorgeous spring day. Finally, they'd gotten the weather they deserved.

She knew that labeling was an important way for babies to learn language, and she was careful to point out the trees, the grass, the dog across the street as they walked.

"Do you hear the birdies singing?" she asked.

Benjamin kicked his baby-stockinged feet, and she could swear she saw a glint of recognition in his eyes as he turned his face upward. She laughed to see him riding around so confidently, holding on to the stroller's front tray, as if he were mayor of their little neighborhood.

She imagined him as a hockey player one day or a baseball player, if his dad had anything to say about it. He was solid, stocky, with those fat baby hands that looked as if they were attached at the arms like a baby doll's, no wrists. Snap-on hands, Rob called them.

When she and Rob had brought him home from the hospital, Benjamin weighed only 4 pounds, 10 ounces. He seemed so fragile with his wobbly head, his tiny feet. He tugged at her arms no more than a flour sack.

Now that it was spring and Benjamin nearly a year old, she could let herself breathe more easily. She reminded herself of how far they'd come. The feelings of joy she'd been waiting to open like a present at the hospital hadn't arrived during those first weeks. Instead, her days and near-sleepless nights were checkered with heart-stopping fear, with the sickening uncertainty of not knowing if Benjamin, a preemie, would be all right. Every movement, every noise he made, was analyzed by them for "normalcy." But really, what did she and Rob know?

The physical therapist came for weekly visits in the early months to keep an eye on the baby's development. She saw things they didn't notice, good things. He could bring his hands together; he would track their movements with his eyes; he gradually was pushing up higher on his tummy. With each pronouncement Lanie let herself calm a bit more. But above all, she sensed—could it be motherly intuition?—that her little boy was a social being, a little person hungry to interact with the world, who seemed never to miss a beat. Ellen joked he'd be a newspaper reporter one day; he was constantly gulping in the world. But this was a few months later, after Lanie's heart stopped quickening with every mid-night cry. When it seemed as if everything might, really, be okay.

Still, in a moment, she could call up that first wrenching week in the maternity wing, the palpable ache that had come when she woke every few hours to hear babies being wheeled back and forth in the middle of the night from the nursery to their mothers' breasts. She could feel the tears rising, the lump in her throat with every hammering of wheels on the tiled floor. Her baby couldn't come to her; she couldn't go to him, miles away in a pediatric hospital, not until her blood count had reached certain levels and some of her strength returned.

She, herself, had lost a tremendous amount of blood, her uterus rupturing to push Benjamin out into the world much too soon. And so, what she had looked forward to as a few leisurely days at the hospital, her last chance for sleep, with food ferried to her on trays, had turned into a relentless check-your-vitals, wheel-you-down-for-more-tests kind of visit. She couldn't wait to go home, fall into her own bed, and quiet the wheels that kept spinning in her head.

During those first painful, scary days, Rob had jockeyed back and forth between hospitals, giving her updates. "Benjamin's off the ventilator," he called, in tears, after they'd released him from the machine that had been breathing life into his lungs for the first three days. "You should see him, Lanie. He's beautiful. Big blue eyes, a spray of hair, perfect little lips."

All she had managed in that call, between her own tears, was, "Be sure he knows we love him, okay? Tell him."

Slowly, other good news began to follow. Benjamin was drinking from a bottle; he was off the feeding tubes. His heart and lungs seemed to be working just fine. Now he only needed to gain some weight and beat the jaundice that had set in. She knew from Rob that Ellen had stayed with their baby every night after work, sleeping by his crib, during those first few days. Rob would arrive early in the morning to release Ellen from her shift, having just slept by Lanie's side himself. The NICU doctors kept saying their son was a fighter; the nurses dubbed him cutest baby in the NICU. It wasn't much to go on, but for the moment it was enough. It had to be. Enough to know her little guy was breathing, responding, being watched over.

Still, the thought of not having once held him, that he lay somewhere where she couldn't even stroke his arm, his leg, give him a binky to suck on, was almost unbearable. The nurses, Rob, Ellen, all told her that she'd see her baby as soon as she was able. In the meantime, Rob brought her a cloth ragdoll especially designed to absorb her scent, which he took to Benjamin. She'd read that babies recognized a mother's scent immediately, that they knew it instinctively from being inside the womb. She hoped her sweet boy would take some small comfort from her smell, know that she was nearby even if she couldn't yet hold him.

When at last the hospital released her to go greet him for the first time, five days had gone by. Already she'd missed so much. When she arrived, still in a wheelchair because she was too weak to walk, she was breathless; here was her miracle boy. What looked like a million tiny tubes protruded from his miniature body. Blinking monitors flashed and beeped all around him. Two blankets propped him up on either side, and his eyes fluttered open when she stood over him and said, "Hi, baby. It's momma." Her voice broke with tears.

"Here she is, little guy. The lady you've been waiting for."

Benjamin looked up at her with the most intense eyes she'd ever seen, dark, dark blue, she could barely detect the irises. A blue blanket swaddled him tightly. She reached out to stroke his cheek. *His skin was so soft!* She peered in more closely and saw that he had little rosebud lips and a slip of an upturned nose, like her mother's, like his grandmother's. Even the swirl of his ears was amazingly beautiful. Rob had said it, but it was true. *Their little guy was perfect.*

"He's still working on his hair," Rob joked. Only a few wisps of brown wove around his head.

She started sobbing then, loud gut-wrenching sobs that surprised them both. Was it the release of finally being able to see her son, touch him, love him close at hand? Or was it the pain of seeing her child tethered to so many machines that worked furiously to help him get better? She supposed it was a combination of the two. She felt Rob's arms around her, his breath on her neck.

"Shhh. It's okay. It's all gonna be okay. He's got his momma now." She nodded, wiped her face with the back of her hand.

"Hi, my little lovebug." She stroked Benjamin's delicate cheek again.

"Do you want to hold him?" The nurse had come back to check on them.

"I'd love to." She paused. "Is it okay?"

"Oh sure, let me help you get him out and settled in your arms." Gently she lifted Benjamin from the incubator, a tangle of wires and cords hanging from the bottom of his blanket, and placed him in her arms. She helped Lanie to position him so that his small head, seemingly balanced so precariously on the rest of his body, was cradled in the crook of her arm.

"You're just a peanut," she whispered, then kissed his forehead. At that moment Benjamin gave a big, air-slurping yawn that made them all laugh.

"Just another typical day in the NICU," Rob said.

"Glad to see you're so excited to meet your momma." Lanie laughed at her little boy's nonchalance while he looked up at her with bright, quizzical eyes, as if to ask, "So, what are we doing next?"

When at last they got the call saying they could bring their son home (Lanie had been home for two days herself, the wait for Benjamin excruciating), she and Rob repacked the bag they'd carefully filled when they'd first been expecting to return home, a happy family of three. Diapers, diaper cream, pacifiers, burp towels, and a chime toy to hang from the car seat. On top Lanie lay the baby's homecoming outfit, a soft onesie with big yellow ducks parading across it. They looked like happy ducks to her, ones that would quack in a cacophony of joy if they could. Rob locked the car seat into the back, and they held hands for the entire drive, hardly speaking a word.

The doctors, not known for their bedside manner, were anything but reassuring at Benjamin's prerelease meeting. Lanie and Rob were elated that their son was finally well enough to come home, to sleep in his very own bassinet. But she felt that elation come crashing down as she listened to the doctors tick off possible signs of concern to look for, to worry over. They had to make sure Benjamin continued to gain weight, that the yellow hue didn't return to his skin, that he was responding "normally" to them.

How could the doctors be so heartless? she wondered. She didn't want to think about those things. She simply wanted someone to tell her that her little boy would soon be clapping his hands, eating goldfish crackers, that he'd be running in the open stretch of their yard one day, that she'd note in his baby book the first day he said "mama." Couldn't they see she was trying to imagine a life for the child she had just given birth to?

When they got home, Ellen opened their blue door wide, welcoming them as "the Taylor family," shooting pictures all the while. Their little guy was home at last. For a moment, as Rob carried Benjamin across the threshold, saying, "Welcome home, buddy," Lanie was seized with panic. How on earth would she take care of this child? Was she even capable in her current state? She turned to Rob who, expecting to see delight on her face, discerned worry in her eyes instead.

"What? What is it? Did we forget something at the hospital?"

"What if I'm no good at this? At being a mom?"

He smiled, put his arm around her, and walked with her to the living room.

"Oh, honey," Rob said.

He set the baby's car seat down on the living room rug and beamed at her.

"How can you not be good at it? You're wonderful. I love you. You're going to be an amazing mom."

She felt her lungs expand. He was right. They were going to be all right. And while her own mother had been taken from her much too soon, she knew how to love fiercely, change a diaper, cradle a child who needed as much touch as possible right now. That was what was needed from her at this moment. She could do all those things.

The memory stuck with her as she wheeled Benjamin around the neighborhood, still bundled up in his sweatshirt and wool hat. Yes, she could do all those things. She *was* doing all those things, she reminded herself now. How she wished her mother were here to see it, to meet her grandson. How she would love this child!

If only her mom could swoop in, like a fairy godmother, and guide her through the next seventeen years. Lanie was filled with both practical questions and questions only her mother could know: When had Lanie's first tooth popped through? How would she make sure that Benjamin started talking and walking at the right age? How did her mother quiet her during her colicky periods? Had she been a napper? (Benjamin decidedly was *not*.) What were her favorite books? She could remember her mom reading *Bedtime for Frances* and *Corduroy*. But what came before that? What had been her favorite lullaby? These were the questions she would ask her mother now but that had never occurred to her in the six short years she'd had with her.

Harriet McClarety often told her girls, on nights when they'd try to imagine their lives' paths, that motherhood was the greatest joy in life. She said it, Lanie always felt, not to discourage them from careers—for her mother was an elementary school teacher herself—but to remind them that they were and always would be her life's purpose.

As she reached down to get Benjamin now, she thought back to that first day, seemingly so long ago, when Rob had bent down to release the baby from his car seat, then handed him to her. He was so impossibly small, so incredibly beautiful, this baby of theirs. Benjamin looked up at her, tightly swaddled, wide awake with bright eyes, much as they were on this crisp spring afternoon, as if to say, once again, "Well, what's next?"

She carried him back into the house, checked the machine for messages. There were three. One from her friend Audrey, mother of three, asking when they could get together again. "Save me!" she shouted from the machine. "I need to get out of the house, and I don't know if I'm ever coming back!" Lanie smiled. Audrey was the queen of melodrama, which made Lanie love her all the more. The second was from Naomi Griffin, calling about "a few early details for the Big Brother benefit" held every fall. Lanie's firm helped the foundation with odds and ends as part of its pro bono work. She sighed. Autumn seemed so far away, but she knew that there were things they had to get started on—donors, volunteers, venue, a theme to bring it all together. She'd call Naomi later when she had the energy.

The third message was from Rob. Things at work were even crazier than expected, and he doubted he'd be home before suppertime. On a Saturday! Lanie felt a pinch of anger; as happy as she was to have her time with Benjamin, she wanted them all together on the weekends. Was that so greedy of her? It hurt sometimes when Rob didn't seem to share her desire to spend time together as a family. Wasn't that what the whole marriage thing had been about?

"Looks like it's just you and me, baby," she said to Benjamin as she pulled off his cap and jacket. She walked over to his high chair and strapped him in. "We'll have our picnic another day. It's too cold out anyway."

She went to the fridge to get cheese and fruit for his lunch. At the back of the refrigerator, she spied some old beers. Would it hurt to have just one? She pushed it aside, just like the thought of Rob's working another Saturday. Benjamin was banging on his high-chair tray with a spoon, "singing for his supper," as they'd begun to call it.

"I'm coming, baby," she called, as she gathered up the food in her arms and turned to give him all her love.

4

"All fine architectural values are
human values, else not valuable."
—Frank Lloyd Wright

Rob checked his watch, then his cell again. No messages. The last
call from Lanie had been to say that she'd meet him at the restaurant. Ellen had agreed to pinch-hit as a babysitter, but Lanie wanted
to go home first, get changed, get Benjamin settled into his pajamas.
Rob had lucked out with last-minute reservations at La Lumière,
one of the nicest restaurants in Madison, and ideal for an anniversary dinner. The waitress had already refilled his scotch, and he'd
managed to shred the cocktail napkin into tiny bits now sitting at his
glass's edge.

He looked out the windows onto the cold, glassy face of Lake
Mendota. The restaurant sat on the other side of the lake from the
office, and the view just one hundred and eighty degrees east was
surprisingly different. The evening light played off the lake, little
pools of shimmering gold and rose, as the sun sunk in the west.
The place was nestled back among tall maples and pines, and a
person could walk twenty paces from the restaurant's windows and
be standing at the water's edge. A small bench waited at the end of
the path, and Rob watched as a bird landed at the nearby feeder,

in plain sight for customers while they sipped wine and nibbled on escargot.

It was a beautiful spot, as Gill had promised when he handed over the reservations to Rob this morning, saying "You're going to be a happy man if you take Lanie here tonight." He'd winked in a conspiratorial way, as if Rob were one of the guys, though Rob didn't think of himself that way. He was in a bit of a no-man's-land at work, the way he saw it. Not old enough to be partner, not young enough to hang out with the swinging bachelors. He was certainly smart and experienced enough to make partner, and it had become a thorn in his side the past year, wanting to get recognized for his contribution to and long hours at the firm. Lanie liked to tease him that work was his mistress, but he failed to see the humor in it. Work was taking time away from his family, from Benjamin. If it were up to Greenough himself, he was sure he would have made partner a year ago. But with Hobbs running most of the day-to-day show, it didn't look as if anything was going to change soon.

His dad, a shoe salesman, would chuckle at Rob's unrest. The man had possessed a coal miner's work ethic, every day in, every day out of the shop without complaint. Vanity, reward for hard work weren't things Midwesterners spoke of. You were expected to provide for your family. Of course, his old man, just like his grandfather, had been his own boss, doing everything from ordering the shoes to writing out the customers' sales receipt on the carbon copy. Rob's dad had loved everything about the business and seemed to get true pleasure out of fitting a customer with the right style, the appropriate arch. He prided himself on knowing the architecture of a foot, the way the bones connected, of providing the necessary support and cushion in a shoe's sole. "The soul lies in the sole," he was fond of saying.

At the back of the store, customers could place a foot inside an old fluoroscope machine to measure size precisely. It was touted as the most scientific way to get the "right fit," and as a child, Rob loved to see the X-rays illuminate the white lines of his bones. His dad would name them for him: "That's your big toe. It's known as a phalange in the medical world. The longer bones are your metatarsals, and that there is your calcaneus, also known as your heel. Did you know your heel is the largest bone in the foot, Robbie? Isn't it a thing of art?" And Rob would nod in agreement, in amazement. That was, until the seventies, when the machines were banned for their high radiation dosage. Rob had placed his small foot in the device countless times, so many that he was probably a prime candidate for cancer. But the machine had been incredible to his young eyes. Funny how his dad had focused on the architecture of the foot, and Rob on something slightly bigger, faintly grander. He'd never thought of it that way before.

He twirled the ice in his glass, took another sip. The scotch was smooth and strong. Thank God Gill had handed over his reservation. People typically booked reservations here months in advance, and it had become a running joke between Lanie and Rob over the years. "If you really loved me, you'd take me to La Lumière," she'd tease every now and then. Rob would counter, "When you've earned it, babe." And she'd rightly smack him.

Except lately he'd been missing his wife. Not the first blush of romance, the excitement over a new e-mail, a new voice mail; he had figured those early butterflies would fade eventually. But he missed the silly things, stuff that no one else in his right mind would find funny but that had thrown them into laughing spasms. He thought back to one night early in their marriage when Lanie had confessed to slight OCD tendencies and said she couldn't sleep with their sliding closet doors open. Rob had left his side slightly ajar, and she asked him to close it before crawling into bed. When he jokingly refused, Lanie wouldn't let him into bed. She made snow angels in the sheets, stretching out her arms and legs, giggling as Rob tried to push his way over. "No way!" she'd screamed. "Not until you close that door!" They were both in hysterics by then, though why it had been so funny at the time, he couldn't really say.

Lanie had won, of course; she had a way of getting what she

wanted. Rob just wished she wanted *him* more these days. Was that selfish? Probably. But how he craved that balance—being a respected colleague at work, a devoted dad, a loving and loved husband. When would it all come?

He took another sip and surveyed the other couples in the dining room. On the rare occasion that they went out these days, Lanie liked to imagine the backstories of the people around them. Rob loved that about her—that she would wonder in the first place—when it never occurred to him to consider what type of day the person in the seat next to him had had. But that was his wife, always wanting to know—and fix—people's problems.

To his right sat a young couple probably on their third or fourth date, the young man working hard to impress the blonde across from him. Every so often he would lean forward to say something too soft to be heard, and his date would giggle, as if on cue. Kitty-corner to Rob's left sat an elderly couple who said little, though what they did say, he could hear clearly since they talked in a tone ten decibels higher than everybody else. At the moment, they were arguing about whether the guy had ordered carrots or potatoes as his side and if he should send back the carrots, as he was certain he'd asked for potatoes. His wife kept shushing him, telling him not to make a scene. Rob exchanged amused glances with a few other diners when the waitress finally brought over a plate of steaming potatoes au gratin, placing it in front of the old man and saying, "Our compliments, Monsieur."

And somewhat disconcertingly, at the table directly to his left sat another man, around his age, sipping a whiskey. When Rob glanced up, the stranger apparently took it as an invitation to conversation.

"Let me guess? Stood up?" Rob laughed and shook his head. He supposed that's what it looked like. "Nah. Waiting for my wife."

"Oh?" The man raised an eyebrow. He was handsome in a traditional kind of way, Rob supposed. Dark hair, thick eyebrows, unusually tan skin for April. "Been there, done that," he added with a wave of his hand.

Rob nodded, uncertain how to respond.

"No thanks. It's the single guy's life for me. No hassle, no needing to be home by a certain time, you know what I'm saying?"

Rob started to commiserate, but the guy cut him off. "Divorced seven years. Much better that way . . ." He paused. "For me, anyway." He took another drink. Then, as if Rob's words had just sunk in, he offered, "Sorry, man. I'm sure you're happily married, taking your wife to a swank place like this. Didn't mean to rain on your parade."

"Not at all," Rob tried. "I've got plenty of friends in your boat," he lied. "So, you've been here before?"

"Once a month, I treat myself. I've got reservations booked for the entire year. Sometimes I bring a date, but usually I'm solo or with my pal, Jim Beam." He tipped his glass, looked out the window thoughtfully. "It's a great place," he gestured to the view, "and you can't beat the food—or the booze."

"Good to know," Rob said, as he spied Lanie walking into the dining room. She looked glowing, radiant. Her hair was swept up in a loose twist at the back and a few stray strands framed her face. She knew Rob had a weakness for eyeliner, and he smiled to see that tonight her eyes were etched in smoky tints of gray. She was wearing a new dress he'd never seen before, a flimsy pink slip-like silhouette with spaghetti straps. He watched as her eyes scanned the room for him. She looked so pretty, smart, and vulnerable all at once. He thought proudly to himself that he would definitely try to pick her up in a bar.

"Your lady?" the guy guessed.

"She's the one," Rob confirmed and stood up to get Lanie's attention.

"Very pretty."

"Thanks." Rob stepped aside to pull out a chair as she walked toward him.

"You made it." He gave her a quick kiss. Her cheek shimmered with a pale pink. "You look amazing."

"Sorry I'm so late," she began. Rob pushed in her chair, then noticed the man at the table next to him, raising his glass.

"To true love," he said with a wink and took a swallow.

"Thanks, man," Rob tried, then sat down opposite Lanie, his back to the congenial stranger.

Lanie raised an eyebrow. "A friend?"

"New friend," Rob explained with a roll of his eyes.

"Ah."

"I would have ordered you a drink but I wasn't sure what you'd like . . ." But Lanie had already caught the waitress's attention.

"Hi, there. Can I have a glass of Merlot, please?" There was something both friendly and matter-of-fact about the way his wife ordered, and he found it oddly alluring.

"Of course." Their waitress turned on her heel perkily, as if she'd been waiting all night for his wife to arrive.

"Why is it that you always end up with the hot waitress when you're waiting alone?" Lanie asked, unfolding her napkin in her lap.

"Do I? Is she?" He genuinely hadn't noticed, a circumstance that, his wife was right, would have usually warranted his attention. "Come *on*. Don't pretend you didn't notice."

"Honestly, I didn't. It's our anniversary. I have eyes only for you."

It was Lanie's turn to roll her eyes.

"Anyway, it took a lot longer than I thought to get home and changed and get Benjamin ready. He was a little bit of a pill tonight. I hope he's okay for Ellen."

"Are you kidding me?" Rob laughed. "He loves it when his aunt spoils him. I'll bet he wishes we'd go out more often."

Lanie sighed, smiled. "You're probably right. It is nice to be out like real adults, isn't it?" She took in the view from their table for the first time. "This place is beautiful. No wonder it costs an arm and a leg."

He nodded and took her hand, squeezing it tightly just as the waitress delivered Lanie's drink, a fresh scotch for him beside it.

She smiled as she lifted the huge wine tumbler from the tray, and he saw now that his wife wasn't far off: their waitress was a bit of a looker. Tall, blond, bleached-white teeth. He sensed Lanie watching him.

"See? I told you so." She hit his knee under the table as their waitress walked away.

"She's not that special." He grinned.

"Nice try." She twirled the wine in her glass and took a sip. "Mmm . . . now *that's* a French wine."

"I wish I knew what that meant."

"Expensive and delicious." She clinked his glass. "Here's to five wonderful years with my honey. May there be many more in our future together."

"Hear, hear," he chimed in.

"God, we sound so cliché."

"Like an old married couple." This made her smile.

How he had ended up with Lanie, he couldn't quite fathom. None of his buddies could make sense of it. She was the whole package: cute, smart, funny, the kind of girl you could bring home to mom—and, as the guys would say, take to a bender. That he'd ended up with her seemed a ringing confirmation that karma did exist in the universe. Meeting Lanie, he liked to think, was his payback for having lost both parents when he was just in high school. In fact, he was certain his parents had played a spiritual hand in the matchmaking. Otherwise how else to explain it?

"Do you ever think that maybe my folks and your folks are up in heaven playing cards together and having the last laugh?" he asked between sips.

"What do you mean?" She raised an eyebrow, smoothed the tablecloth by her plate.

"Like how unlikely it is that we'd ever end up together. It's like they were playing matchmaker up above, and my dad probably said to yours, 'Hey, Stan, your daughter's a real looker. Mind if I match her up with my loser son?'"

This made Lanie laugh, and it made Rob smile. Lately, she seemed so stressed out.

"Not bad. But my guess is that our *moms* would have played matchmaker. Harriet McClarety would not let her daughter marry just any old guy."

Rob grinned at the thought. He wished his parents could have met Lanie, wished he could have met Lanie's folks. He knew his mom and dad would have been instantly charmed. It made him sad to think that they'd never be able to bring Benjamin to a big Thanksgiving dinner, all the grandparents gathered around the dining room table, the homemade place cards and centerpiece set out on the white table cloth.

It didn't feel like five years since they'd taken off for Paris for their honeymoon, Lanie sick all the way, mumbling, "Welcome to married life." Thankfully, things had taken a turn for the better once they landed, the vaulted expanse of Notre Dame as breathtaking as promised, the sweep of the Louvre more awe-inspiring than they'd imagined. They'd found a quaint bistro along the Seine one night, not so unlike La Lumière, with a droll French waiter who teased Lanie with her high school French. When she passed on the appetizer but not the dessert, the waiter joked with her: "*La soupe, non, mais la crepe, oui?*" And they had laughed over Lanie's sweet tooth, not to be denied even after an enormous French meal.

Now Rob tipped back in his chair, feeling like a giddy schoolboy. Their meal had arrived, coq au vin for Lanie, filet mignon for him, succulent and rare. Their waitress was doing a fine job of keeping their glasses filled. He took it all in. He and Lanie were due a meal like this, a real date night at last. How tired he'd been of feeling as if, when he got home, Lanie turned off and he turned on. She'd throw in a load of laundry, take a bath, pick up the toys with Rob home to watch Benjamin. He didn't get a lot of time with the baby, so he didn't mind the hour he had with him before Lanie swept him up again to rock him to sleep. In fact, he kind of loved the down time. It reminded him of why he was working at a job he didn't necessarily love. It reminded him of what was important; sometimes, he'd swear he could feel his heart and Benjamin's beating in unison. He just wished that Lanie wanted to do more than go to sleep at nine o'clock. If the gods were willing, tonight would promise more than a delicious dinner.

Lanie set down her knife and fork on the edge of her plate, as if readying for an announcement, and wiped a bit of sauce from her chin. She leaned in to grab his hand. "I love you so much. You know that, right?" He could feel her breath on his cheek.

Unlike a lot of other people he knew, his wife made a good drunk. He remembered being impressed by this fact when he first met her. He'd once heard that alcohol brought out a person's true colors, and for Lanie, the colors were all vibrant. When she'd had one too many, her tough lawyer façade slipped away to reveal the sweet Midwestern girl he'd fallen in love with. Like tonight, her words might slur a bit, her eyes turn a little glassy, and she might, as she was now, start caressing his knee under the table, as if the floodgates had opened to drown the drought of touch in their relationship over the past months.

"I love you, too, babe," he grabbed at her hand before it reached indiscreet places.

"And we're okay, right? You and me?"

He swallowed his steak. "Of course, we're okay. Aren't we? Why do you ask?"

She twirled her napkin in her hands, shook her head. "Oh, it's nothing. I just know it's hard when there's a baby in the house. And, I know things have been a little crazy at work lately."

"Yeah, but that's called living, right?"

"I think so," said Lanie. "At least I hope so."

"That wine's going straight to your head."

"I know. I can't remember the last time I've been this drunk!" She said it loudly, and a few people turned to look. Rob smiled. Lanie remained blissfully unaware.

"So, I have to tell you something . . . a secret," she began. She leaned over.

"Really?" He waited. He hoped to hell it was something dirty, maybe something about what she was wearing underneath her dress.

"I love you so much, but . . ." She paused.

"But?" What was she trying to tell him? There were no *buts* allowed in this conversation.

"But I love Benjamin even more. I didn't think it was possible to love someone more than I love you. Isn't it amazing?"

He stopped a beat. He hadn't seen that coming. He was relieved, though, that the conversation hadn't gone in an entirely different direction—the "I-love-you-but-I-need-a-break" direction.

"I mean couldn't you just eat him up, he's so lovable!"

"Sure, honey. He's amazing." He signaled to their waitress to bring the check. It was time to get Lanie home, before she passed out. Of course, he meant it. He loved Benjamin with all his heart. Especially after everything the little guy had been through, hell, after everything they'd all been through together. He had never thought of their family as a love sweepstakes, though, one person being more deserving of love than another. He loved Benjamin completely, but differently from the way he loved Lanie. It wasn't the same; the two weren't comparable in his mind.

"Honey?"

"Yes?" He was trying to focus on the arithmetic of the bill in front of him, making sure he left the waitress a generous tip. The food, the service, the view, the drinks, everything had been spectacular, as advertised.

"I don't want to die."

"Lanie, for God's sake. Don't be so morbid. You're not going to die."

"Someday I am. But I mean now. I really, *really* don't want to die. I want to be around for Benjamin. I can't imagine ever leaving him." When Rob looked up, her face was turned toward the window. "I don't know how my mother ever let us go. She made it seem like it could be okay, that it wouldn't be the worst possible thing for a mother to die before her children. But it is. It would be."

Her voice caught, and Rob was unnerved as tears began to run down her cheeks.

"Honey, stop this. You've had too much to drink. Everything's fine, just fine. Benjamin's all right; you're okay; I'm okay. Don't worry. Don't do this to yourself, especially on our anniversary night." He slid his chair over and put his arm around her, squeezed her hard.

She wiped the tears away with the back of her hand, sniffled. "I'm sorry. I don't know what's come over me." She laughed and pointed at her empty glass. "Well, except that, of course."

"Hon, it's all good."

She nodded, blew her nose into her napkin. "Look at me. I'm a mess." She sniffed and wiped at her eyes, black mascara smudges streaking underneath.

"You look pretty cute, actually." He kissed the top of her head.

"Forgive me for being so maudlin?"

He nodded. "Of course. Let's get you home, okay?"

She nodded. "See, this is what happens when you take me out in public," she joked. He looked around the nearly empty restaurant. Only one other couple, deep in conversation at the far side of the room, remained. Their bachelor neighbor had long since left.

He helped Lanie pull her wrap around her shoulders and grabbed her purse off the back of her chair, nodding a thank you to their waitress on the way out. He put his hand on the small of his wife's back and guided her to the car.

"Watch your step," he cautioned as she tried to navigate the rocky parking lot that was rustic but not very practical after a few drinks. He realized with some surprise that he wasn't exactly smooth on his feet either. They laughed as they both almost tumbled, hanging on to each other for balance.

"Are you okay to drive?" Lanie asked.

"Of course. I only had a few."

"Sure?"

"Absolutely." He opened the car door for her and kept his arm around her while she slipped into the seat. She buckled herself in, laughing, saying, "I can buckle myself, you know."

He went around to his side, slipped into the supple leather seat, clipped his seatbelt, and turned on the engine. He gave it a few seconds to warm up in the cool night air, and pushed the buttons on the radio, looking for something a little softer than sports radio for the ride home. Before pulling out, he turned and said, "Happy anniversary, honey."

But when he leaned over to kiss his wife, she'd already fallen asleep.

5

"Notion for the day: If everyone had *kringle* for breakfast,
the world would be a happier place."
—*The Book of Kringle*

Before Henry came over for supper, Ellen set the table with the wedding china she'd never had the heart to give away. She rinsed the ivory plates in the sink, admiring the way the delicate pink flowers twirled around the borders. She had always loved the pattern, if not the marriage it represented. Next to the plates she laid a full set of silverware and couldn't recall the last time she'd had to use it. It seemed lately she needed only a spare spoon for her tea, an extra fork for a rare treat when Lanie stopped by. Had it really been that long since she'd had anything close to a date?

She wiped the edges of two wine glasses that had been languishing in her top cupboard and gently set them on the placemats. She wondered if Henry would prefer beer, but no matter, she didn't have it. Wine would have to do.

She had warned him that her culinary expertise stopped at the bakery door, but Henry laughed and said anything other than franks and beans would be a cut above what he was accustomed to.

So she'd decided to go with something easy, penne pasta and a salad. While she contemplated making her own sauce, she bet in the end that Henry wouldn't notice if she used a store-bought brand. To it she added red peppers, celery, a touch of onion, and a sprinkle of oregano. It certainly smelled delicious. She hoped it would simulate the homemade thing.

She wondered if Gretchen, the woman her Fowler's first edition was inscribed to, had cooked pasta for Anthony. Surely, her sauce would have been the authentic stuff—no Ragu or Prego for her suitor. Then again, theirs had probably been a clandestine affair, of the Romeo and Juliet variety. *What was the equivalent of a pool boy in the early 1900s?* she wondered. Anthony would have been intimidated by Gretchen's wealth and intellect, and short of writing his own prose, he would have given her the book. The stories that must lurk between its pages! She was sure Gretchen didn't have to deal with an immature ex-husband who wanted her back.

When the doorbell rang, Ellen quickly straightened the pillows on the couch and took one last look at herself in the entryway mirror. Her powder blue cashmere sweater (her only cashmere) seemed tasteful enough. Not overtly revealing and yet cut enough at the neckline to suggest a hint of something underneath. She'd pulled out her favorite jeans last night, retired in her bottom drawer for months, and was secretly delighted to see that she could still slide them over her hips. And heels. Lanie had insisted she wear some kind of heels, dropping off multiple strappy sandals for her to choose from.

"It's too cold for sandals," she'd protested, but Lanie said, "It's never too cold for a strappy sandal with jeans. Just like it's never too cold for something else."

"Oh please," Ellen had rolled her eyes, but she chose the black two-inch-heeled sandals for good measure. Lanie smiled triumphantly.

Now when she opened the door she felt the rewards of her sister's influence immediately. Henry stood on the front stoop, looking slightly stunned to see her in something other than an apron. She was happy to see that he was dressed in a dapper red golf shirt and faded jeans with a belt that had small boats sailing across it. He held out a bottle of wine and flowers.

"Ellen," he said and stepped forward, her name lingering in the air. "For you." He handed her the bouquet of soft pink tulips and the wine. "I hope white is okay."

She was confused for a moment. "Oh, the wine, yes, perfect. Come on in." She took the gifts from him. "And the flowers are absolutely beautiful, Henry. Thank you."

"Flowers are words which even a baby can understand. That's Bishop Arthur Cleveland Coxe," he said when she raised an eyebrow. He stepped into the foyer and noticed the wide staircase winding around at the back. "Nice place."

"Thank you." She gestured for him to follow her down the foyer to the living room.

Ellen loved the house's wide, open spaces. It was an old Victorian that had been up for foreclosure and she'd gotten it for a song, shortly after she and Max had parted ways. She'd seen it through a lover's eyes, imagining what could be, how with a little paint it could become the house she'd always dreamed of. She'd hung a swing on the wide wraparound porch, painted the rooms in muted earth tones, and polished the ornate wooden banister on the staircase till it gleamed in the sun from the skylight above.

She watched now as Henry surveyed the living room, a landscape of couches and bookcases with their titles tucked in sideways. It was decorated in neutral tones, tans and whites, in her attempt to create a reading room feel. When she looked at it through Henry's eyes, though, she noticed the tan corduroy couch looked a bit dreary, its antimacassars worn through, and her bookshelves, a messy assemblage, as if the titles had been stuffed in at all angles instead of placed there with great care and thought.

"Very Ellen-like," he pronounced. "Comfy and classy."

She couldn't help but laugh. "Well, I try. I'm sure if Laura Lowry saw it, she'd have a thing or two to say." Laura Lowry was the bigshot realtor in town whom Ellen couldn't bear. The woman, who

60

had a flair for gossip, never had anything nice to say. Ellen got an earful every time Laura stopped by the kringle shop, declaring her kringles "the best pastries ever." But Ellen suspected she was full of it, and wondered what Laura said about her behind her back since, as far as she could tell, Laura shot a barbed dart at anyone she knew.

Henry laughed immediately and easily, his eyes crinkling at the sides. "Yes, she would, wouldn't she? She'd probably load up the moving truck herself and remodel the whole place in hot pink batik pillows before she put it on the market." Ellen was glad to see he shared her disdain.

"So, have a seat and make yourself at home. I'll pour us some glasses."

She went into the kitchen, put the flowers in a vase, and dug through her top drawer for the bottle opener. Where had the darned thing gone to? If that wasn't a sign she'd been single too long, she didn't know what was. As she poured the wine, nicely chilled, into the glasses, she noticed that her hands were shaking.

Henry was flipping through her collection of Flannery O'Connor stories when she came back into the living room. "'A Good Man Is Hard to Find.' One of my favorites." He turned to her now, set the book on the table.

"Really?" Ellen couldn't hide her surprise.

"What? You think I don't read? My wife was a Southerner, don't forget. She loved Miss O'Connor."

Ellen wasn't sure if she should feel flattered, impressed, or worried by that information. She simply said, "She's one of my favorites, too. Doesn't beat around the bush."

"No, she sure doesn't. Reminds me of someone else." He grinned.

"How funny." Ellen took a sip of wine and smiled. She actually enjoyed having a man in her house again. It was . . . unanticipated.

When she heard the lid on the sauce pot start to rattle, she excused herself and hurried into the kitchen. Henry followed behind. Once she'd rescued the pot from the stove, she caught him eyeing her tattered copy of *The Book of Kringle,* which sat open on her cookbook stand.

"What's this?" he asked.

"Ah, the whole inspiration behind my little store." She dabbed at the spilled sauce on the stove, still hot to the touch.

"No kidding?"

"It was my mother's originally. I rediscovered it in the attic one day when I was feeling lonely and it was like a lightbulb went off."

"Wow. Isn't that something? Why are Montgomery and Phoenix underlined next to these contributors' names?" He pointed to the highlighter marks, pink and yellow, on a recipe for apricot kringle that had been submitted by readers from those cities.

"Oh, that." She could feel herself blushing. "I was just paging through it for some new recipes the other day, and I decided to try and crack the riddle at the end of the book. I've yet to solve it but when I do, you'll be the first to know. Something about a secret ingredient that will make my kringles to die for."

The truth was, she'd been puzzling over it, on and off, for more than a few weeks now. The riddle went like this: *"Look back, fair reader, and reflect on what you've read / A secret ingredient hides in its stead / For if you like capitals first and seven, you'll quickly see / That two teaspoonsful make all the difference in your* kringle *and tea."*

She knew decoding it had something to do with the state capitals peppered throughout the book's pages. People from all across the country had submitted their favorite kringle recipes, with their hometowns listed after their names: Montgomery, Alabama; Phoenix, Arizona; Juneau, Alaska. Originally, Ellen thought the riddle must have something to do with capital cities from the states beginning with A: *Alabama, Arizona, Alaska.* Perhaps the first seven "A" state capitals? But closer inspection revealed a recipe submitted by a chef from Columbus, Ohio. What on earth was Columbus, Ohio, doing in the string of "A" capitals she'd found mentioned thus far? She hadn't the foggiest.

"But they already are," Henry said. "Your kringles . . . To die for."

It had been a long while since anyone had so much as cast a glance her way, let alone compliment her outright. Ellen thought she could get used to it.

"Stop it," she said instead. "Now, go sit down."

He went to take a seat at the long farmer's table in the dining room, while Ellen watched from the kitchen, noticing how he ran his hand gently over the wood. "Maple, right?" he called out.

"Right! I forgot I have a horticulturist in my house," she said and scooped the pasta into huge bowls. "Or is it botanist?"

"Horticulturist," he confirmed. She carried everything out to the table.

She had been in Henry's store a few times over the years. Each visit reminded her of walking into a field of wildflowers. The fragrant smells jumped out at her, a honeysuckle here, a planter of sweet peas there. And always, tucked in between the rows, was Henry, bent over a plant, caressing its leaves, plucking a stray bloom. He reminded her of Toad in the childhood *Frog and Toad* stories, where Toad sang to his plants and played the violin, saying "Now plants, start growing!" She figured it took a man with a good heart to pour his soul into raising things that didn't give a person the satisfaction of a response.

When she told him this now, sitting down across from him, he smiled and said, "But they *do* talk."

The pasta steamed up from their bowls.

For a moment, she thought she'd found herself another man who'd gone off the deep end, too late to rescue. She raised her eyebrows as she reached for the salad tongs and served Henry, then herself.

"Plants talk to you with their flowers, the way they either dance or wilt, and with their leaves, if they're upturned toward the light or hiding in the dark."

"Oh." She was pleased now. The man was a poet, not a nut.

Henry took what seemed like an overly cautious bite.

"So, what do you think? Do you like the sauce?"

He swallowed, seemed to think for a second. "It's rambunctious."

"Rambunctious? Is that good or bad?"

"You decide," he said with a wink, and she noticed for the first time that his eyes weren't brown, but more of a soft hazel.

"I'm going to take that as a compliment."

They discussed books, the wonder of getting lost in a story. Henry, it seemed, liked a good tale just as much as she did.

"Don't you love that smell when you first crack open a brand new book?" he asked.

"Yes! Or, just the feel of the pages, the weight and heft of a novel in your hands," Ellen added.

Henry nodded in agreement. "It almost casts a spell over you, doesn't it?"

When she pressed him on some of his favorites, she was surprised they were mostly classics: *Moby Dick*; *To Kill A Mockingbird*; *War and Peace*, along with some Wendell Berry and Henry David Thoreau thrown in.

Another glass of wine later, the talk turned to the bakery and all the folks who came in; Henry confessed that work wasn't what it used to be for him. He'd inherited the store from his dad, who'd inherited it from his father.

"I never thought I'd run a nursery, but after working a few summers, I got hooked despite myself," he explained between bites. "Before I knew it, I was taking horticulture classes at the extension school and advising my dad on the latest in seed hybrids. These days it's all about organic gardening." He paused. "Never did get my diploma, though. Guess I have more of what you'd call street smarts." He smiled at Ellen. "Or garden smarts."

"There's nothing wrong with that." She took a sip of wine, though she caught herself wondering if she really believed that. Still, the man loved books. How dumb could he be?

"To be honest, I've been feeling a little stuck lately. Do you ever feel that way at the store, like you just keeping doing the same old thing over and over?"

Ellen thought for a moment. "Sometimes. But then I try to imagine that it's all new. That tomorrow is my first day of work. I'll move the tables around to give it a new look. Or, I'll challenge myself to something silly, like say one nice thing to every customer today." She took another bite of the sauce, proud of her own cleverness on two glasses of wine no less.

"I like that." He nodded, looking off at the dining room window, as if imagining Ellen's advice taking flight. "Kind of like when you trick yourself into believing that everything around you is great. The power of positive thinking, right?"

"I'm not sure about that." Ellen paused. "That positive thinking talk always seemed suspect to me. But I don't see anything wrong with giving yourself a fresh start in your mind's eye."

Henry took a sip of wine, rubbed his lips together. "Hmm . . . I told myself I'd make a fresh start at Charlotte's one-year anniversary, but it was tougher than I thought." His finger traced a pattern in the wood grain. She hadn't noticed his large, weathered hands before, the skin tanned, even in early spring. Ellen was tempted to reach out and grab one. "The anniversary of her death, I mean."

"Oh Henry," she offered. "I'm so sorry. I read about it in the papers, of course, but I'm sorry that I never knew your wife. I'm sure she was amazing."

He nodded. "The thing is, you think you're over someone and then you find out you're really not, you know?" He looked beseechingly into her eyes, and she was darned if she didn't think he was looking straight into her heart. Had someone told him about Max's e-mail?

"I guess so," she said instead.

"Charlotte was one of a kind. She was smart and funny and gracious, all rolled into one. She never quite lost her Southern drawl, even though she'd been here since college. I loved that about her."

"I'll bet."

"And that Southern sense of humor. Didn't take things quite so seriously as we Midwesterners do."

"Well, that's a virtue."

"I used to tease her that she was my Southern belle."

"That's so sweet." But Ellen was trying to figure out how to change the direction of the conversation. She really didn't care to spend the rest of the evening talking about Henry's dead wife.

She got up to clear the plates.

"Here, let me help you with that." He pushed back his chair.

"No, you stay. I'll be right back."

The evening was going better than expected, the talk of Charlotte aside, but then, what *had* she expected? Ellen couldn't remember through the haze of wine. True, she was nicely dressed, but that was more for her own vanity than for Henry's sake. Or was it?

She sighed to herself then grinned to think she was like a nervous teenager right here in her own grown-up kitchen. She squeezed the amber beads of dish soap into the sink and watched as the basin filled with steaming water, then slid the plates in gently. Frankly, she was just happy for Henry's company. Lanie had teased her that maybe she'd get lucky tonight, but Ellen smiled at how ridiculous the thought was. Henry was still in mourning. Like her, he was hungry for company, for conversation.

She dried her hands on the kitchen towel, then grabbed the bottle of wine off the counter and walked back into the dining room. "Some more?" she asked, as she started to tip the bottle over his glass.

Henry looked up and smiled.

"Yes, please. I think I will."

6

"The mother's day is not an eight-hour day.
It is a twenty-four-hour day. She is never free.
No wonder she is tired and impatient sometimes."
—*Talks to Mothers* (1920)

Lanie arrived late to work, where stacks of paper were spilling off her desk. She checked her BlackBerry and groaned to see her schedule as she scrolled down. This week alone she had two depositions, a discovery due, and a motion to file for a guardian ad litem for a foster child. There was always an uptick in cases in the springtime; her secret theory was that the fresh air finally gave some very unhappy women the confidence to imagine a better life without their cheating or otherwise delinquent husbands. She asked Hannah to cancel lunch with a client on Wednesday; it was her turn to bring peanut-free, gluten-free treats to Benjamin's day care for a snack. Considering most of the kids didn't have a full set of teeth yet, her options were even more limited. *Did applesauce count?* she wondered. There simply weren't enough hours in the day to do her job well and be a loving mom and wife all at once.

Lately she'd been thinking maybe she should take some time off from the law, slow down. But she knew that she and Rob lived more or less from paycheck to paycheck. Cutting her monthly income would likely send their lifestyle into a tailspin. Not that they were living wealthy lives in a McMansion. Far from it. But they did own two cars and a four-bedroom home in a good neighborhood. They took a few vacations during the year; they paid their bills and put food on the table. It was the American dream, right?

Her newbie drive to help all the unhappy divorcing wives of Madison was wavering though. She could feel it like a palpable lack of vitamin D in her diet; six years in and she was already weary, as much as she hated to admit it. And, though she'd never say it aloud, she was secretly starting to worry that she might become one of *them*. She could feel herself growing resentful of Rob's late nights at the office, the weekends spent away from her and Benjamin. As nice as their anniversary night out had been, it was just that: one night of abandon, then back to the same old drill. Both of them being stretched to the limit so they could have everything they'd ever wanted. What happened if everything they wanted turned out not to be enough?

She took out the Sullivan file, papers and receipts spilling out. Hadn't she asked the intern to organize all of this last week? It looked barely touched. Receipts for car repairs were tucked into the "Groceries" file, worn slips for mortgages filed under "General." If she was going to help Mrs. Sullivan get more than her fair share from her wealthy accountant husband, Lanie needed to have an insanely organized case.

The shabby record-keeping habits of her more affluent clients often surprised her. Supposedly being a lady of leisure meant you were excused from such petty details, but Lanie couldn't fathom such disorganization. Each month, money in and money out was ticked off in her checkbook. Her desk at home was filled with color-coded folders for house expenses, vacations, car expenses, child care, entertainment, and groceries. That's how she knew that she and Rob were living precisely at their means; one tip in either direction and their lives would be markedly different.

She sighed as she began the tedious work of organizing the file.

She should really just hand the file back to the intern and insist she start over, but there was no time. The deposition with Steve Sullivan was in three days, and she had to know exactly how much money his soon-to-be ex-wife needed each month to continue the lifestyle she was accustomed to. The irony of fighting for women who already had so much wasn't lost on Lanie. In her pro bono cases, her clients were typically looking for nominal child support payments, or in the worst-case scenarios, a restraining order to make sure their creepy ex-husbands didn't step foot within one hundred yards of them.

But the common thread that tied all her clients together (her sister included), no matter their stature or financial standing, was an aura of sadness. She watched, a witness to their hurt, as they sat on her couch and ripped tissues, confiding their stories, nursing wounds of betrayal, anger, exasperation. It was as if they were surprised to see their lives become the opposite of what they'd imagined. Sometimes she felt she was billing by the hour to be a therapist as much as a litigator.

She was reading a receipt for a hair salon visit for a whopping three hundred and fifty dollars when Hannah, her assistant, stepped in.

"Special delivery for a Ms. Lanie Taylor." In her hands was an enormous bouquet of yellow spring tulips. "You must have done something right or else Rob's in the doghouse."

"It's May first—our anniversary," she explained, taking the vase and inhaling the sweet scent. She felt a slight pang that she'd just been feeling resentful of all his time at the office. He'd already left for work when she woke up this morning.

"Happy anniversary! How many years?"

"Can it already be five?"

Lanie noticed a small envelope attached to the front of the vase. She pulled out the note and read, "For Lanie, my X and my O, who makes every day a gift. All my love, Rob."

"So sweet. I always said that Rob is a romantic guy." Hannah pointed to a small card that fluttered to the ground. "What's that?"

Lanie picked it up and read: "Ooh, it's a certificate for Spa

Sensations. Massage, facials, body wraps, whatever I want. That's the place I was telling Rob about last week. I guess he does listen from time to time," she joked. "Ellen mentioned it to me. Have you ever been?"

"No, but I hear it's supposed to be great. When are you going?"

Lanie flipped over the card. "There's no date here. Guess whenever I want . . . once life settles down."

Hannah smirked.

"What?"

"The whole point of a spa retreat is that you *get away* from the rat race for a while. Life won't settle down for about, oh, another seventeen years."

"Thanks for the reminder." Lanie sighed. "Like I needed it."

But she knew Hannah was right. She wasn't juggling motherhood and a sixty-hour workweek as gracefully as she'd hoped. "You're right, of course," she said now. "I'd like to think I'm the Jackie O. of my generation, hobnobbing with the rich and famous, raising a beautiful child, while my husband saves the world and I look glamorous."

"Don't forget Jackie had a nanny she hid from the press."

"She did?"

"You bet. Not to mention a philandering husband."

"Oh, right."

"And if anyone should know that the façade isn't always what it seems, it's you," Hannah said matter-of-factly.

When Lanie raised an eyebrow, she quickly added, "Because of the clients you work with, of course."

Lanie admired Hannah's directness; she found it worked to her advantage when it came to evaluating clients, getting things done. Hannah was probably fifty pounds overweight, but again, Lanie found that to be a plus. One look at her assistant and you knew she meant business. Not to mention she was a wizard of efficiency. But every so often, Lanie bristled at her young assistant's matter-of-factness, the divining rod she seemed to wield for the personal lives of those around her. Lanie didn't need advice from a twenty-eight-year-old on her personal life right now, thank you very much. She turned her back, setting the vase of flowers on her desk.

"Anyway, I hope you're leaving early to share a nice dinner with your husband."

"Not exactly," Lanie started, "but before you criticize, it just so happens that Rob and I went out for a lovely dinner at La Lumière last week. A sort of pre-anniversary celebration."

"Wow. I'm impressed. *Very* romantic." Hannah clicked her tongue.

Lanie didn't mention that Rob had lucked out with a last-minute reservation.

"So, can you take the Sullivan file home tonight and try to whip it into shape? I need it for tomorrow and it's a total mess."

"I told Marty that new intern isn't worth a hill of beans," Hannah confirmed.

"How old are you again?" Lanie laughed. "Honestly, sometimes I think you're channeling my mother."

"Glad to help out, and I'll let that comment slide." She picked up the folders and held them close to her chest as she turned in her flats. Sometimes Lanie wished she could sign Hannah up for one of those makeover shows, one that would steer her toward clothes with a waist, shoes with a hint of heel.

She shut the door and returned to her desk. When she tapped in Rob's number on her cell, his voice mail picked up. "Thanks for the flowers, honey. They're gorgeous. Happy anniversary! Love you."

Then she called Ellen.

"What should I get Rob for our anniversary?"

There was a pause. "That's right! May Day! Happy anniversary."

"Rob got me a gift certificate to Spa Sensations. You interested in going?"

"Absolutely." Another pause. "But wouldn't you rather go with your husband? Get a couples' massage or something?"

"Rob doesn't do spas. All that peace and quiet, no sports channel to watch. I'm pretty sure it's his idea of purgatory."

"Then I'm in."

"So, ideas for my husband. Please?" She could hear the whine in her voice. How was it that she could bill a sixty- to seventy-hour workweek and yet not handle her own anniversary?

"How about a kringle in the shape of a heart?"

Lanie laughed. Somehow Ellen always managed to make her feel less stressed. "Try again." She walked over to the window. It was a beautiful spring day, the apple tree just beyond reach sparked with tiny pink buds. "Hey, I meant to ask: How did your dinner go with that Henry guy?"

"What?" Ellen asked, talking to a customer on the other end. "Oh that. I'll fill you in later. Gotta go. Bye."

Lanie hung up the phone and grabbed her wallet. At the very least, she could purchase a heartfelt card for her husband.

After she'd run to the grocery store, she picked up Benjamin early from day care. Hannah was right: it was her anniversary. To hell with work today! When she arrived, Benjamin sat in an ExerSaucer, his attention rapt on another boy who was loudly banging blocks together. The room was littered with colorful toys, and a handful of young women smiled at her.

She loved to sneak up on her little guy and surprise him so that when he turned his head and then looked back, she'd be crouching down beside him. She thought it must be confusing for a baby to have no sense of real time, no sense of when someone was going to meet you at the end of the day. After all, babies didn't wear watches that told them when five o'clock was approaching.

"Hello, lovebug," she whispered now. It always took him a moment to process that a familiar face was in the room, but once he did, he cracked a wide smile and started bouncing like a crazy person in his ExerSaucer. Her heart clapped in her chest. "Did you have a good day in school?"

She pulled him from the ExerSaucer, causing the cushion seat to stick up like a red umbrella, and hugged him hard. Benjamin kicked his feet. His T-shirt was splattered with remnants of his lunch of squash and sweet potato; his chin glistened with drool.

He held his head back and looked at her, as if to get a better view and be sure it was his momma. Then he opened his mouth wide and planted a big, sloppy kiss on her cheek, baby-style. It was her new favorite thing in life.

"You are *such* a lovebug." She gave him another squeeze.

She gathered up his lunchbox and bottles and they said bye-bye to the staff. When they stepped outside, Benjamin squinted in the sun, as if he'd been holed up in a cave all day. Lanie broke into her usual routine of whispering in his ear, "We're busting out. Ready, buddy? We're busting out of school!" And he giggled with a great conspiratorial laugh, the best laugh of any baby, ever.

She had once joked with Rob that their child possessed a sixth sense, privy to their every thought. When Benjamin had been home only a few nights and woke up crying mad, she discovered he'd wet through his onesie. It was the middle of the night, she was half-asleep, Rob was still snoring in bed, and she struggled to get the soaking garment over the baby's head in the nursery's dim light. After she got the diaper off and a fresh one on, she looked into his big eyes, staring at her knowingly, as if to say, "The jig is up, lady. I know you don't have a clue."

She talked to him, saying, "We're going to do this together, okay? You help mommy figure out how to get this fresh onesie over your head, and then she'll sing you a pretty lullaby, okay?"

Benjamin stared at her, his bottom lip starting to quiver, gearing up for full-throttle hollering. She cupped his head, quickly stretching the shirt over. It got stuck halfway, the baby screaming, but eventually she got the thing on, the tiny snaps at the bottom fastened. Only after she'd picked him up and rubbed his back, cooing to him that all was right with the world, did she realize she'd forgotten to use the wipes or the diaper cream.

As she sang "Little hands and little feet, little nose and little toes" that night, she breathed his scent in deep and hugged him tight till he surprised her with a big football player's belch that made her laugh. Then she watched in awe, his head cradled in her elbow, as he slowly let his lids close under long, dark lashes, soft little breaths emanating from his parted baby lips. Perfection.

She let herself and Benjamin into the house. She needed to slow down, she could hear her mother's voice inside her head: "You're doing too much; take your time; breathe." Harriet McClarety would scold her for not taking a moment to appreciate what was wonderful about the here and now. "Lanie, you live for the forest, not the trees," she'd told her young daughter once, and Lanie, only six, hadn't understood what she meant at the time. Of course, now she knew.

Tonight she would savor the trees. She would cook her husband a mouth-watering dinner, a rare treat.

After she'd unpacked the chicken, rice, carrots, ginger, and broccoli, she poured herself a glass of wine and carried Benjamin into the living room, a sea of toys. Lately he was fascinated by the way things came together, putting the lid on a jar, taking it off again. He could do this a hundred times and never tire of it. Eventually, though, he crawled across the living room to the bay window, where the late afternoon light fell in slats across the window seat. The baby pulled himself up, holding on to the seat's edge with one hand. He grabbed at the streaks of sunlight in the air, as if they were something to catch and bottle up. Each time his hand came up empty he looked surprised, opening and closing his fingers, searching for where the beams could have disappeared.

"It's magic," she explained in her best surprised voice. "Catch the sun, baby. You can do it."

He tried again, then shaped his lips into an O and made a noise that reminded her of Al Pacino in *Scent of a Woman*. It was a big "Oooh-ahh!" that sounded as if he'd joined the baby mafia, this its clarion call.

She took the imaginary beam from his open hand, his fat fingers splayed wide.

"Thank you, baby. I've been looking for that sunlight all day."

Benjamin beamed with pride. She wanted so much for this child; she would give him the sun if she could.

"Come here now. Be careful." She grabbed him under the arms and carried him, his legs kicking all the way, to the pile of blocks on the living room floor. Instead of playing, though, he pulled himself up on a nearby walker with an electronic voice that spewed forth jingles like, "Keep going! Nice job! Don't stop now!" It reminded her of a bad aerobics instructor. Benjamin, on the other hand, seemed charmed by the woman's singsong voice. He pushed the yellow contraption forward as he lifted up each foot, pointing his toes like a little ballerina, before placing the foot gently down before him.

"You've got to start somewhere, don't you?" she asked as she followed behind him, crossing the living room rug.

"Ba," said Benjamin.

Here was her anniversary present, taking baby steps before her. *Picking up Benjamin early from day care. A husband who sends flowers on our anniversary. Catching the sun.* Three good things. Her mother had always told them to count three goods things at the end of every day. "You can always find three," she would say, "and if you can't, you're not looking." Lanie had plenty of time, she reminded herself. Plenty of time to enjoy with her little man before she had to get dinner going, get case files read.

She smiled as she wondered how many baby miles they'd walk before the sun slipped away and her husband walked through the door, the scent of homemade cooking greeting him for the first time in weeks.

7

"The physician can bury his mistakes, but the architect
can only advise his clients to plant vines."
—Frank Lloyd Wright

As many times as he replayed it in his mind, he didn't see how he
was guilty. Of anything. With anyone. Rob was in love with his
wife, totally whipped, as his friends liked to say. He'd sent Lanie an
avalanche of tulips on their anniversary, taken her to La Lumière.
Things were good. Sure, she told him she loved his son more than
him, but so what? That was natural. And if he had a stray eye every
now and then, that was just the way the male species was wired.
It was no crime to look, he told himself. No crime if an attractive
woman happened to walk into the room in a slightly revealing
blouse, a hint of lace showing underneath, and he looked twice.
And, if that woman happened to be someone he was working with,
he couldn't be blamed, could he?

Rob was working late again, and it was all he could do to keep his
eyes open. His desk was littered with coffee cups and soda cans. He
had consumed enough caffeine to fuel an entire little league team
for at least one week. He hoped Lanie would forgive him. He'd
been late for the dinner she'd cooked on their anniversary night.
And now, here he was again, two weeks later, pulling the same crap.

Or rather, Eli was pulling the same crap. Rob had lost track of how many times he'd redrawn the west wing for the art institute, trying to devise a layout that would suit both Eli's and his own sensibility. He refused to be a sell-out; at the same time, he didn't want to be a martyr.

He stared at the plans that lay spread over his desk. Everything was beginning to look the same—uninspired, each new draft bereft of any sense of style that would set it apart. Going into it, he'd known this would be the toughest part to design; the guy who'd ponied up the money for it had stipulated that this wing be for and by children. That meant plenty of room for interactive displays, for art that wouldn't necessarily be framed or behind glass like that in the rest of the museum. Rob had originally imagined the rooms unfolding like a train with connecting cars, each car with its own theme. But Eli wasn't buying it, thought the whole idea was hokey. If he took a few steps back, Rob supposed Eli was right; he was planning a wing with his son in mind, something that would appeal to toddlers. Did five-year-olds care about choo-choo trains? Perhaps. But eleven- and twelve-year-olds? Probably not. Still, it irked Rob to have to take pointers from Eli, who didn't even have kids.

"I've got eight nieces and nephews," Eli began, when he'd weighed in on yet another conference call last week. "I think I know what would appeal to them."

Rob hated his snippy, know-it-all tone. But it became clear that Walter Greenough didn't want to step into their foursquare.

"You fellas figure it out. I'm sure it will be spectacular."

When Rob reminded Eli that Madison already had a children's museum and they couldn't possibly compete with it, Eli replied with a quick "*Pfft.*" As if he'd thought of it months ago.

"What we want is something classy that will stand on its own, a place that will be a wonderful home for children's artwork for years to come—paintings, drawings, sculpture—but that will be hip enough to appeal to today's Internet-savvy kid. We need more electronic-driven exhibits, more interactive displays, that kind of thing."

As if he were the wizard of hip. Rob heard Walter nodding on the other end. "Mmm hmm."

"Geez, my understanding, Eli, was that the museum's board of directors will figure out those details. We're just supposed to provide the *space*. Are you telling me we need to do more?" Rob felt his face turning red. If Eli was going to play the prick here, he could play the bigger prick.

"Of course not. No one's implying we do the museum's work. But we have to give them a space that will make a good home for those kinds of things."

"All right, all right. Let me go back to the drawing board," Rob offered, wanting the conversation to be over, unable to disguise his annoyance. "I'll see what I can get you. But it will be at least a week."

"Rob, why don't you bring Samantha in on the job," Walter offered at the end of the call, his one piece of constructive advice, as far as Rob was concerned. Samantha was an associate architect in her late twenties; she'd no doubt have something to offer on the project. She was, after all, closer in age to their potential viewers than any of them were.

And, in fact, Samantha had proved a huge help in the last week— tweaking Rob's ideas, diplomatically incorporating Eli's without Rob having to deal with the man directly. It was nice, he had to admit, to have a go-between. It was their first project together, and Rob had been impressed. The girl had a sense of humor, thank God, something Eli sorely lacked. She was the one who had suggested going with a more traditional layout but sticking with Rob's ideas to give each room its own thematic architectural style.

More brainstorming had led to one area that would feature a mosaic of children's artwork from the city's schools, glazed into the wall's ceramic tiles. Another would feature a wall with stenciled quotes from famous artists and leaders meant to inspire kids' creativity. And, in a nod to Eli, there would be a room dedicated to "interactive art," whatever the museum's board deemed that to be, electronic or otherwise. Two more rooms would remain open for rotating displays of current artwork from children in the city's schools.

Rob was pleased with what they'd accomplished, holding true to their original vision for a building designed in the style of Frank Lloyd Wright. The museum would be built in a beautiful spot near the lake, and an entire wall would be devoted to windows looking out on it. *Nature as art.* Rob admired the simplicity of the Wisconsin architect's vision, the marriage of design and nature, the smooth lines and connected spaces that would now define the art institute.

The deadline to show the final draft plans to the board and donor was looming, and he and Samantha had been working their tails off to make sure it was a shoe-in. Eli, on the other hand, had left the building promptly at five tonight to catch a premier of a new Bruce Willis movie. *Just as well,* Rob thought, as the guy had a knack for getting in the way.

"Eli and Bruce Willis?" Kate asked on her way out the door at seven. "Who knew?"

"Don't ask me. I'm just glad he's left the building."

"He doesn't seem like the Bruce Willis type, does he? Maybe he's really Superman on his night shift." Kate giggled at the preposterous image. "I better get out of here before I get myself in trouble."

"Agreed," Rob said with a grin. "Have a good night, and thanks for all your help." He turned back to his sketch board, pencil in hand.

About a half hour later, Samantha poked her head into his office, holding out two wrapped sandwiches. "Turkey and cheese on white or tuna and tomato on rye?"

"Oh man, how did you know my stomach was growling? Turkey and cheese sounds great, thanks."

She handed over one of the bundles wrapped in waxy paper. "I trust you've got your drink there?" She eyed the mess of cups scattered across his desk.

"Yeah, no shortage of caffeine here. Can I get you anything?" He gestured to the soda cans from the vending machine that Kate had set on his desk before heading out.

"No thanks. Brought my own medicine." She held up a can of Red Bull.

"That stuff really work? I've never tried it."

"Like a charm. It keeps me up for hours. Only drawback is that I probably won't sleep a wink tonight." She pulled up a chair and sat down at the table, unfolding the wrapper, and took a bite of her sandwich. A bit of tuna spilled out the back. She wiped at her mouth as she cast an eye over the plans. "Mind if I take a look?" Rob smelled a scent he couldn't quite recognize. It reminded him of a shampoo he'd loved in high school. Was it Agree?

"I don't think either one of us is going to get much sleep till this thing is done." The nervous feeling he'd had about the project was pretty much gone, but he still worried that the board would nix some detail in the end. At least they seemed to have Eli on board at last. Thanks, largely, to Samantha. He took a bite of the turkey sandwich.

"Is that the mosaic room?" She pointed her neatly manicured nail to one of the squares on the drawing.

"Yeah, and the mosaics will be illuminated with these soft spotlights overhead."

"Nice." She nodded as a slip of hair fell past her cheek. It was no surprise that the guys in the firm talked about Samantha as if she were one of the unattainable girls in high school. She was way out of their league. Her wavy blond hair hung loosely around her shoulders. Her green eyes were framed by long, dark lashes, and her body was obviously toned, free of any mommy tummy. Kate, who was no fan of competition in the office, had sniffed to Rob that all the girls in the office knew Samantha wasn't a natural blonde. "Look at her eyebrows. Why are *they* brown?" Kate had gone so far as to look up Sam's graduation photos in her high school yearbook. "She was nothing to look at then," Kate had informed him smugly. "Highlights," she added with a dismissive wave of her hand.

But Sam Wilcox had grown into herself. She was, he supposed, the kind of woman who turned heads when she walked into a room not because she was outrageously attractive, but because she exuded confidence, an air of "I can't be fooled" coupled with a certain coyness.

"Looks like we're almost there," she said now and looked up at him with a smile. She took a sip of Red Bull.

"I sure hope so." He shook his head. He couldn't take much more of this project. "And, thanks to you, we got there a lot sooner than we might have otherwise."

"Ah, you flatter me." She waved him off, but she looked pleased.

"No, really. You're not bad for a young whippersnapper." He liked to pull the age card when he could on the associates. It made him feel wiser, despite his paltry thirty-seven years.

"Thanks. That means a lot. Sincerely." She played with the tab on her soda can. "You know, I heard a rumor about you."

"Really?" *What could possibly be interesting enough about my life to start the rumor mill turning?* he wondered.

"I hope you won't think it's too personal a question," she paused, gave him the once-over to see if he was about to object, "but is it true that you're color-blind?"

"Oh, that." He felt himself deflate slightly at the fact that *that* was the salacious rumor circulating about him. "Yeah, it's true."

"Isn't that kind of, I don't know, an oxymoron? A color-blind architect?"

"Not exactly. I can see colors . . . I just don't see a whole spectrum like you do."

"What do you mean?"

Did she really want to hear this or was she just being polite to her superior? Rob couldn't tell.

"*Color-blind* is kind of a misnomer. I have what they call a red deficiency. I can't see it. So, when I'm looking at red or orange or yellow, I see a pale green. When I'm looking at purple, I see more of a blue."

"Because no red."

"Exactly."

"Huh." She thought about it for a moment. He couldn't help but notice again the hint of lace that poked out from behind her top button. "Doesn't that make practical stuff hard? Like traffic lights?"

He cleared his throat. "Nah. My parents figured out early on that I was color deficient, so I learned how to make allowances over the years—like red light on top, green light on bottom."

"And architecture?"

"You'd be surprised how you learn to accommodate. Still, my wife has to lay out my tie for me every night to make sure it doesn't clash with what I'm wearing."

"Interesting. I don't think I've ever known anyone who's color-blind."

"Interesting for about five seconds," he added, and they shared a laugh.

"Anyway, shall we get to work, add the final touches?" he asked and rolled up his sleeves.

"We shall," she said, wiping her mouth and throwing her wrapper into the wastebasket. "And seriously, Rob, who says *shall* anymore?"

8

"It's important to remember when twisting
the traditional Danish knot, if you twist too tightly,
the center filling will burst through."
—*The Book of Kringle*

Ellen had brought her cookbook to the store. She'd been puzzling over the riddle long enough and thought perhaps if she considered it in the ambience of the shop, she would be inspired, crack the secret wide open. She'd added a few other capitals to her list—a recipe sent in from Atlanta, Georgia, and another from Tallahassee, Florida—but they stumped her even more. What on earth could be the secret ingredient tying these places together? Or maybe she was meant to focus on just *one* state capital with seven letters? After all, the riddle had said: *For if you like capitals first and seven.* Was it Atlanta and therefore a Georgia peach? But what could *first* refer to? She sighed. She was getting nowhere.

It was then that she looked up from the cash register and saw him. Sitting at the table, his hat in his hands, a goofy grin on his face. His face was tanned, his hair lighter, whether from the sun or high-lights she couldn't guess. He wore a denim jacket over his T-shirt, a bit of a non sequitur for a fifty-year-old man, she thought. And a little gold hoop in his left ear.

"Ellen," he said with a mix of what sounded like sweetness and regret.

Her hand shot up to her neck. She could feel it turning a deep crimson. For the first time in a long time, she was speechless.

"Ellen," he said again. "I was just in the area and thought I'd drop by to say 'hi.'"

"Well, hello." She had found her voice. She hated that it came out so small, so girlish. She cleared her throat. "Can I get you something? A coffee?" She wiped her hands on her apron.

"That would be nice." She grabbed the coffee pot, ducked out from behind the counter, turned over his cup and poured it for him, black.

"Lookee that. You remembered how I like it."

"Don't get too excited," she said. "I just haven't offered you any cream or sugar yet."

He laughed. "That's my Ellen."

Ellen bit her tongue, refrained from telling him she wasn't anyone's Ellen and most especially not his anymore. A customer in the corner looked up from his paper. He wasn't a regular, though, so she couldn't know if he understood the gravity of the situation.

"So, how've you been?"

Just another typical Monday, she thought to herself. Your ex-husband walks into your store after eighteen months and asks you how you've been.

"I'm fine, Max. Just fine. You?"

"Did you read my e-mail? You never responded."

"Oh, I got it all right. Sorry for the delay in getting back to you. I've been busy with the store." She waved her hand in the air, gesturing around her as if no one could imagine all the work the place required.

"Right. I figured," he said and took a sip.

"Are you back for good?"

He raised his eyebrows.

"From Sint Maarten or Martinique or whatever it's called."

"No, no. Like I said, I'm just visiting. Wanted to say hi to my sister, check in on some old friends. Here for just a few more days, then I'm headed back to paradise."

"Good." Ellen caught herself. "I mean it's good that you're visiting your sister. I'm sure she appreciates it." Max's younger sister, Lily, had been in and out of relationships with one guy after another. Last Ellen heard, she was seeing a minor league baseball player from Dubuque, a long distance relationship that sounded slightly serious for a change. For her sake, Ellen hoped it would stick.

Max nodded, looked around. "So, business has been good, I take it?"

"Oh, fabulous. We got written up in *Isthmus* the other day, and apparently a writer from the *New York Times* saw it. He called to say he was thinking of flying out to interview me about the finer points of kringle-making." It was only partially a lie. The Singular Kringle *had* been included in *Isthmus* the other day among a roundup of recently anointed bakeries in the area. And a fact-checker from the *New York Times* had called to confirm the spelling of *kringle* in one of its articles.

"Well, isn't that remarkable?" Max asked. He sounded sincerely pleased for her. "That's great. Congratulations. Good for you."

She couldn't remember one time in their marriage when he'd congratulated her on anything.

"Kringle, huh? You always liked your Sunday morning kringle." She was surprised he remembered that she'd kept up her mother's tradition of buying kringles after church.

"And you? How did you end up in Sint Maarten?" She couldn't help herself. She really was curious.

"Oh, you know me. Always something up my sleeve. I've always wanted to live down there, just never imagined it was possible. Then an old buddy of mine from college called to say he was opening this scuba store and did I want to go in on it with him? I figured I'd better jump before I got too old. And so, that's where I am now. It's like *Fantasy Island,* I'm telling you."

She smiled to think of her old favorite television show. She loved watching the seaplane land at the beginning of every episode, the passengers deplaning, full of hope and possibility. She doubted Sint Maarten, or at least Max's version of it, was anything close.

"Sounds like good living." She went back to the counter, cut a few slices of raspberry kringle and brought them over to the table, sitting down across from him. With only one other customer in the store, it couldn't hurt to take a moment to be civil and regain her composure.

When she looked up from her plate, though, she had to catch her breath. Damn him, the man was still heart-stoppingly handsome. Those bright blue eyes, the chiseled cheekbones. It was all too much, blinding. And a smell that could only be Max's, some kind of shaving lotion mixed with what she'd always thought of as his own personal brand of pheromones. It was intoxicating.

"Why don't you join me?" He said the words and they hung in the air for her to claim or not. Did he mean what she thought he meant, or was he just belatedly asking her to join him at the table? Ellen could hear the man in the corner breathing, a sort of asthmatic wheeze, while she watched the invisible words cross the table to her. From the intense look on Max's face, she could tell he meant the former.

Where to begin?

Funny, how shortly after the divorce she'd found herself overcome with sadness, wondering what on earth she'd done. Had Max really been *that* bad? She was so sure when she signed on the dotted line, making the divorce final, only to be wracked with second-guessing a few weeks later. Was she destined to be a spinster with cats? (The fact that she was allergic to cats gave her hope that that particular fate wasn't in the cards for her.) But still. She hadn't really wanted to be alone for the rest of her life. Then the pizza joint had gone up for sale and she'd snagged it, poured all her energy into it. There was no more time for self-doubting and second-guessing.

Except now here he was, sitting in her store, asking her to question the very thing she'd wondered after he'd gone. When his e-mail arrived, a little door in her heart had, admittedly, squeaked open. Here he was trying to pry it open further.

She laughed a little. "Oh, Max." The kringle crumbled between her fingers, dropped to her plate. "You've always had a good sense of humor."

He reached across to lay his hand over hers. "I'm not kidding. Come with me. You'd love it down there. I'm a changed man, with a real job and a real nice place that I call home."

"And give up all this?" She pulled her hand away and gestured to the walls around her.

"I'm sure you could sell it for a pretty penny."

Where was Lanie when she needed her? On their last date, Henry had told Ellen that a sapling shoots off myriad seeds to signal when it's in trouble; Ellen imagined herself sprouting miniature seeded helicopters by the dozen right now, but no one seemed to notice.

All the "what-ifs" came flooding back. What if she was never going to meet another man who'd bring the kind of adventure and excitement to her life that Max had, even if it wasn't always the good kind? She had had fun with Henry that first night, so much so that she'd agreed to his invitation for a second "date," and then a trip to the movies and dinner out. But with Max across from her, she felt her ground shifting in a way that it hadn't in months.

"Isn't it iconic, how you loved kringle and now you've created all this?" He grinned.

She didn't have the heart to tell him that he meant *ironic* and that it wasn't even the proper use of the word. But it was enough to snap her back to reality.

She pushed up from the table. "I appreciate your stopping by to say hello," she said. "But I don't see how things have changed."

He looked crestfallen. "You're the one who was always faulting me for not keeping a job, and now I have one."

"Max, I'm sorry, but I just don't think it's a good idea, do you?" She tried more gently now.

"Did you get my gift?"

She searched her mind. "Your gift?"

"Yeah, the Fowler's thing or whatever it's called."

"That was you?" She felt the romance of Gretchen and Anthony come crashing down around her feet. She was a balloon, deflated. So Max had been in town for a few weeks. Why had it taken him so long to stop by?

"Sure, I stopped by the store late one afternoon. You'd already closed up for the day, so I dropped it through the mail slot in the door. I know how much you love that grammar stuff and when I saw it at a used bookstore, it had your name written all over it. I figured you'd know it was me since I always used to give you such a hard time about being a word freak."

"But that was weeks ago."

"Yeah, took me a while to work up the nerve to come by again."

She was momentarily stunned. It wasn't like Max to do something, well, thoughtful like that. She thought back to when she thanked Larry for the book. He *had* played it off as if he'd no idea what she was talking about, but she'd assumed it was part of the lark. And perhaps a small part of her, she was surprised to admit, was disappointed it hadn't been Henry after all.

"Thank you. It was very thoughtful of you."

"Come on. Don't be such a fuddy-duddy. How about we start with something small? Like dinner? It'll be just like old times."

She felt something spark inside her. "Let's not do this. It won't end well, you know that, right?" The words came out softly.

"Unlike you, Ellen, I'm an optimist. Call me a fool, but that's what I am."

About that, he was right. He was never short of optimism. It had been a good counterpoint for her more dour moods.

Max pushed back his chair and stood up.

"Is there someone else?" he asked.

She inhaled sharply. What to say? That she'd had a few dates with a horticulturist who seemed nice enough but who had yet to kiss her? Max would laugh.

"In a manner of speaking," she said. "I mean there might be. I'm, well, I'm not quite sure." Why was she showing any hesitation to Max of all people?

"Might be?" Max raised an eyebrow. He buttoned up his denim jacket. "Well, I'm in town a few more days if you change your mind." He walked to the front and paused to look back before heading out. "You've got a nice shop here, Ellen. Good luck with it."

And with that, he walked through the door. And out of her life once again.

Except. Except that he showed up at her house later that night, cradling paper cartons of Chinese beef and broccoli, her favorite, and a six-pack in his tanned, muscular arms.

"I know you said no, but we both know that sometimes it just takes a little arm-twisting. I thought if you won't go to dinner with me, I could bring dinner to you. This way you won't have to be seen in public with me."

She knew in that moment that she should shoo him away, hold strong. But instead she found herself looking across the yard to see if anyone was around to notice her ex-husband standing on her porch. All clear.

She showed him in, against her better judgment.

"Dinner, but that's all, got it?" She wasn't one to turn down free beef and broccoli. There was a practical side to all of this, she told herself. Dinner *gratis*.

Three helpings of beef and broccoli and a six-pack later, she rolled over and half-smiled to see his familiar shape lying next to her. She had forgotten how nice it was to be close to someone, had forgotten the contours of his body, the freckles that swam across his back like schools of fish, the slightly raised mole on his left arm. The tan lines that ran across the top of his waist and circled his upper thighs were new. And his hair was sandier now—lighter in color and rougher, as if the southern seas and all that salt had added texture.

With Max, she had to admit, it was comfortable. She knew him, inside and out, good and bad. There wasn't much mystery to him, aside from not knowing where his next adventure would lead him. And perhaps that was what had made her cave in earlier tonight, follow him after he took her by the hand to lead her up to a bedroom that he had, ironically, never set foot in. The clothes had come off on the way up the stairs; she'd almost tumbled over his pants in midstep. She had forgotten passion, what it felt like, tasted like.

Max was comfortable in his own skin wherever he landed. Ellen missed that. She missed feeling wanted, missed feeling as if it was fine to forget everything and throw herself into the moment. Max had been good at getting her to do that. And here she was, seduced again.

She ran her finger over his shoulder and down his arm. He was always the first to fall asleep after they'd made love. She envied him that quick, deep dive into the ocean of dreams. His eyelids fluttered every so often as she imagined the dreams playing out behind them.

Did she still love him?

Yes, she supposed she did. She could feel it as she lay there looking at him.

But people didn't just stop loving each other, did they? And for all the reasons why they had divorced she had only to look at the folded piece of paper in her bedside table that outlined those very reasons, scribbled down over a year ago. How absurd, how ridiculous that Max was back in her bed again! Lanie would never believe it. No, she wouldn't want to hear about it. Ellen wouldn't be able to tell anyone about this night.

She got up and tied on her robe. Her first instinct was to call Henry, say hello, right her world to a position of normalcy. But then she saw that it was one thirty in the morning. She'd startle him if she called so late. And, honestly, what would she say? "Hello, Henry, I just slept with my ex-husband, and I thought you should know." Crazier things happened in those Lifetime movie specials, but this was her life. She wasn't a complete idiot.

She brushed her teeth and ran a brush through her hair. She

wasn't going to begrudge herself the fun she'd had with Max tonight. She deserved this much, after such a long dry spell. But in the morning she would make it clear where they stood: it had been an enjoyable night; thanks for the dinner and the memories; have a safe trip back to the island. Simple and straightforward. She owed it to herself, to Max, to Lanie. And in some small way, she hoped she owed it to Henry.

9

"The child who has had a happy day with simple food, sunlight, and good air, and proper work and play, will slumber well. The angels of good-health and good-will guard his bed."
—*Talks to Mothers* (1920)

Lanie dreaded Rob's work banquets. Supposedly meant to bring everyone together in brotherly love, they were, as far as she could tell, occasions for thinly veiled attempts at hobnobbing and brown-nosing. The only thing that made them slightly bearable was that she knew Rob detested them as much as she did, if not more. And to atone for dragging her to this one, he would soon enough be attending a similar function, no doubt, for her firm. On the drive over they agreed to grin and bear it.

"So I'm not going to complain, only pretty please don't make me talk to that misogynistic jerk who's been at your firm forever. What's his name, again?" she turned to Rob in the car.

"I think you're referring to Earl Norman, one of the most brilliant architects in the tri-state area." A small smile played across his lips.

"Brilliant, schmilliant. I hate him."

"Honey!" Rob exclaimed. "He's not such a bad guy."

"Oh yeah? How come every time I see him he talks to my

breasts? You'd think his wife wasn't standing right next to him. Then again, she always seems oblivious."

"I think you're imagining things."

"Right." She knew Rob was trying to make light of Earl's reputation as a womanizer, an especially ironic moniker seeing as Earl was a portly, balding sixty-five-year-old man, not to mention someone who thought all women still belonged in the kitchen. Lanie always felt a stab of pity for his wife, Eleanor. She usually looked as if she'd been airlifted right out of a 1950s magazine spread, her auburn hair perfectly coiffed in an up-do, her plump body wedged into a shimmery dress that only accentuated her heavy midriff and asymmetrical calves. Lanie had yet to hear her say anything other than "How lovely to see you again, dear."

She knew she shouldn't be offended; they were an old-fashioned couple stuck in their old-fashioned ways. Still, it irked her every time she had to stand next to the guy and his wife, nodding her head in agreement to each asinine comment that came out of his mouth. She wanted to grab Eleanor by the elbow and whisper in her ear, "What do you say we go get skunk drunk on appletinis?"

She'd never do it, but the thought made her smile while she looked down into her gin and tonic now, predictably standing next to Rob in a small group that included the Normans, making small talk about the Brewers and the Cubs.

"I remain a Cubs fan, loyal to the bitter end," one of the young architects was saying. He was cute in a Hugh Grant kind of way, minus the accent. A slight build with floppy hair and a thin nose, he struck Lanie as someone she might have dated in her twenties. But he was probably also the type who courted one-night stands, avoided commitment. She wondered if his date tonight knew that about him. The woman was pretty enough in an understated way: gray suit, brownish hair that fell to her shoulders in loose waves, warm brown eyes. She smiled at Lanie when she glanced her way.

Why did Lanie always assume the worst about these guys? After all, they were her husband's colleagues, some would argue among the most eligible bachelors in the city—smart, well educated, articulate, good earners, fully groomed, and washed.

"I second that, buddy," Rob said and clinked his glass of scotch in camaraderie. "Honey, this is Craig. New to the firm two months ago."

"Hi, Mrs. Taylor." His voice gushed with youthful enthusiasm.

Lanie smiled back. Even after all these years, she wasn't accustomed to being called Mrs. Taylor. "Very nice to meet you. I've heard a lot about you," she lied diplomatically.

When the conversation quickly shifted to the even more mundane topics of building permits, she turned to Craig's girlfriend for an escape.

"So, have you been to a lot of these?"

"No, this is my first, actually."

"Oh really?" Lanie raised an eyebrow. "Lucky you," she whispered. "I'm sure you'll be attending a lot more as Craig's girlfriend."

"Oh, I'm not his girlfriend." She laughed and shook her head. "Definitely not his type. I'm his sister."

"Oh?" Lanie felt double-duped. She would have never guessed it. The two couldn't have looked more different.

"No worries," the woman who introduced herself as Jennifer said now. "Happens all the time. We look nothing alike. He got all the looks in the family; I got all the brains."

Lanie laughed. "I think you're selling yourself short."

"So, what do you do?" Jennifer looked at her earnestly, brushing off the compliment.

"Lawyer. One in a million, right?" Lanie twirled the lime in her drink. "Go ahead if you want to share your favorite lawyer joke. I think I've heard them all."

"Actually," she said under her breath, "I was thinking I could use a few good architect jokes. These guys are a serious bunch, aren't they?"

Lanie felt herself warming to this woman, and how could she not? At last, a kindred spirit, maybe ten years her junior, but instantly likable.

"Thank goodness you said it and not me. My husband, after all, is one of them," she quipped, feeling ungenerous as soon as the words flew out of her mouth. She hated it when spouses put down their husbands or wives teasingly, as if all marriages were good fodder for jokes. And here she'd done it with a total stranger.

She leaned in closer to Jennifer. "So are you from Madison?"

"No, Chicago. I'm just visiting for a few days, and Craig asked me if I wanted to come along. He promised free booze and food. It sounded like too good of a deal to pass up."

"Got to love a practical woman," Rob said, joining their circle.

"Oh, I'm sorry, I didn't really mean that." Jennifer's face colored slightly.

"Don't worry about offending me." Rob put his arm around Lanie. She could smell the scotch on his breath, tell he was already on his second or third. "My wife has already given me every gibe in the book." Lanie smiled.

"Anyway, it's very nice to meet you." She suddenly felt the need to escape and get her husband to a place where he couldn't embarrass them. "Honey, I think I need another drink. Come with me?"

"Nice meeting you," Jennifer said and turned back to her brother.

"What was that all about?" Rob asked.

"Nothing. I just thought we should circulate, not to mention get some food."

They found the buffet table, laden with vegetable ravioli, beef stroganoff, cheese fondue, and chicken fingers. Lanie helped herself to the ravioli and fondue. Rob dove into the beef stroganoff. Hands full, they made their way to two empty seats at a table near the bar. Lanie set her plate down next to Rob's and nodded a hello to the familiar faces as well as to a few she didn't recognize. A wave of good-to-see-yous made its way around the table before Lanie said, "Would you all excuse me, please? I'm just going to refresh my cocktail."

"Oh, I'll come with you!" Samantha, the lovely blonde who could double as a model but, damn her, was as smart and capable as she was gorgeous, volunteered a little too loudly. It was clear she'd discovered the bar a few hours ago.

"Okay," Lanie tried, for the sake of civility. She actually felt a little sorry for Samantha. Here was a talented young architect trying to fit into a mostly boys' club; maybe she thought by matching them in drinks she would earn their respect. But Lanie already knew from Rob that Samantha had the respect of the firm's elders if not also the attentions of the young men at Hobbs & Greenough. She had graduated top of her class from the University of Illinois at Chicago's College of Architecture and the Arts and had gotten her masters there as well. Every firm in the Midwest wanted her. Somehow Rob's firm managed to woo her back to Madison, her hometown, where she'd been her high school's valedictorian.

She saw Rob cast a worried glance at Samantha, and Lanie whispered, "Don't worry, I've got her back." He nodded when she rested her hand on Samantha's shoulder and guided her toward the bar, wondering how she'd convince her to switch to ice water.

As they navigated the tables and waiters with full trays, Samantha started talking over her shoulder. "Your husband," she began, and Lanie couldn't help notice the way Samantha's sleek gold dress clung to every curve of her body. Surely every man in the room had taken note and commented on it by now. "Is the coolest," she finished, when they reached the bar, slurring her words at the end.

"I'm glad you think so." Lanie ordered a gin and tonic and a scotch.

"Definitely. He's so great. How did you ever shag him?"

Lanie stopped short, then realized she had misheard *shag* for *snag*. She wasn't sure if an insult was intended but she decided to let it slide and shrugged. "Pure luck, I guess."

It was an entirely inappropriate conversation for Samantha to be having and if she remembered any of it in the morning, the poor girl would be mortified. But Lanie could feel the gin working on her own brain cells, and she didn't really care. Screw etiquette.

"Seriously, though, he's been such a great mentor to me,"

Samantha continued. "I don't think I would have lasted a week without his reassuring me that I have *some* talent."

Lanie nodded, thinking it odd that Rob had never mentioned how he was "mentoring" Samantha. But she also knew the only reason she cared was because of the incontrovertible evidence before her: Samantha was gorgeous. What guy could look at her and *not* think about the architecture of her body?

"Please tell him. Be sure he knows, okay, like how grateful I am." She leaned on Lanie now, fresh wine sloshing out of her glass. "I'd be embarrassed to tell him, but he should know, you know?"

"Sure, honey, I'll do that." One thing Lanie had on this woman was the wisdom of her years—not to mention relative sobriety. Right now she just wanted to make sure she got Samantha back to their table without her stumbling and making a complete ass of herself.

When they returned, the discussion had turned to the recent volatility in the stock market. Samantha clumsily lowered herself into her seat, and Lanie began devouring her ravioli, not realizing how much she'd been starving. When she looked up a few minutes later, Samantha was staring blankly into her plate of food, her wine glass drained. As someone pontificated on international markets, Samantha let a half-hiccup, half-burp escape. She covered her mouth and giggled.

"Excuse me, I think I'd better use the ladies' room." She pushed herself up from the table.

Rob looked at Lanie, as if to say, "Should you do something?"

But Lanie just shrugged this time. Samantha was a grown woman; she could take care of herself. Funny how she'd been dreading this dinner. It had actually turned out to be quite entertaining. Earl Norman was climbing up on stage to say a few words when Samantha returned to the table, her eye makeup slightly smudged, her hair tousled. She wiped at the corners of her mouth and smoothed her dress, seemingly more composed.

But then Rob whispered in Lanie's ear. "Honey, help." He nodded toward Samantha.

In turning to look at the stage, Samantha had fallen partly out of her halter dress—and had yet to notice that fact herself. There was her young breast in full bloom, beautifully shaped with a perfect pink aureole at its tip. Lanie took a quick inventory of the table. Only a few of the wives, mouths agape, appeared to have caught on; their husbands' eyes still focused on Earl Norman. But she could feel the wave of nudges starting to make its way around the table.

Samantha was too far out of reach for Lanie to help. She couldn't exactly walk over and tuck the girl's boob back in without the rest of the banquet hall noticing.

"Samantha!" she whispered loudly.

She looked over, doe-eyed.

Lanie gestured madly to her top. When Samantha looked down, she gasped and covered the blooming breast with her hand. Then she discreetly leaned over and tucked it back in. She flipped her hair and looked up, eyes trained on Lanie.

"Thank you," she mouthed.

"You're welcome," Lanie mouthed back. How could the girl not be fazed by what had just happened? If it were her, Lanie would have crawled under the table, made some excuse to leave. Perhaps the alcohol had sufficiently dulled Samantha's common sense? It all seemed a little too easy to Lanie, but then she supposed Samantha was one of those people for whom everything in life was easy.

Which was why Lanie couldn't help but notice with some satisfaction, as her husband patted her knee, that Samantha's beautiful breasts, while fully-sheathed, now sat oddly lopsided in her halter with a smear of something—was it vomit?—on the top of her right breast.

10

"Lars, an old man on his deathbed, said to his wife,
'Get me some *kringle* before I die. That way I can go to heaven
a happy man.' His wife turned to him and said, 'Sorry, honey,
but we're saving it for your funeral.'"
— *The Book of Kringle,* recounting a kringle folktale

"Come." He held out his hand.

Ellen followed Henry through the rows of arching, fragrant greenery. Lush pink, orange, and purple blooms spilled over into the aisles. She was trying to absorb the sweet scents and delicious calm around them, but it had been a tougher week than most. In the span of a few days, she had managed to break a crown on her tooth, flatten a tire, and crack the garage door window with a broom handle. Now the tooth was re-cemented, the tire patched, the window taped. But it was just like Max: wherever he showed up, a tsunami was sure to follow.

When her sister called, it was all Ellen could do not to spill the beans about her ex's surprise appearance. But she didn't trust herself. Once she revealed Max had stopped by the store, she'd be a short skip from disclosing the night that followed. And true to her resolution, she'd said good-bye to Max that morning. Perhaps it wasn't as final a good-bye as she'd planned (Max's words: "Hope to see you soon"), but she made the point that there was no way she could leave her shop now. He seemed to understand that reasoning, take it less personally. How she really felt about Max, well, apparently she still needed to work through that; but she was pretty sure it had been a one-night stand. Nothing more, nothing less.

And now here she was on what was supposed to be a private showing of Henry's greenhouse, with a tour by the owner himself, and her mind was spinning with thoughts . . . of her ex-husband's soft skin.

They'd just come from dinner at Henry's favorite Chinese restaurant downtown, and Ellen could feel the sweet-and-sour chicken sitting in her stomach. She wore a silk halter top, black capris, and the same strappy sandals she'd worn the first night Henry came over, but she couldn't help think she should be in flowing white linens, her hair done up with braided flowers. She was better dressed for a night at a cheap dance club than a nursery tour.

"That's a honeysuckle. And this is an anemone." Henry said, interrupting her thoughts. "They're ostentatious flowers." He plucked a big pink flower that looked like a daisy and handed it to her. She liked that he called flowers ostentatious. "They bloom best in August and September. This one's early."

She twirled the flower in her hand. "You know, I used to think forsythia were called ForCynthia," she conceded. "I'd think to myself, how nice that all the Cynthias in the world have a beautiful yellow spring flower named after them. What a dummy, huh?"

He stopped and smiled at her. "That would be better, wouldn't it? Maybe you should go into the business of naming flowers like those guys who come up with names for cars: Highlander; Cross-Country; Autumn Breeze. I hear they get paid a bundle."

She laughed. "I'm pretty sure there's no car named Autumn Breeze, but you're right that it would make a nice name for a flower—or a drink, for that matter." They turned down another row, past hyssops, long purple summer stalks that reminded her of salvia but gave off a strong, sweet licorice smell. "Mmm, that smells delicious."

"It's a good one. Butterflies love it, too." At the end of one row, somewhere around the hostas, he stopped.

"Stand right here. . . ." he said, grabbing her hips all of a sudden and moving her into place. She felt a small shiver of anticipation. "Now look up."

When she tilted her head skyward, she took in a sharp breath. Through the paned glass of the nursery, she could make out the slip of the moon and a scattering of stars across the night sky, the Big Dipper just at its edge.

"It's breathtaking, Henry. Truly beautiful." His arms circled around her, a move that he'd yet to practice on her. It felt comfortable, right.

"I used to come here a lot, sit a spell, and look up at the night. Not so much anymore."

"Why not?"

"I'm not sure."

He let go of her then and produced a blue cushion resembling a yoga mat from the corner.

"You're like a magician, Henry. Pulling flowers and mats out of your hat. If I didn't know better, I'd think you were trying to impress me."

"Don't get a big head now." He patted the mat for her to sit down with him, and she eased herself onto the cushiony foam, lying back in his arms and setting the flower aside. *That's how Max and Henry are different,* she thought. Max would have been rolling around with her by now, if he'd even bothered to lay down a mat at all.

"Is this how you seduced Charlotte?" she asked, looking up at him. She regretted the words as soon as they left her mouth. She could see Henry's face blanch, even in the moonlight.

"I'm sorry. That just came out. I didn't mean it." What on earth was she thinking?

"No, it's okay." Henry's face softened. "It's about time I turn over a new page. I loved her with all my heart, but I know she'd scold me for living in the past."

"I guess we all tend to dwell on the past, don't we? It's natural."
Then quietly she asked: "What do you miss the most about her?"

He sighed. "Good question. There's just so much—the way she
loved our children, the sense of calm she brought to our lives. And
then there's all the silly stuff, you know? Like the egg-on-toast she'd
make, with a hole cut out in the center for the egg. Or the way she
looked forward to a good thunderstorm, or how I could always tell
if she'd read a book because the corners of her favorite pages would
be turned over."

Ellen was silent. *How lovely* was all she could think. How lovely
and how in love this man had been with his wife. Was he still?

He cleared his throat. "How about you? Do you ever miss Max?"

She paused. "Not like that, Henry. Not like that, that's for sure." If
she had answered in full truth, she might have said, *I miss the smell of
his skin, his certainty that everything will work out all right, his bright
blue eyes that pierce you as soon as you look at him, his easy laugh.*

They listened to the wind blowing outside for a moment, their
faces tilted skyward. She did miss Max, but if she pressed herself
to consider, it wasn't a healthy kind of missing. It was more of a
quick-fix missing. Max was wonderful in the moment, less so in the
long haul. She felt herself relax against Henry's body as she leaned
farther back. If there were ever a moment to enjoy, this was it: being
held by this sweet man, whom she'd known for only a short while,
but who seemed to offer solace, a balm in her life without even trying. Her mother always said that still waters run deep. Henry Moon
was the embodiment of that phrase. Quiet, constant, he continued
to surprise Ellen with his love for nature, for literature, and yes, even
his deceased wife.

"You know," he interrupted her thoughts, "I'm a firm believer
that people's true selves are reflected in the kinds of flowers or trees
they're drawn to. I've seen husbands and wives get into some nasty
fights over what tree they'll plant. One wants a sugar maple, the
other a white paper birch."

"Really? I never thought about it. What are you?"

"Oh, I'm a sugar maple all the way."

She smiled. That seemed about right. "What's an impulsive, live-in-the-moment kind of tree?" she asked.

"Let's see. That could be an aspen. Quick grower. Likes to rustle its leaves in the wind for attention. Definitely not an oak or an evergreen. Those are your sturdy, reliable types. I don't see you as an aspen, though. Maybe a holly tree?"

"Oh, not for me. Just someone I know," she added quickly. "A holly tree? Why's that?"

"You know, a nice shape, a bit of a show-off, a tad prickly."

"Oh, really? A tad prickly?"

"I mean that in the best possible way, of course."

"Of course," she chided.

"I don't know how to put it . . . but sometimes you seem a little, what's the word, guarded?"

She thought about it. Had he picked up on all her ruminating over Max? She decided it was unlikely. "It probably has something to do with the fact that my mom died when I was sixteen. You quickly learn to put up walls."

He pulled away and sat up beside her. "You're kidding me. I mean, that's terrible. I had no idea."

"Why would you?"

"You never said anything about it. What a huge loss—and burden—for you."

"It forced me to grow up quickly, that's for sure. Someone had to look out for Lanie; she was only six. And, yes, I suppose it's not something I bring up often."

Ellen nuzzled her way back into his arms and looked at the spray of stars above. She thought back to when her mother, Lanie, and she used to do the same thing on cool summer nights, spread out on a blanket in the backyard and count the stars till they could no longer bear the mosquitoes.

"But as my dad always told us, my mother gave us more love in a short time than most mothers give their daughters in a lifetime."

Henry sighed. She wondered if he was thinking about Charlotte. She knew they had three children, but they'd gone off in far-flung directions after college: a daughter in China; a son in San Francisco; another in Seattle. From what she could glean, Henry talked to his children infrequently, a once-a-month check-in call. It didn't surprise her, given that grown children were bound to grow apart, but it did make her a little sorry for him. He'd gone from a full family of five, to just him and Charlotte, and now only him. She wondered if his house got lonely at night, the way hers did.

"You know how people say someone's larger than life, and you think, well, how can that be? Well, if you'd met my mom, you'd know. She *was* larger than life. In fact, I don't believe our dad ever let her go."

"Did he remarry?"

"No. It's something I worried about. What if some horrible woman became our stepmom? But he didn't. He never really recovered from her death, I don't think. He just turned inward more and more. He'd always been quiet and loved his books—he was a librarian. But his books became his new wife. We didn't really see much of him, but then we never did even when my mother was around. He died fifteen years later, when I was thirty-one. It's what brought me back home."

"You had to take care of him?"

"No. Thankfully his was a quick passing—heart attack. But some-one from the family had to get our affairs in order, sell the house, figure things out. Lanie was a senior in college at the time, so it fell to me. And, well, I kind of never left."

"I'm so sorry. I didn't know." He kissed the top of her head.

"Don't apologize. There's no rhyme or reason to some things. And you?"

"What about me?"

"What's your checkered history?"

"Not very interesting, I'm afraid. My dad was a farmer, as you know, and ran the greenhouse here. My mother was a great woman, but I don't think she ever got to see the world much. She pretty much was my dad's right-hand man on the farm, always canning or cooking something. She loved to bake—you would have liked that about her. They died within a year of each other."

"I'm sorry." If Henry were a tree, she decided, he would be an oak, not a maple. Steady and strong. She liked the rush of his breath across her bare shoulder while he talked. His breath smelled sweet, like the peppermint he'd taken from the restaurant.

"No brothers or sisters?" she asked.

"No. That's why I told Charlotte we had to have at least three kids. I wanted a loud, busy family." He was quiet for a moment and then pulled his arms away. Slowly he began to push himself up, and Ellen almost fell backward. "Well, that's plenty of sharing for one night, don't you think?"

He smiled at her but she felt as if the tenor of the evening had shifted ever so slightly. She stood up and brushed herself off as well. The scenes she'd been imagining for them earlier in his warm embrace evaporated into the humid air, twirling filaments of lust.

He picked up her flower and handed it to her, then folded the mat, and led her gently by the hand to the front. "I'm going to stay and finish up a few things here, if that's okay."

"Oh, all right." She was taken aback. Hadn't they been on their way to his house or hers? "Good night then, I guess." What else was there to say?

"G'night, my holly tree."

They stood there awkwardly for a moment before he leaned in to kiss her. She felt his lips searching around, as if they didn't quite remember how the whole thing worked. She dropped her flower. He pulled back after a few seconds.

"I'm sorry. I didn't mean to be so forward."

"You're joking, right?" She was tingling.

He looked at her curiously.

"Henry, I think it's about time you kissed me."

"Oh?" He kissed her again, wrapped his arms around her. She felt the heat rising in her cheeks. His kisses were sweet, tender.

"I've been wondering what that would feel like," he said, pulling away.

"And?"

"Pretty spectacular." He kissed her again, then pulled back. "I better let you get home before this gets out of control." He gave her a small peck on the forehead.

"Right, we wouldn't want that, would we?" She dug her keys out of her purse, buying time. "Talk to you tomorrow?" She so wanted to give him long, wet kisses, run her fingers through his hair. She didn't know what exactly had come over her, but then again, it had been something like a million years since she'd been with a man. Not counting her ex, of course.

"You bet."

She walked to her car, confused. Did Henry really like her or was she just his rebound girl? She wasn't used to men playing it so coy. Max would have at least followed her out to the car for some fooling around. Henry, on the other hand, had shut the greenhouse door behind him.

Maybe that was a good thing. She and Max had eloped on a whim. Maybe she needed a more pensive, reserved man like Henry for a relationship to work. Maybe she needed still waters.

As she turned the key in the ignition, she wondered if small details about Charlotte came to Henry's mind unexpectedly, touching all sides of a day, like the concentric circles of a pebble tossed in a puddle. Certainly memories of her mother did, and at the oddest times, like when she was making a peanut butter and jelly sandwich and she heard her mom's voice telling her to spread each on separate sides of the bread.

Ellen knew that the love for a mother and the love for a spouse were not the same. But she suspected the loss of both hurt with a similar ache and that each healed over with a puffy scab, one that eventually fell off but forever left its mark. She eased her car out of the lot, the darkness leading her home.

11

"To enjoy good health, to bring true happiness
to one's family, to bring peace to all, one must first
discipline and control one's own mind."
—Buddha

Lanie could feel her muscles unfurl as the masseuse worked her way down her back.

"That . . . feels . . . so . . . incredible."

She barely managed to get the words out. She'd forgotten how amazing a massage could be, the cucumber-scented lotion, the soothing rain music, the methodic drumming on her back. She'd at last slated some time to redeem her certificate at Spa Sensations with Ellen. Rob was watching Benjamin for the day, and she and Ellen had started with a relaxing lunch over a glass of wine at Pomodino's. It had been, so far, nothing short of divine.

Ellen was in the room next to her, getting some kind of sea wrap that promised smooth skin, toned muscles, and instant weight loss. They'd both been skeptical about the weight loss part, but figured it couldn't hurt. "I'll see you when I'm a new woman," Ellen, bundled in a white robe, called over her shoulder, a glass of ice water with lemon in her hand. "I can already feel the years coming off."

"Lucky Henry!" Lanie shouted. Over lunch, Ellen had finally

filled her in on some of the events of the past weeks. Henry was a "good man," Ellen said; she "liked him." He was apparently still a little "stuck on his wife" but that was to be expected, her sister explained. They'd shared some nice dates so far, though Ellen joked that the romance had better heat up soon or they'd be in trouble. It was the most Lanie had heard her sister talk about anyone since Max. And, oh, how Lanie had loved to see Max go his own way! He'd never deserved her sister; the fact that Ellen had fallen for him so hard, like a drunken sailor over the side of a ship, had been terrific luck on his part. Lanie only hoped her sister would finally meet someone worthy of her wonderful mind, her big soul, her giving heart. She was excited to think that Henry might be the one.

"You've got some awfully big knots here," Kristin, the masseuse, was saying as she poked her fingers in between Lanie's shoulder blades and spine.

"Feel free to work them all out," Lanie encouraged. "I think it's been about two years since my last massage."

"Yikes. You need a massage every month, if not every week. You're very tense."

"Tell my husband that." She laughed, then felt a small stab of guilt for making it sound as though Rob were her prison warden. "Actually, he's a good guy," she tried to redeem herself. "He's the one who gave me the gift certificate for a massage in the first place."

"He should buy you more, I think."

"Hmm," was all she could muster. Her muscles were so relaxed she'd lost the ability to speak. And, honestly, what did she care what this girl thought of her or her relationship with Rob? Kristin probably got an earful of relationship stories all day long, one running into another. Lanie told herself to *let go*, at least for the next sixty minutes, to stop worrying, caring about anyone else or what anyone thought. She was thirty-five! When on earth was she going to give herself free license to be herself?

The thing was, she wasn't sure if she knew who that self was. For so long she'd been trying to get to the next flag, add it to her belt, that sometimes she felt like she'd forgotten why she was chasing down all these flags in the first place. The first flag had been honor roll, then valedictorian of her high school class; then it was admission to college; Phi Beta Kappa; law school and law review; then top jobs across the country till she'd landed both her current job and Rob, her best and brightest flag up till that point. And then there was Benjamin, sweet, chubby, wonderful Benjamin. He was her whole belt of flags, multicolored, flying wildly and happily around her waist.

Some part of her, she supposed, was always trying to make Harriet McClarety proud. At every major event in her life—whether graduations, her wedding, Benjamin's birth—she had imagined her mother in the audience or at her side, applauding and smiling, nodding her head, as if to say, "I knew you could do it. I'm so proud of you." As a young girl, Lanie had gotten little praise from her father, he'd been so lost in his own world, and Ellen had lent as much support and encouragement as a sister could. But it would never fill the gaping hole of her mother's absence, her voice, her hug, or a pat on the back. Lanie had been short-changed in life.

There, she'd said it. And she supposed all the bitterness, sadness, and toughness that grew out of that realization had also helped fuel her many accomplishments. The acknowledgment was bittersweet, though. If for just one minute, she could have her mother back to say, "Honey, you've turned out to be the most wonderful woman. I couldn't have dreamed of all you'd accomplish. You're an amazing mom. I love you. I love you all," she thought she could at last move on with her second-guessing, her self-doubt. All would be okay.

But who was she kidding? She was never going to get that kind of endorsement. She imagined her mom saying to her now instead, "You were waiting all that time just for me to swoop down and tell you everything is okay? Lanie, how silly of you! You should know better. Look around you: You already *have* everything and everyone you need to make a happy life. Now, just be yourself."

She had nearly dozed off, and Lanie roused herself with a start. She realized, with her head in the donut hole, that she'd started to drool and a big splotch of saliva had landed on the floor below her. She could see it. And she didn't care. Not one iota. She was buck naked, full of knots, and drooling on the floor. It was not her best moment. And yet, so what? Who cared? She was getting the most wonderful massage of her life. She could feel Kristin's fingers digging into her skin, unlocking knot after knot, her shoulders adjusting to a level half an inch lower than before. She imagined her muscles yelling out in glee, "Thank you! Thank you! We've been cooped up for so long. It's so nice to relax."

She didn't need any more flags. She had all that she wanted. She was happy, and yet she was driving herself crazy. How was it possible to be both at once? She suspected plenty of other women felt this way. No, she *knew* plenty of other women who felt this way, trying to juggle fifteen million balls at once. It was too much, and someone ultimately was going to get short-changed, whether it was her clients, Rob, Benjamin, or herself. She didn't want more flags, but she sure as hell didn't want to lose the ones she had.

A week and a half later the baby spiked a fever of 103 in the middle of the night. He was screaming, his sleeper drenched with sweat, his curls pasted to his forehead—and Lanie was terrified. After she'd called, the pediatrician said not to worry, that babies spiked fevers quickly, but they should give Benjamin some Tylenol and get him to the ER just in case he needed antibiotics. "Probably an ear infection," she guessed. "But I wouldn't want to diagnose it over the phone, especially given how little he is."

She squeezed a thimbleful of the liquid medicine into Benjamin's mouth, but it was hard to know if he got enough when some pink liquid leaked out at the corners. He calmed eventually, but when she rocked him in her arms, saying, "It's gonna be okay, little guy," he seemed not even to respond. That scared her the most. How she craved her mother's advice right now! If only she could reassure Lanie over the phone that Benjamin was going to be fine, not to worry.

Rob got the car going and now they were headed to the hospital, the baby strapped into his car seat, a light blanket covering him. Lanie sat next to him in the back. He had been fighting a little cold, but nothing major. When she laid him down to sleep tonight, he hadn't even felt warm. Or had he? She tried to remember if she had checked his forehead. What kind of a mother didn't feel her baby's head before she put him down to sleep?

"Stop it," she said out loud now.

"What?" Rob looked back at her, his pasty face even whiter in the glow of the car's fluorescent dashboard.

"Me. I'm telling myself to stop blaming myself."

"For what?"

"Not noticing that Benjamin was so sick. He seemed fine, he really did, when I rocked him to sleep tonight."

"And he was fine. Babies spike high fevers all the time. The doctor said."

Of course, Rob wouldn't know. She couldn't ask him how Benjamin seemed to him tonight, because, par for the course, he hadn't been home before Benjamin fell asleep. Another late night. On top of a string of late nights.

Technically, she wasn't talking to Rob. Not since he'd skipped out on the fancy dinner she'd prepared for him. After their anniversary dinner at La Lumière, she'd made a vow to cook at least one nice meal a week. She'd forgotten how much she enjoyed relaxing over a good dinner, no babies to tend to. A late-night Friday supper each week, the baby in bed, copious amounts of booze at their disposal, seemed like a marvelous idea. That is, until she'd called him at the office to ask when he'd be home, already angry that it was nine o'clock and still no Rob. When someone else picked up, she first thought it was Kate. Then she realized: Samantha. One-boob-wonder Samantha.

And she hardly sounded stressed. As a matter of fact, Samantha was in mid-laugh, as she said "Hello?" It was more of a question than a greeting, as if she couldn't fathom who would be calling the office at this hour.

Lanie was so stunned she couldn't speak.

"Hello? Who's this?" Samantha tried again.

"Um, Samantha? It's Lanie Taylor. Rob's wife."

"Oh, Lanie, hi! We were just talking about you."

"Really?"

"Yeah, Rob was saying how in grad school you used to make sure he wouldn't drink more than three Cokes a night when he had to pull an all-nighter. Otherwise he'd get sick. Is that true?"

Lanie didn't know what to think or feel. She felt slightly sick that Rob and Samantha had been discussing a personal detail of their married life at nine o'clock on a Friday night.

"Um, yeah. I guess that's right. I haven't thought about that in a long time."

"You're a good wife, Lanie. Here he is." She could hear the phone being passed to Rob, something mumbled out of earshot.

"Hey, honey, what's up? Everything okay?"

Her mind was quickly flipping through the possibilities. For one, what the hell was Samantha doing answering his phone? Where was Kate? She typically helped Rob on his late nights. And Kate was safe, with a steady boyfriend, practically engaged. Samantha, on the other hand, was annoyingly untethered. Untethered and in her husband's office. A woman whose *boob* her husband had seen, for God's sake. She felt the accusation layered thick as the words flew out of her mouth.

"Gee, I don't know. I was just calling to see when my husband might be coming home. Or maybe you won't be? Shall I just lock the doors and go to bed?"

There was a pause on the other end. "Lanie."

"Don't talk to me when she's standing right there, Rob. Have a little decency and respect, please." She could feel the flush in her face. How dare he try to smooth things over with Samantha right there?

A sigh, then, "Lanie. Okay, I'm by myself now. Why are you being so weird?"

"I think you should ask the same question of yourself!"

"Excuse me?"

"I call to check in and find out when you'll be home for the lovely dinner I've been slaving over for you. And what do I find out? That you're having a rollicking good time with Samantha." She spit out the name.

"Lanie, you gotta stop this. Please. You're being ridiculous."

She almost hung up right there. "*I'm* being ridiculous? I think I'm being pretty fucking tolerant, wouldn't you? When's the last time you've been home for dinner, Rob? Did you forget you have a wife and a son?"

She let the words hang in the air and could feel their sting, even on the other end.

"I'm not having this conversation right now," he said softly, firmly.

"You're not? Well, I sure as hell am." She was pissed, but she couldn't stop herself. How dare he assume she'd be all right with his working late with the most attractive colleague in the office? A colleague, who for all intents and purposes, he'd seen *nude*. Funny how he never thought to mention it. Funny how it never came up. "Is there anyone else there with you two?"

"I'll talk to you when I get home."

"That says it all, doesn't it? I'll be asleep. Good night, Rob. I hope you and Samantha have a wonderful night." She slammed down the phone.

She dumped the steak and the bread for the fondue into the trash. Poured the oil into an old soup can and shoved the Sterno can in the back of the cupboard. They wouldn't be having fondue anytime soon. She climbed the stairs to bed, but not before throwing up in the toilet. When Rob finally came home at eleven, she feigned sleep, her back turned. He leaned over and kissed her on the cheek, then got his pillow and headed downstairs to the couch.

The rest of the weekend had been hell, both talking only when it was required, each taking Benjamin out to run errands, doing everything possible to avoid the other. The Zen-like calm Lanie had achieved on the massage table the other weekend, ready to give herself over to the world, not to worry so much, had flown right out the window—and she'd given it a huge shove on the way. Sure, it was fine to have balance in your life *when your husband wasn't having an affair.* No amount of massage or rain music or Zen training could fix those things.

Rob had tried a few times to start a conversation: "Lanie, there's *nothing* going on." For a brief moment she heard her lawyer's voice in her head: "Your honor, this is pure hearsay. The case should be dismissed." But she didn't want to hear it. Her husband, she was certain with a wifely intuition, was having an affair. She didn't want to hear him confirm it or for that matter, deny it. Somehow that was worse.

Because mostly, as mad as she was at Rob, she was mad at herself. What a fool she'd been to miss the signs, not to spot the obvious! Rob's not telling her that Samantha was working on the museum project in the first place—a convenient omission; all the late nights at the office; Samantha's trying to befriend her at the party and tell her what a wonderful mentor Rob was. Just the thought of it made Lanie want to throw up again.

She was exhausted from the turmoil of it all, the sleepless nights that had followed later that week. She'd shared her suspicions with Ellen and nothing else. Because what else was there to say? *I'm such a bad wife that I missed all the signs. My husband is in love with another woman? Who by the way happens to be a dead ringer for Cameron Diaz?*

But now, she was praying madly that her little guy be okay.

"Just please, God, let him be all right," she whispered. She felt the tears coming. Nothing mattered if Benjamin wasn't okay. She reached for a tissue from her bag. Plenty of moms had sick babies, she told herself. Sick babies got better. No big deal. Still, she hated the thought of stepping back into the children's hospital, where she hadn't set foot since Benjamin's release at birth. Just the thought gave her goose bumps.

When they arrived, the hospital's fluorescent lights cut through the dark, and an ambulance had pulled up ahead of them, its red lights flashing back to eleven months ago. Rob pulled the car up and Lanie unstrapped Benjamin. His eyes were half-closed, whether because he was half-asleep or despondent, she couldn't tell. She pressed him tightly to her chest while Rob handed the keys to the valet and took the ticket for their car.

She felt herself breaking into little pieces, as if her body parts were spiraling into the air around her. An elbow over here, an eyebrow over there, a bent knee floating over there. She didn't think she could take anymore. Who was she fooling? Her marriage was breaking down; work sucked; and now the only thing in the world that really mattered to her . . . well, she couldn't even think past the immediate fever.

"Let's go," Rob said firmly, giving her a little push while Lanie stood frozen, the revolving doors beckoning. "C'mon, hon. We need to get Benjamin inside," and with those words her legs were moving again, her body whole once more.

They checked in as friendly nurses milled around him, taking the baby's vitals with cheery voices. Their pediatrician had called ahead.

"We've been expecting you, little guy." Dr. Lisa looked to be in her early thirties. She gently unfastened the top snaps on Benjamin's sleeper and laid a stethoscope on his chest. He howled at its coldness.

"Well, at least we know you're feeling well enough to protest." She looked at Lanie as she listened to his heartbeat. "That's a good sign, Mom." Lanie nodded, breathed for what felt like the first time since they'd gotten to the ER.

"His heart sounds good." She made a note on her chart. "Why don't you fill me in on when he started feeling lousy."

"I don't really know, that's the scary thing," Lanie began. "It all came on so fast. He seemed fine, a little sniffly when I put him down tonight, but nothing out of the ordinary. He certainly wasn't hot like this."

The doctor glanced at the chart. "One hundred two point five, so the Tylenol seems to be helping."

"That's still high, though, isn't it?" Lanie asked.

"High, but not atypical in babies. Let's take a look at his throat and ears. Those are typically the culprits when babies spike fevers."

While Lanie held him, the doctor took a quick swab of Benjamin's throat and sent it off for a strep culture. Then she looked inside. Benjamin was furious now, kicking his feet and pushing the doctor's hand away. "Just hold his head still, please." She looked again, then pulled back. "Some postnasal drip but it doesn't look like strep to me. Still, I've been proven wrong before. We'll see what the test results say."

"How long does that take?"

"About half an hour. Plus we'll want to make sure that fever comes down before you guys leave the hospital."

"Okay. Good." As much as Lanie hated hospitals, she felt a twinge of relief that people who were qualified were now looking after her son.

"And now let's take a look at those ears of yours." She got out her otoscope. "Has he been tugging on his ears at all?"

"Not that I've noticed." Lanie looked at Rob, who shook his head. As if he would know. "But a lot of kids at his day care are sick right now."

"Oh, day care. The petri dish of infections."

Was the doctor trying to make her feel bad? she wondered. But no, Lanie decided this was a young woman who had charted a career path for herself. She was in no position to judge. She was simply stating a fact.

"So we hear," Rob affirmed. Lanie shot him a look. *That* felt judgmental.

Benjamin proceeded to holler more loudly as the doctor looked first in his right ear, then in his left. "Yup. You've got a double ear infection, buddy. No doubt about it." She rubbed Benjamin's head. "That's why you're feeling so yucky. We'll get you better in no time."

She went to the wall dispenser of antibacterial lotion and squirted a dollop onto her hands and rubbed them together. "If you could just wait around till we get the strep results and the fever comes down, that would be great. I'll write up a prescription for the antibiotic and maybe, Mr. Taylor, you could go pick it up at the pharmacy downstairs in the meantime?"

"Sure." It was the first time Lanie detected worry in Rob's voice, as if the seriousness of the situation were just dawning on him.

"Our nurses will check back every so often to monitor the fever." She pulled back the curtain that lent their bed an air of privacy. "Don't worry. I understand you folks have had some tough times here, but Benjamin is going to be fine. This is a typical ear infection. Babies get them all the time."

Lanie could have kissed her as she pulled the curtain behind her. Those were the words she needed to hear: *Benjamin is going to be fine.*

When the strep results came back negative and the fever had diminished to 99.5, Dr. Lisa returned to sign Benjamin out. He was sitting up in bed now, giggling as he banged together two tongue dispensers that one of the nurses had given him. He didn't seem fazed by the rough patch he'd been through just hours ago. Lanie and Rob, however, looked exactly like the tired, frazzled parents that they were. Rob's stubble was already poking through, and his hair was flat against his head on one side, the side he'd been sleeping on, Lanie suspected. She hadn't noticed that he had a small cut above his eye. When had that happened? Lanie knew she looked like hell, but she didn't care. She could be the laughing stock of the whole ER, for all she cared, so long as Benjamin was all right.

"So, it looks like you're feeling a little better, Benjamin," the doctor said as she came in to check his charts one last time. It was 4:04 in the morning. "Glad to see the fever came down. Keep giving him Tylenol every four to six hours as needed. And that antibiotic should start to make him feel much better in about twenty-four hours, if not sooner."

She signed off on the sheet and handed it to Lanie. "Thank you so much, doctor. You've been great."

"Happy to help. Give us a call or your pediatrician a call if anything else comes up, okay? Especially if that fever doesn't break completely in a couple of days."

"We will."

"And I'd keep him home from day care for a couple of days."

"Of course," Lanie said. "Of course." She didn't care if she was expected to litigate the Paul McCartney divorce in court tomorrow. She wasn't leaving Benjamin's side. She started to bundle him up in his coat to protect against the early-morning chill. He fought it, but it made her smile. At least her little guy was getting some of his gumption back. She'd take it—happily.

"Let's go, shall we?" She turned to Rob, who was pulling on his own coat. He smiled at her.

"What?"

"I was wondering where I got that from."

"Got what?"

"Oh nothing. Let's go, okay?" He gave Benjamin a kiss on his head.

"Whatever. Yes, let's go, *please*." Suddenly she couldn't wait to get home.

12

"An architect's most useful tools are an eraser
at the drafting board and a wrecking ball at the site."
—Frank Lloyd Wright

By the time they got home, Benjamin had fallen asleep. Rob managed to move him from his car seat to the crib without waking him.

"Well, that was a little more drama than we needed for one night," he said as they watched their son sleeping peacefully.

Lanie looked up at him, and for a moment he thought she was about to launch another one of the barbed arrows she'd been shooting for the past days. But she refrained. Maybe the all-too-real reminder of what they'd been through at the children's hospital almost a year ago was enough to make her drop her weapons for a few hours. He hoped so.

At the hospital tonight when he'd watched Lanie holding Benjamin, he felt the anger and accusations of days past slip away. His family meant more than anything in the world to him. How could Lanie think for one minute that he'd fool around with Samantha? At first, when he'd hung up the phone that fateful night, he'd taken her anger as just that: She was pissed because he was late again and she'd made a nice dinner. The fact that Samantha was there added insult to injury, but nothing more. Lanie knew Samantha, had told him on the way home from the company banquet that she liked her, even felt a wee bit sorry for her after the whole breast-falling-out-of-the-dress incident.

"She's never going to live that one down no matter how smart and successful she is," Lanie said. "That's the thing that totally sucks."

"A thing you'd know something about," Rob teased.

"I'd like to think so. Because no matter how smart you are, you're still just a sex symbol to guys. Did you see how the husbands at the table all tried to look away but couldn't help themselves?"

"Honey, it *was* a little hard to overlook."

"You know what I mean. Samantha will forever be known as 'that woman whose boob popped out.' She'll probably quit next week, it's that humiliating."

"You really think so?" Rob hoped that wasn't the case. "She didn't seem that bothered by it." He still needed Sam for the museum project.

"She was too drunk to care, but trust me, it will bother her in the morning."

"I think Samantha may have earned a little *more* respect with some of the guys after tonight," Rob had joked. Though when he thought back on it now, he regretted the comment. Maybe he'd planted the seed for his own wife's suspicions.

And now when he reconsidered, maybe he was a little guilty even. Maybe he secretly *had* hoped that Samantha would find him attractive. Not that he'd ever act on it, but it would redeem his manhood in a way. His wife hardly looked at him twice these days. If someone young and attractive like Samantha found him appealing, then he must still have something going on. He tried not to spend much time thinking about his sex life—what was the point?—and in that way, work had been a convenient distraction. How ironic that it was now getting in the way.

He'd spent more than a few nights sleeping on the couch, listening to Coltrane, Miles Davis, Billie Holiday, a cool glass of scotch in hand. God, he loved that music, the way the saxophone ran up and down the scales in "I Cried for You," or the trill of the piano in "I Wished on the Moon." His mom first introduced him to jazz as a kid, and he'd thought Holiday's voice was the most amazing thing he'd ever heard, so ethereal. He used to joke with Lanie that he would have been better suited to an earlier era, the twenties or thirties, frequenting jazz clubs, tipping back whiskey during Prohibition. He'd never had a gift for the piano, like his mom, but he still loved the music. And the lyrics—all about love, betrayal, heartbreak—seemed so right, so true. Ella singing "Summertime" still gave him goose bumps. He thought back to their wedding night, Lanie twirling in his arms to Billie Holiday's "The Very Thought of You." She had smiled up at him and whispered, "This is just the beginning, honey." How little did they know then what lay ahead for them. He certainly never thought he'd find himself in the predicament he was in right now, his wife accusing him of cheating.

He still wasn't sure why he hadn't mentioned Samantha's joining the project in the first place. At the time, he didn't think it a necessary detail. He wouldn't normally fill Lanie in on the details of who was working on what project. But he got that Samantha was different. Did he also know, if he were being completely honest with himself, that Lanie would be upset? Especially since the project required so many late nights at the office?

So he'd conveniently deleted certain details from his workday life. But, then again, he and Lanie didn't have a lot of time to talk these days, aside from matters having to do with Benjamin. Rob heard plenty about the baby doldrums from his friends, but Ben was almost one year old now. How much longer did they have to wait till they could resume their normal relationship? Or was this the new normal?

Of course, there was one big detail he'd neglected to mention: Samantha *had* come on to him, in a manner of speaking. It was as if Lanie had been gifted with a premonition. Two days ago, after the museum board had signed off on the plans with applause and a shower of compliments, a small group of them decided to go out for drinks to celebrate. Rob called Lanie to pass along the good news. "Congratulations," she'd said icily. "We'll see you when you get home."

It was after the blowup over Samantha, before Benjamin had gotten sick. He knew he should go home, but it was the last place he wanted to be. Samantha would be with them, but so would Craig, Eli, Kate, and a few others from the firm; Rob made sure Lanie knew this. Frankly, he was more than a little ticked that his wife couldn't be happy for him. All those late nights had been worth it! He'd taken Lanie's icy remove, her accusatory looks and had filed them away with something like resentment. How quickly his disbelief had turned to a simmering anger. He was doing all this work for his family. How dare she accuse him of being disloyal! What he'd assumed would be a fight that would blow over had lasted what felt like an eternity. But he didn't say anything except, "Okay, I'll be home as soon as I can."

Then one round of shots led to another, and before long they were all singing bad karaoke out of tune. Rob had pulled Rupert Holmes's "Escape" from the tumbler, and they belted out the chorus line. Before he was done, a very drunk Samantha looped her arm over his shoulder, singing along. When the song finished, he excused himself to the men's room to "regain my dignity." As he headed to the restroom, he heard footsteps behind him, a sultry laugh.

When he turned, he saw it was Samantha, looking fabulously drunk. Her blazer was off, revealing a cream blouse with a camisole underneath. Her tight black skirt hugged her in all the right places. And she was still in her pumps, her Jimmy Choo's. Everyone in the office teased her about her expensive taste in shoes, but she countered that if she got hit by a truck she'd rather be wearing expensive shoes than expensive underwear. *A bit provocative, but clever,* Rob thought. In short, Samantha was the embodiment of all his vices, something his wife had realized long before him.

She came up to him and rubbed his shoulders. "Someone's a

little tense," she said. He wondered if she'd picked up on the trouble at home.

"Samantha, you're drunk. *Very* drunk." He could smell the vodka on her, could see her pores in the harsh light. He lifted her hands off his shoulders.

"So?" She tilted her head to the side, as if she couldn't quite focus on his face. "We worked hard. We deserve a few cocktails."

"I agree. But you don't want to go there." He hoped the innuendo was obvious enough.

"Go where?" She smirked. "Hey, your tie doesn't match."

At that moment, Kate walked up. "Looks like someone didn't make it to the girls' room. C'mon. I'll go with you." She took Sam by the arm and whispered to Rob, "Someone's had a little too much."

"Thanks," was all he could get out.

In the bathroom, he stood at the sink and splashed cold water onto his face. What the hell was he doing? Had he led Samantha on somehow? Was he sending her subtle signals even he wasn't aware of?

He looked like crap. Then he laughed. Of course, he did. They'd been working like maniacs to get the final drawings done. But what on earth was he doing? He loved his wife. He loved Benjamin. Then it dawned on him: He'd really fucked up by coming out tonight. What kind of idiot goes out to celebrate with the woman his wife suspects him of having an affair with? Even if she had no evidence that he'd been cheating, Lanie didn't trust him. He could feel it. He needed to get that trust back somehow.

There was no point mentioning Samantha's hallway escapades to Lanie now. Nothing had happened. His wife would just read layers and layers of subtext into a little shoulder rub.

Still, one thought plagued him: *Did a lascivious thought a cheater make?*

He hoped he and Lanie could get back to normal, whatever that was. In just a few more hours, he'd have to go into work. Lanie had already called in sick after the night's escapades with the baby. He heard the buzz of her electric toothbrush in the bathroom and moved to go downstairs, catch a few hours of sleep on the couch before his alarm woke him. But on his way down, he heard her voice.

"Honey?"

He turned, pillow in hand.

"Come to bed." She held out her hand. "I want you to be close to us. Just in case Benjamin needs anything."

It wasn't quite forgiveness, but Rob reminded himself he didn't need forgiveness. Whatever it was, he'd take it.

He followed her soft footsteps down the hall and fell into bed next to his wife, his girl.

13

"Lemon betwixt buttery layers makes for an unbeatable
combination. For summertime, think tart, light, fresh."
—*The Book of Kringle*

Ellen, Lanie, and Benjamin sat under the big oak tree on the Union
Terrace, eating overstuffed crepes from the Golden Pan. It was a warm
day in early June, and the trees danced with bright greens and yellows.
Orange, red, and yellow chairs bedecked the terrace, like colorful
piñatas stretching out to the lake. She and Lanie were planning the
details of Benjamin's first birthday party to be hosted in a few weeks at
The Singular Kringle. As they talked, Lanie broke off small pieces of
her ham and cheese for the baby, who sat buckled in his stroller.

"I can't believe you're almost one, baby!" Ellen tickled his toes
while Benjamin kicked and cooed.

"I like the Winnie-the-Pooh theme. You're sure you don't mind
being on cake duty?"

"Not at all. I want to," Ellen said. She hummed a few bars of the
Winnie-the-Pooh theme song and Benjamin smiled in recognition.
"It's so funny that he knows that already. He's like a little sponge."

"Hmm . . ." Lanie said in mid-swallow. "So true. So, I was hoping
to keep the party small. You know, just close friends and family. Will
you bring Henry?"

Ellen grinned. "I suppose I should. You could finally meet him. Might not be such a bad thing."

"I'm beginning to think he doesn't exist, kind of like Snuffle-upagus."

Ellen laughed. "Oh, he most definitely exists. You just don't hang out in the cool corners of town."

"Well, bring him. We'd love to meet him."

"And you and Rob? Things better on that front?" She couldn't help herself. She needed to know. Just the other day Lanie had divulged her suspicions that Rob was having an affair. With Samantha. At the office. Go figure. This was before Benjamin's fever had given them all a good scare.

Ellen had tried to talk Lanie down off the ledge: "No way is Rob having an affair. He's way too busy and exhausted to pull it off practically, let alone emotionally."

Ellen couldn't fathom it. As far as she could tell, the only incriminating evidence Lanie had was that this woman answered the phone in Rob's office on a Friday night. But they were work partners. A late night wasn't so unusual, was it? She supposed the failure to mention it to Lanie in the first place was Rob's biggest mistake in the whole mess.

"I don't know. I honestly don't. He still denies it. Maybe it was just a one-night stand, maybe it was nothing. Maybe my imagination is getting the best of me. It's almost beside the point, though. He was spending all this time with Samantha—work or otherwise—and he felt the need to hide it from me. Isn't that saying something?"

Ellen thought about it, took another bite. Her stomach churned. Lately, she'd been having indigestion and something that felt a lot like how she imagined hot flashes feeling. It was hell getting old. "I suppose if I hadn't known Rob for six years and loved him like a brother," she began, "I'd agree. But, I just can't imagine him doing anything so seedy. He probably didn't mention it because he assumed you'd get mad, or worse, jealous."

"Which I would have." Lanie paused. "Which I am."

"See?"

"So what's your point? I'm in the wrong here? I swear, Ellen, if it weren't for Benjamin, I would have kicked him out of the house that night."

"Of course not. It's just that I don't think you have anything to worry about. At a certain point, you have to take your husband's word for it. Unless, of course, you're planning to become Samantha's stalker."

"Don't count me out," Lanie said sternly, then started to laugh. "God, now who sounds ridiculous? I think I've lost my mind." She crumpled up the rest of her crepe and tossed it into the trash barrel next to them. "It's so weird. I've gone from being completely pissed, to denying it, to being plain sad about it all. How could we have become such a cliché? Husband goes off and has a fling after his wife gets fat and has a baby."

Ellen almost spit her water out. "First of all, you don't get to call yourself fat around me. Got it?" Lanie shrugged. "Second of all, you guys have had a lot going on lately. You're both working long hours, you've got a new baby—it takes a toll."

Benjamin banged his stroller tray, as if in agreement.

"It's all about balance, honey," Ellen tried again. "Just like in a good kringle, no one ingredient should overwhelm another."

"I don't know." Lanie sighed. "Maybe we just need a break, a vacation or something. Work has been so incredibly stressful. Something's got to give. The other week I lost out on a restraining order for a guy who I *know* is going to keep stalking his ex-wife. And I feel personally responsible. That takes a toll, too."

Ellen held Benjamin's juice cup and looked at Lanie.

"What? Why are you smirking at me like that?"

"Henry and I were just talking about that very thing—vacation, that is, not restraining orders."

Lanie shot her a look. "I've always wanted to go back to Nantucket and Henry's never been . . ."

"But I've never even met him!"

"What? You don't trust my taste in men?" She regretted the question instantly; Lanie had never been a fan of Max's.

"I'm not going to answer that. Suffice it to say I don't think you should be traveling across the country with a man I've never met. What if he's a mass murderer?"

"If Henry is a mass murderer, we're all pretty safe."

Benjamin started to fuss in his stroller. Ellen set down his cup and pulled him out, perching him on her lap. Melted cheese stuck out on tufts of his hair. Lanie dabbed her napkin on her water bottle and wiped his hands clean, then tried her best to pull the sticky mess out of his brown curls. She dug the pacifier out of her purse and plopped it into his mouth. Benjamin happily sucked away.

"Wow. I wish I had a body like that." Lanie nodded toward a lithe girl in cut-off shorts and a bright pink tube top walking by with a beer in hand. Her body was toned and tanned, muscular in all the right places.

"But you do!"

"Hah." Lanie grabbed at her belly. "My mommy tummy has yet to go away, and my thighs were mommy thighs *before* the baby." They both took in the young coeds walking around them. It was too discouraging. Ellen wanted to get back to the vacation.

"If you're so worried about Henry and me, why don't you all come along?"

"So now you're definitely going with Henry?"

"I'm just saying, think it over. It could be fun."

"And what would your date think if you brought your sister and her husband and her toddler along? Kind of a buzz kill, if you ask me."

"Who cares what Henry thinks? If he wants me as his tour guide, he'll have to accept it. Besides, it'll be more fun if you're there."

Ellen stopped herself. Maybe she was selling Henry short. She liked him, didn't she? Why else would she be talking about a long weekend in Nantucket? Things seemed to be moving in the right direction, ever since the night of their first awkward kiss. In fact, Henry had slept over at Ellen's place a few nights in the guestroom.

And over dinner, when the talk turned to places they'd like to visit before they died, Henry mentioned Nantucket.

"But I love Nantucket!" Ellen had said. "I worked there one summer in college."

"Well, then, what better thing for two lost souls than to spend a few days on Nantucket?" he'd joked. But when she asked him the next day if he were serious, he'd said absolutely. So serious that he had already looked into possible plane fares and ferry times in August.

"He's a good man. I think you'll like him," she said now in his defense.

"Maybe a vacation is a good idea. I could really use a break. Besides, if Rob *is* having an affair, he won't want to go away with us."

"How's that?"

"He wouldn't want to be apart from Samantha. Or maybe we could bring the slut with us. She could be our nanny!" Lanie giggled.

"Glad to have my sister back." Ellen handed the baby to her. "Now stop with this affair craziness, would you? Come to Nantucket. I'm telling Henry that we're going and you're coming, too."

Ellen looked into Benjamin's big eyes. "Can you say Nantucket, baby?" She pulled out his paci. He lifted his arms in a "So Big!" response and said, "Dah."

"Close enough." Ellen smiled at her sister. "Close enough, sweet boy."

Summer

14

"[The] art of *kringle*-making demands a fine sense
of balance. No one element—whether dough, filling,
or topping—should overwhelm another."
—*The Book of Kringle*

The cape roses were in full bloom. All along the roadside, vibrant pink blossoms dotted green bouquets, like fuchsia butterflies aloft in the air. Ellen hadn't been back this way since college, when she had worked one summer on Nantucket for a cleaning company that readied rental homes between tenants. Her father liked to joke that it was the one job that had instilled a work ethic in her. She knew what it meant to have dirt underneath her nails, knew what it felt like to have her knees rubbed so raw from scrubbing floors that only thick aloe creams could soothe the burn. She remembered the smell of suntan lotion, left over from Sundays on the beach, mixed in with the ammonia of cleaning emollients on Mondays. How hard it had been to make those eight o'clock morning shifts back then, clearing out the detritus of one family and making room for the next, due to arrive that very afternoon on the ferry.

She was always surprised by how messy rich people could be. They left behind, after just a week, old magazines and newspapers, too many beer bottles and wine decanters to count, energy bar wrappers, broken plastic pails and shovels, abandoned suntan lotion, flip-flops, a trail of sand through the house, and discarded shells that evidently hadn't made the final cut for the trip back to Boston or New York or D.C.

It was the bathrooms she hated the most, though. Apparently, the wealthy never cleaned out their tubs. Inevitably, a big swath of dyed blond hair would be pooling in the drain. Ellen would pick it up with her rubber gloves and discard it quickly, imagining the older woman from whose head it had come. Naturally thin, her wrinkles Botoxed, her unnaturally white teeth dazzling.

It was funny to think that now she was here on the flip side of things, coming to Nantucket as a consumer, not a cleaner, as clientele as opposed to the help. It was nicer this way. As fun as those booze-filled, sun-drenched summers had been, there'd never been a love interest, at least not more than a fleeting one. Back then she had been filled with dreams of where life would take her. Would she fly to Paris to live with her friend Julia, who had stayed on after spending sophomore year abroad? Would she go back to Boston and find a job in the advertising industry? Or, would the pull of her childhood home be too great to resist? There was nothing quite like Midwestern hospitality, especially when she held it up against the more austere East Coast veneer. This was before her father had been felled by his heart, her choices suddenly narrowed to one.

She and Max had never traveled out east. *Odd,* she thought to herself now, as she dragged her suitcase on wheels over the cobblestoned street. Not once in ten years. For all his big dreams, he rarely ventured farther than a two-hundred-mile radius of their town. In fact, come to think of it, she wasn't sure he had ever left the Midwest when they were married. Once, when he was selling pharmaceuticals out of a suitcase, a job that lasted a brief two months before he got fired for siphoning off extra pills to friends, he traveled every few months to the Twin Cities, Minneapolis and St. Paul. But he never invited Ellen to join him. It was as if they had shared an unspoken rule that business and pleasure couldn't mix.

She walked next to Henry now as she pointed out The Juice Bar on the corner that served out-of-this-island smoothies, the whaling museum, and the bike store where they would rent bikes for the weekend. A sign, WHEELS AND DEALS, was posted in the window. They zigzagged between the other travelers just off the ferry, a sea of brightly colored polo shirts and shorts. Young children with packs strapped to their tiny backs wandered around, their eyes wide.

She loved being back. She'd forgotten how charming it was, the feel of being on the island, somehow a part of it, yet removed, an outsider come to visit.

She inhaled deeply. "Can you smell it?"

"Smell what?" Henry asked. He sniffed the air.

"The ocean . . . saltwater . . . roses . . . vacation." She turned to him and smiled.

"Mmm . . ." He breathed in deeply. "Amazing."

She wasn't sure if he was humoring her, but she didn't really care. She finally felt as if she was back in her element, a place where she could unwind but also pretend she was as refined and elegant as the vacationing women around her. She'd gotten a manicure and a pedicure in hot pink before leaving Wisconsin. Now all she needed was a tan and a few Nantucket mudslides.

They followed South Beach Street all the way down to a side street, where a charming, gray-shingled colonial with arms of deep red roses stretching around it awaited them. The Inn at Forty-One-Seventy, it was called on its web site, where she'd booked their room. Ellen liked the geographical coordinates of the inn's name; she thought it lent it an appealing authenticity.

Henry squeezed her hand.

"Looks like this is it." He held the screen door open for her. "You are as fair as a rose in May, my love."

"Bernard Shaw?" she guessed.

"Chaucer." Henry winked at her as she stepped inside.

A spry man with a dash of gray hair jumped up from his chair to greet them. He was nicely tanned, wearing navy shorts and a short-sleeved pink oxford shirt.

"Welcome, welcome," he said, extending his hand with a smile. "You must be . . ." he paused.

"Ellen McClarety and Henry Moon," she filled in for him.

"Oh, right! You're the couple from Wisconsin." He beamed with what seemed genuine enthusiasm. "There's some great country out there. I used to go to summer camp up by Manitowish Lake when I was a kid."

"You're kidding." Now it was Ellen's turn to be genuinely enthusiastic. "That's where my dad went to summer camp. Camp Manitowish. Now that's what I call a coincidence."

He looked at her as if they were long lost friends, and then at Henry, as if trying to ascertain their relationship to each other. *Did she and Henry appear married?* she wondered. *Maybe recently single? Or maybe never married but in love?*

"Sorry, I've forgotten my manners. I'm Wes Crowley, your innkeeper. Very pleased to meet you." He gave a little bow. "Let me take you to your room." He grabbed a key off a hook and took Ellen's bag from her. "You'll be staying in the Nautilus Room, my favorite. It has spectacular views of the island."

They followed him up a winding staircase to a blue wooden door, where he ushered them into a room framed by windows looking out onto a blue sliver of water. The wallpaper danced with whimsical silver sailboats. Nautical maps of Nantucket and the Cape dotted the walls. So charming! Her heart sunk a bit, though, when she saw the two single beds with their matching compass quilts; she'd assumed when she checked the "double occupancy" box online that they'd get a queen-size bed. But to say anything now would be inappropriate.

"Wow! This is fantastic!" Henry said. "Look at that view." He walked over to the window.

"It really is. Thank you," Ellen chimed in. Henry reached for his wallet to give Wes a tip, but Wes held up his hand.

"No, that isn't necessary. Keep your money for the restaurants and the shops."

"All right then. Thanks." Henry slipped his wallet back into his pocket.

"Oh, and look, Henry, there are chocolate-covered cranberries." Ellen was holding up a basket stuffed with candies and brochures.

"An island treasure," Wes said. "Well, I'll leave you two to your vacation." He handed Henry the room key, hanging from a sailor's knot. "Please don't hesitate to ask if there's anything we can do for you. You'll find maps of the island in the basket. Breakfast is served downstairs from eight to ten in the morning. Join us anytime."

"Thank you," she said, turning to him with a smile. "This is lovely."

"Enjoy."

When he shut the door behind him, she flung herself onto the bed like a child. Henry did the same on the other bed. "I love vacation!"

"And you haven't even seen the stores yet," she added.

"We're not here to shop, remember?"

"Whatever you say." She plopped a chocolate into her mouth, enjoying the sweetness melting on her tongue. "You really should try one of these."

She threw one in his general direction and Henry lunged to the side of his bed, hopelessly missing and nearly falling to the floor. They looked at each other and burst out laughing, as if already high on the champagne they'd drink later that night.

The long weekend unfolded at a languid pace. She checked in with Larry twice a day, but each time he chastised her for worrying.

"We're *fine* here. Don't worry. Have fun. Enjoy Nantucket. Enjoy Henry." She could almost hear the wink in his voice.

"And how's Erin?" She winked back.

"Erin's fine, too. Don't you worry about her." Before she left, Ellen had caught the two of them in an embrace in the back room. They were embarrassed, trying to hide their budding romance from her all summer, but she already knew. She had caught the sideways glances and smiles, the cup of coffee that Larry poured for Erin each morning, how they made a special point of leaving the store separately, as if Ellen were a bloodhound who had to be thrown off their scent.

"And the board? You're keeping up on the drips and tips?"

"Absolutely. We've had some real doozies from the glass bowl." Ellen smiled to think of it. "Today it's the difference between *forgo* and *forego* with a 'e,'" he added.

"A good one!" She couldn't help herself. It was a common error, using *forego* to indicate abstaining from something, when really a person meant they'd *forgo*. She knew the store was in good hands.

For the rest of the day, she and Henry people-watched, taking in the sights and sounds of those who "summered" on the island. He raised an eyebrow at the rudeness of one man who complained that the sandwich line was taking too long, asking, "Who the hell is in charge of this place?"

"Guess someone's not accustomed to waiting," Ellen said under her breath. "Some people pack a sense of entitlement in their suitcases along with their sunblock."

"What an ass," Henry said, surprising her with his vehemence.

She thought to herself then and there that she could like this man—a lot. Even if they hadn't slept together yet. Even if she was beginning to wonder if he and Charlotte had made a deathbed pact that Henry would never have sex again. How else to explain his passionate kisses *sans* anything else? Max had been at her house for three hours and had bedded her; Ellen figured she'd logged more than a hundred hours with Henry so far and nary a move. Nantucket would be the linchpin. If sandy beaches and the scent of suntan lotion couldn't inspire romance, what would?

The first night, however, had been a complete bust. Back at their room, Henry made a fuss about how tired he was. "The jet lag, the champagne," he'd explained. In the bathroom, Ellen debated whether to leave her makeup on or take it off. She didn't want Henry to think she slept with the stuff on; then again, she wasn't sure if she was prepared to show him her "natural" face. If the circumstances had been different, if he had, for instance, immediately thrown her down on his bed and started kissing her, she wouldn't have cared. She would have fallen asleep in his arms, makeup kissed off by his gentle lips. Instead, she knew for a fact that as she stood in the bathroom getting ready for bed, Henry was in his very single bed, reading glasses on.

She decided to wash her face. The man would have to love her the way God made her or it wasn't worth pursuing this relationship. With one last swoosh of mouthwash, she opened the bathroom door, hoping beyond hope that maybe he had dimmed the lights, pulled back his comforter for her.

But no.

"This is an incredible book. Have you read him?" he asked, without looking up, a Patrick O'Brian novel in his hands.

"No, I've always meant to though."

"Great seafaring drama when you're all cozy in your bed on an island."

"Hmm," Ellen said as she slipped underneath her own covers.

"I always like to have a few good books with me on vacation," he added.

Ellen put her head on the pillow, looked up at the ceiling. "Yes, it's a good idea." She waited.

At last, she heard Henry turn in his bed, set his glasses down. She braced herself for the warmth of his body against hers and felt a shiver of anticipation travel down her spine.

"Well, g'night, my holly tree. Thank you for a wonderful first day of vacation." He flipped off the light. She heard him blow a kiss across the yawning chasm between their beds.

Really? She'd traveled hundreds of miles for a blown kiss? She couldn't believe her bad luck. What had happened to all the lovey-dovey sayings back home, entwined arms and legs that promised more to come on vacation? Had Max turned her into a sex-crazed

ninny? Was Henry truly tired? A noble bunkmate? Was he waiting for her to make a move? When she heard him snoring after a
few minutes, she knew the latter was not the case. She said a silent
prayer for help. Apparently it was going to take some kind of divine
intervention for things to go any further.

On the second day, they toured Nantucket by bus, taking in sea
captains' homes, Sankaty Head golf course and lighthouse, and the
so-called Serengeti of Nantucket. Around noon they hopped off to
get a bite to eat in 'Sconset. At a restaurant perched by the ocean,
they sat and held hands across the table. Ellen had decided to let
last night slide. Better just to enjoy today. Henry ordered buttery,
mouth-watering lobster while she savored every bite of a grilled
salmon salad.

"Heaven on earth," Henry pronounced as they traded bites.
"We've found it."

"I think you're right."

Afterwards, they walked along a stretch of beach below. The crisp
waves whipped up to the shore as the tide moved in. Every so often
Henry would try to pull Ellen into the ice-cold water, tickling her,
ducking around her, grabbing her, and finally throwing her down on
the sand for a kiss. It was romantic and wonderful in a way that last
night had decidedly not been. She could feel the sand in her hair, a
rock poking in her back. She didn't care.

When they continued walking, she stopped at the water's edge to
retrieve a black rock with a faint white mark running through it.

"See this?"

"A rock?" Henry looked at her quizzically.

"It's not just a rock; it's a friendship rock, Henry."

He stared at her blankly.

"You've never heard of a friendship rock?"

"Should I have? Is that one of those things in the trashy magazines
you were reading on the ferry?"

She ignored the jab. "When you find a black rock with a white stripe running all the way around, it's a friendship rock. It's supposed to bring you good luck—and friends, of course."

He threw his head back and laughed, a good-natured, relaxed laugh. "You believe that? If so, I have a boat with a hole in it to sell you."

She grabbed his hand and started walking with him along the shoreline. "But the line has to go all the way around, uninterrupted. Otherwise it doesn't count. That's what makes them so rare." She gave the stone to him so he could rub his thumb over it.

He wandered off to comb the beach by himself. About five minutes later, he called out: "Hey, look! I think I found another one."

She made her way over and grabbed both stones from his hands for inspection, incredulous at their good fortune.

"Henry." He grinned at her sheepishly. "You big cheat! You've scratched a white line around this rock with another. That doesn't count."

He laughed, then kissed the top of her head.

"That's my Ellen. Can't get anything past her."

She felt a pang of familiarity. That's what Max had called her: "my Ellen." Except here, on Nantucket with Henry, it felt right.

"It was clever, I'll give you that. I've never known anyone to make his own friendship rock."

"Well, sometimes, you have to make your own luck, you know?"

"Don't I know it," she said under her breath. As far as she was concerned, she'd been trying to make her own luck her entire life. She'd come to think of it as selective serendipity.

She handed the true friendship rock back and Henry slipped it into his shirt pocket.

"We better head back to catch the next bus if we want dinner in town."

Henry reached over and held her hand as they walked up the beach. Lanie, Rob, and Benjamin would arrive tomorrow (Lanie had insisted that Ellen and Henry have at least two days to themselves on the island), and Ellen could hardly wait.

. . . .

The next day they met her sister and her family at the ferry. Ellen was high from the night before; Henry had finally shed his island shyness, if that's what she could call it. While he hadn't pushed their beds together, he had climbed into hers, where she had discovered the freckles running along his ribs, the funny little bruise above his right ankle, the small, rosy birthmark hiding behind his ear. If fireworks hadn't exactly gone off, a sense of well-being had swept over her, like a cool wave. To think that she might actually be falling in love with a man other than Max, well, it made her feel slightly unmoored—in a good way.

Ellen was replaying the night in her mind when she saw Lanie waving to her from the boat deck. She wore a bright floral sundress, her bob still styled even after the long flight and ferry ride, with Benjamin bouncing on her hip. Rob, dressed in a Green Bay Packers shirt and tan shorts, waved to them like a crazy man.

"Ahoy there, sailor!" Henry shouted out.

As they walked down the ramp, Ellen overheard her sister saying, "Boat. That's a boat." She scooped the baby out of Lanie's arms.

"Lovebug. You made it!" She threw Benjamin up in the air, who squealed with delight, his sun hat tipping slightly to the side. She gave Lanie and Rob hugs. "Hi, hi, hi. So great to have you all here! How was the flight out?"

Henry offered to take one of Rob's bags.

"Not bad." Rob gave her a kiss on the cheek. "The stewardess kept bringing Benjamin all sorts of treats, so he was a happy man for most of the flight."

"Except for the landing." Lanie rolled her eyes. "Ouch."

"Did your ears pop?" She asked Benjamin who was now on her hip, his arm around her neck, poking her nose.

"He's into noses being horns now," Lanie explained apologetically.

"Honk, honk!" Ellen shouted. "I missed you buddy. Kisses, lots of kisses for you." She kissed him all over his fat cheeks.

"Henry, hello. Good to see you again." Lanie smiled.

"Good to see you. Glad you made it here all right."

"Me too. This place looks great."

"Can't wait for my first Nantucket lager," Rob added.

"Henry can help you there. He sampled quite a few at dinner last night."

"Rob, my man, I'm at your service," he said with a grin. "Anything I can do to help, you just let me know." He slapped him on the back.

"Good to see you again." Rob shook Henry's hand. They'd all met briefly at Benjamin's birthday party back in June. "Just getting out of these clothes and into my flip-flops will be a good start." Lanie strapped Benjamin into his stroller.

"This place is so cute!"

"I told you you'd love it here," Ellen said as they left the dock and followed the cobblestones into town. Ellen couldn't help but notice that her sister looked relaxed, happy, as if the cloud of suspicion hovering over Rob had lifted. She prayed that was the case. Otherwise how to explain the change from a few weeks ago? Unless, of course, Lanie was secretly plotting her revenge, a murder on the island, a husband gone mysteriously missing like in those television specials. She would have to ask for details later.

"We'll get you guys settled at the inn, and then you can join us at the beach once you've had a chance to change."

"Sounds like a plan. I already *feel* more relaxed." Lanie nodded at a passerby in pink whale shorts. "How can I not feel more relaxed around men who wear shorts with whales on them?"

After they'd left the others with directions to Surfside Beach, Ellen and Henry walked to the bike shop and paid for two three-speeds for the weekend. Hers was seashell white with a wicker basket tied to the front. She stuffed their beach towels, suntan lotion, water bottles, and books into it.

"Is this a long ride?" Henry asked. "I'm not so young anymore, you know."

"No more than an hour's ride," she said spritely.

Henry looked alarmed.

"Kidding," she called over her shoulder, as she angled the bike out the store's door and around the corner. "Where's your sense of humor?"

He smiled and followed behind her. She stood up on the pedals as they traveled over the cobblestones and down side roads till they reached the main stretch leading to the water, where they could cruise on the smooth blacktop path. It was nice to feel her muscles pumping again, the cool breeze on her face. She felt . . . young. On the right they passed one island home after another, some modest gray capes, others with expansive porches stretching around to swimming pools in the back. Their shingles were still a new tan, not yet the weathered gray of older homes. She wondered if these were year-round or summer getaways. She couldn't imagine having such a luxurious place as a part-time retreat.

Henry shouted behind her, pointing to a restaurant on the left, advertising dollar beers before five o'clock. "We should stop there on the way back," he yelled, and she gave him a thumbs-up.

Scarlet beach roses dotted the path all the way to the shore. A red-winged blackbird landed on one bush, calling *"Conk-a-ree! Conk-a-ree!"* She knew from her mother, an avid birdwatcher, that only the males sported the red flash of color with a streak of yellow underneath. Funny how it was reversed in so many species, the male having to be the pretty one, do all the flirting. Henry would never survive as a blackbird.

At last, they pulled their bikes up to the stands and locked them. Ellen took off her sandals, then said "Ouch, ouch!" as she did a little dance on the hot sand, already sizzling in the late-morning heat. She promptly put her shoes back on.

Henry stood looking out at the blue expanse, waves rolling in, as some kids jumped in with their boogie boards. Blue and yellow umbrellas dotted the white sand, like candles on a birthday cake.

"This place is incredible," he said, his voice draped in awe. "I've never seen anything like it."

"Stick with me," she teased and helped him navigate his way over to the umbrella stand, where a young girl, no more than sixteen, gave them two beach chairs and an umbrella for twenty dollars. Thick white zinc oxide coated her nose. Her hair was a shocking blue, and a tiny spider tattoo crawled across her bare shoulder. A young man stood at her side, asking her what she did last night, whether flirting or working, Ellen couldn't tell.

Their chair straps slung over their shoulders, they wandered down the boardwalk to the sand. Henry lugged the yellow-and-white-striped umbrella, while Ellen carried their bag. She steered them to the right, where there was more open sand, and at last they planted their umbrella pole in a patch with a clear view of the water.

He laughed as she tried to undo her beach chair, the thing all elbows to her. He set his down easily then helped her with hers.

"Well, aren't you Mr. Know-It-All," she said, embarrassed that she couldn't figure it out for herself, she the veteran islander.

They looked out on cool reaches of blue, drawing a line against the sky in the distance. "Mmm . . . it smells like the ocean," she said, a stupid thing to say, but true. She loved the smell of saltwater, suntan lotion, and sand. *This* was summer. She smoothed the white lotion, warm to the touch, onto her arms and legs. Her chair sat at the umbrella's edge, her face still in the shade. Henry, however, sat directly in the sun, his hat still on. She had to laugh. "Do you want some sunblock?"

"I'm good for now, thanks."

"You don't need to play macho around me. This is Nantucket. The sun's a little stronger around here."

"I know. I just want to enjoy it for a few minutes."

Her anticipation of rubbing suntan lotion onto his back quickly faded. She pulled out her book instead.

"What've you got there?"

She held it up for him to see. "*Wuthering Heights.* You're not the only one rereading the classics. Thought maybe I'd get more out of the heather imagery a second time around."

Henry laughed. "Ah, a romance to break the heart. . . . Maybe Catherine chooses differently on a second reading?"

Ellen looked sharply at him across the top of her book. What was he implying? But before she could parse his meaning (was Henry supposed to be Heathcliff and Max, Edgar?), he continued.

"You know, on second thought, I think I'll test the water. Looks refreshing."

He pushed up from his chair and jogged over to the water, pulling his shirt and hat off in one swoop. As a wave came up in perfect synchronicity, he plunged in and for a second his body disappeared in the blue. Ellen held her breath until she spied his head, bobbing like a buoy, in the wake of the wave.

"Henry Moon," she called from the water's edge, his hat in her hands and her toes curling at the freezing cold. "I'll admit, you surprise me sometimes."

Around noon, when the sun was straight overhead, the others arrived. They'd ridden their bikes, with Benjamin trailing shotgun in the tent-like attachment that reminded Ellen of a motorcycle pod. She laughed when Lanie pulled him out; his face and tummy, arms and legs, were all streaked in white sunblock. He looked like a little alien.

"Hey, big guy. Nice hat!" Rob set their station up next to Henry—beach towels, chairs, a mini-cooler, an umbrella, and a rope bag teeming with beach pails and shovels.

Ever since Lanie had shared her suspicions, Ellen had been trying to read Rob's tone and expression to detect any insincerity or subterfuge. But she couldn't deny it—Rob still struck her as one of the most sincere, nicest guys she knew. No amount of imagining could get him into another woman's bed in her mind.

"That sun feels wonderful." Lanie stretched out on a bright orange beach blanket, her body framed in a slimming black one-piece. Mommy tummy or not, Ellen's sister was still a knockout. The new bathing suit accentuated her breasts (which, Ellen noted, a few weeks of breast-feeding had done nothing to diminish), and her long legs, shining in oil, shimmered with suggestion.

Ellen suddenly felt fusty in her diamond-print bathing suit with its skirt. Her legs, which she'd thought were all right for a late-fortyish woman, now looked lumpy and spider-veined compared to her sister's. What could Henry possibly see in her? She felt another hot flash coming on, coupled with a wave of nausea.

Rob opened the cooler and pulled out two beers hidden in Styrofoam holders, handing one to Henry.

"Now *this* is what I call living."

"Doesn't get much better," Henry agreed. He didn't know anything about what Lanie had confided to Ellen, only that she and Rob were in desperate need of a vacation. Ellen had said it would be fun to have Benjamin and another couple along—and that it would be a nice thing for them to do. Henry had happily obliged.

She watched while Benjamin busily dropped sand into a bucket. Every so often he'd look up at his mom for approval, who clapped enthusiastically.

"Remember when life was this easy? Just a little sand in a bucket could make your day?" Lanie asked.

"Don't I." Ellen thought back to her pre-Max days. She hadn't heard from or talked to him since his surprise visit.

"Hey, isn't there anything in there for the ladies?" Lanie turned toward her husband.

"I almost forgot." Rob pulled out a juice box from the cooler.

"Very funny," she said. "How about some punch with a kick?"

She poked the straw through the juice box and handed it to the baby, then grabbed a strawberry wine cooler from Rob. "Now that's what I'm talking about."

"My wife continues to live in the eighties," Rob explained to Henry. "And I love her all the more for it." He winked at Lanie, who beamed. "No one else in the world drinks wine coolers. I couldn't believe they still make them!"

They all had a good laugh. Then Ellen asked for a cooler herself, which sparked another round of laughter.

Later, the boys took Benjamin out to the water's edge to search for shells. Lanie shielded her eyes with an upheld palm. "Henry's got a pretty hot bod for a gardener."

"Really? I hadn't noticed." Ellen grinned. "It must be all that heavy lifting of pots and plants."

"Yeah, right. So, it looks like the summer of romance between Ellen and Henry is official, yes?"

"We'll see." Ellen didn't want to give too much away just yet. She fanned herself, sweat pooling at her brow. "Is it just me or is it really hot today?"

"Um, hello? It's summertime? On Nantucket?"

"I swear I'm having hot flashes. Look at me!" A patch of sweat had bloomed on Ellen's stomach.

"Menopause, no question," Lanie joked. "By the way, I'm glad you made us come."

"Well, I didn't exactly *make* you come, but I'm glad you're here."

"Me, too. We've been here only a few hours, but somehow everything just seems better on Nantucket. Simpler, you know?"

"I know what you mean." She wanted to ask if the affair business was resolved, but the boys were heading back to their towels. They unpacked sandwiches and chips from the cooler and shared a picnic, while Henry shared the story of the teenage romance that had played out beside them earlier on the beach.

"You should have seen this girl. She couldn't have acted less interested in the guy, and he was practically drooling on her."

"Poor dude," Rob said. "I feel his pain. Lanie didn't give me the time of day when we first met. She thought I was some poor grad student . . . which I was."

Lanie leaned in to give him a kiss. "Good thing you proved yourself worthy later on."

Ellen played patty-cake with the baby when a young woman in a yellow thong bikini paraded by them. The conversation stalled.

"You know, I *like* Nantucket," Henry said.

"I'll see you that 'like' and raise you one," Rob joked.

"Boys, don't be fresh," Lanie cautioned. "Thank your lucky stars for what you have."

"Oh, I thank my lucky star every day." Henry gave Ellen a quick kiss.

"Very funny." Ellen could tell her sister was impressed though.

Soon they packed their bags, ready to bike back to the inn for showers and an early dinner of lobster and wine on the terrace. In the natural light, Ellen got a better look at Henry. "I hate to say it, Henry, but you look like our dinner tonight."

He held out his arms, which seemed to be turning pinker by the minute. "Does that mean I'm cooked?"

Rob whistled. "Dude, you're going to be in a world of hurt later." Henry looked chagrined.

"Don't worry, we'll get some aloe gel on the way back," Lanie offered.

"I thought my skin was feeling a little tight." He tucked his towel into the basket and eased himself gingerly onto his bicycle seat.

Ellen started to laugh, then Lanie, then Rob. "I'm sorry, Henry, but we can't help it." She was bent over now, hugging her sides. "If you're not the spitting image of a lobster riding a bicycle, I don't know what is!"

15

"There is something else a home needs to make it
a real home and a good place for growing boys and girls.
It needs pleasant surroundings and a cheerful outlook."
—*Talks to Mothers*

Even the *air* felt different on the island, crisp, inviting, fresh. Lanie woke up early and tiptoed around in the dark until she found the running gear she'd laid out last night. Vacation, she figured, was as good a time as any to jumpstart her running again. She shut the door softly behind her, leaving behind her dozing boys. She probably had a good hour before either one stirred.

It was brisk outside, the sun beginning to pink the horizon. She zipped up her running jacket before starting down the cobblestone street, which led out to the main thru-road. She loved going for jogs in new places, unlocking a whole new world each time she set out, her feet rhythmically hitting the pavement. Last night, after a decadent dinner of lobster (and a few jokes at Henry's expense), she looked at the map Wes had given them and highlighted a running loop that was about two miles long. Two miles would be plenty after not having run for months.

Slowly, she felt her blood start to pump again, her breathing grow more labored. She passed the mansions that lined the road, seemingly tucked into every available plot of land on the way out to sea. Except for a few early-morning delivery trucks, the island was quiet. Sprays of roses were slowly opening up along the weathered fences guarding the homes behind, and she watched as a calico cat slipped across the road ahead of her, then ducked behind the shrubs of a day-care center.

Her lungs began to ache, the cold air burning. But it was a good kind of hurt, she told herself, a chill that reminded her of crisp fall cross-country runs back in college. On their late afternoon practices through the Blue Hills, she could always sense when fall was around the corner. Not just from the vibrant crimsons and golds that magically appeared overhead one day but because the air turned so precisely; it was sharp, as if she could cut through the scent of fallen leaves, ripening apples.

It felt good to leave the stress of work behind, the humdrum of their lives. It had been too long. And it felt especially good to be rid of the tension that had been tormenting their marriage over the past few weeks. Oddly enough, it hadn't been Rob who ultimately convinced Lanie of his innocence. It was Samantha.

She took Benjamin into the office one sunny summer afternoon, a rare day off from work, to say hello to his daddy. She figured the least she could do was make sure that her son stayed on "speaking" terms with him. And perhaps she was beginning to feel a smidgen of doubt. What if she was wrong about Rob and Samantha? She thought if she could just catch a glimpse of them working together, unawares, she'd know in an instant if there were anything between them. Maybe that's what she was secretly hoping for when she arrived at his office.

Benjamin ran up and down the long hallways, chirping "Hi!" in his high-pitched voice to all the office assistants. As they found their way to Rob's office at the end of the hall, the baby made a beeline for a closed door. Recently her boy had learned how to turn doorknobs, and the shiny metal of the door handle was too tempting to resist.

Lanie rushed to grab him as soon as she saw what he was up to, but he beat her to it. The door opened as the words, "Benjamin, stop it!" left her mouth. She gasped at what she saw behind it: Samantha, behind her desk, in a kiss. With another woman.

Samantha quickly pulled away. She looked completely flustered. The other woman was petite, probably younger than Samantha, with a pageboy haircut.

"Lanie, hi. Benjamin, hi. What a surprise."

Lanie watched as Samantha searched for words. Which was fine because she had no idea what to say either. She was sure she was blushing as deeply as Samantha. She held Benjamin's hand as he pulled in another direction.

"God, Samantha, I'm so, so sorry. Benjamin just broke loose and he opened the door before I could stop him."

"No worries." She smoothed her jacket and looked out the door to see if anyone else was in the hallway. "This is my friend, Veronica. Veronica, Lanie. Lanie is Rob's wife and a lawyer in her own right."

"Hi. Nice to meet you." She stepped forward to shake Lanie's hand. She had perfect little white teeth.

"We were just going to get some lunch." Samantha tried now for normalcy.

"Oh, right. Good. Don't let us get in your way." Lanie cringed at the false cheerfulness in her voice. What was she supposed to say? She picked up Benjamin and backed out of the doorway. She felt all her anger, pointed at this woman and her husband for days, suddenly melting away. What she wanted to say was: *Don't worry. Your secret's safe with me.* If it even was a secret. But Rob didn't know that Samantha was a lesbian, did he?

As she walked with Benjamin (holding his hand this time!), she couldn't help but smile. Rob's fling was all a figment of her imagination, just as he'd said. The woman all the men in the office were lusting after didn't even like men! Samantha wasn't out to steal her husband or break up her marriage. Samantha was fighting her own battles. Even in the liberated capital of Madison, Lanie knew it was no cakewalk to come out at a firm like Hobbs & Greenough, where many of the older partners were still stuck in another century. And she had no intention of ushering Samantha through that door. It was her choice to make, hers alone.

Lanie felt a momentary stab of guilt, but not so much for wrongly accusing her husband as for assuming the worst about Samantha. Instead of a quick hello, she treated Rob and Benjamin to a pizza lunch. And it was then that she brought up the idea of vacation on Nantucket. Rob had jumped at the chance. He was smart enough not to question his wife's change of heart.

Now, her muscles working, her breathing even, she couldn't believe how insane she'd been over the whole idea of Rob's infidelity. With the distance of Nantucket, she could see clearly that her husband was still the same man she'd married five years ago. That she had him off and running around with some Madison floozy was comical.

After a crazy summer, she was anticipating the fall even more than one short week ago. Because after calculating the numbers again and again and floating the idea past Rob, she had decided she was really going to do it: *slow down*. Her new mantra. Rob had come home one night to find her raving about a new product she'd discovered in the drugstore, a powder to sprinkle in her hair that would miraculously absorb the oil and grease on days when she didn't have time to shower. She thought it ingenious. Forty bucks a bottle. It should last her a few months. Why hadn't she invented it herself? But Rob saw it as the tipping point, the big finger pointing the way to change. "My wife should not have to *pay* to stay dirty," he'd said, after Lanie told him about it, sprinkling some into his hand. "This is insane."

And so they'd had a heart-to-heart. They could trim a few expenses, boost their trips to Costco, cut back on some luxury items, and, after multiple calculations, they agreed they could probably swing it if Lanie worked part-time. On a Tuesday morning, nervous and excited, unable to eat breakfast, she went into her boss's office and told her she wanted to cut back her hours. Her boss had almost rubberstamped the decision with, Lanie thought, an audible sigh of relief. They'd been looking to cut an attorney altogether; now Lanie and one other mom who'd made a similar request would render it possible for everyone to stay onboard. The perfect solution.

Starting in September, Lanie would spend two and a half days at home with Benjamin. Her heart raced at the thought of what lay ahead, days that were sure to unfold at a slower pace but that would be fuller, she imagined, in other ways. She was excited to see if by doing less, she could really have more. All the dozens of self-help books she'd read on simplifying life, organizing and downsizing, neglected to point her to the most obvious answer: *Spend more time doing the things you enjoy.* And for her it meant realizing that the things she enjoyed had changed. She looked forward to, could almost taste, the lazy days ahead with her baby boy, outings to the park, play dates, trips to the children's museum. *Her mother would be proud,* Lanie thought, as her sneakers drummed the pavement. At last, she would take the time to savor her three good things each day. She would begin anew today: *the fresh morning air on Nantucket; the calm that had been reinstated in her marriage; the anticipation of slower days ahead.*

She planned to fill Ellen in on it all, but not till the ferry ride back to Falmouth. She didn't want to distract her from her time with Henry. This vacation was supposed to be about them, after all—Lanie and Rob were just there as sidekicks. And there was something surprisingly satisfying about *not* telling her sister first, for once, about the recent developments in her life. Ellen didn't need to hear every little detail right now.

She began the loop back to the inn, the morning air warming her skin, and passed a few islanders as they walked to their cars for work, their coffee mugs in hand. Thankfully, her only worry today would be making sure Benjamin was wearing enough sunblock. Poor Henry would have to plant himself under an umbrella for the entire afternoon.

16

"Every great architect is—necessarily—a great poet. He must
be a great original interpreter of his time, his day, his age."
—Frank Lloyd Wright

Rob cracked open another beer. He could get used to island living.
The ostentatious homes, the preppy rich who acted as if this lifestyle
was their birthright, the sea-stung air. All of it seemed about right, a
vision of how the other half lived. The winter months were probably
hell, though, isolating and bitter cold. That part might take a little
getting used to. He wondered if there was a market for architects on
the island. Maybe he could start his own business out here, put out a
shingle to build summer homes for the well-to-do. It was a tempting
thought.

The girls had gone off to explore the quaint island shops with
a sleeping Benjamin in his stroller; he and Henry had opted for a
hall pass. "We haven't tried all the excellent lagers the island has to
offer," Henry explained.

The girls rolled their eyes but agreed to meet them back at the
inn around dinnertime.

Rob looked over at Henry now, his face tilted toward the ball
game on the big-screen television above the bar. He'd gone from
the bright pink of the other day to a darker crimson. It still looked

painful as hell, Rob thought, though Henry claimed the burn was feeling much better, layers of aloe later.

"You a big fan?" he asked.

Henry broke his stare. "Of baseball? Sure. Of the Red Sox, not so much."

Rob nodded.

"When I was a kid, I was a nut for baseball, back in the day when the Brewers were fun to watch. Think we had some Boston guys playing for us, too. Wasn't it Lonborg and Billy Conigliaro?"

"That's a touchy subject around here," their bartender, a weathered old gentleman who was wiping up the bar, interjected.

Henry licked some foam off his lip with his tongue. "Yes, I guess I'm showing my age, aren't I?"

"Pretty much anyone from Massachusetts knows those guys' names. Lonborg was part of the dream team back in the 1960s, but the Sox handed the World Series to the Cardinals back in '67. Then the Sox gave up on Lonborg, traded him and Conigliaro in '71. Fatal error." He shook his head and wiped at a stubborn watermark on the counter with his rag.

"I remember that," Henry pitched in now. "That was a historic trade. The Sox lost a couple of games to the Brewers that season when Lonborg was pitching, right? Irony of ironies."

"Right you are. And another one when Conigliaro had four RBIs. Not that anyone was counting." Their bartender stopped cleaning and tucked his rag behind the bar. "Of course, that was the year the Sox finished half a game out of first place. If they'd won just one of those games against your Brewers, well, we'd be having a different conversation."

"Henry, my man, I think maybe we should shut up if we know what's good for us." Rob laid a hand on his back.

"Ah, I'm just having fun. It's nice to meet someone with a genuine love for the game. Cheers." He hoisted his glass up to the bartender.

"To the love of the game, *that* I can drink to." The bartender smiled and clinked a shot glass against Henry's mug.

Rob was trying to figure out if he liked Henry or not. Not that it really mattered. Ellen could do her own choosing. But she'd crashed and burned with Max. Rob knew that Lanie was hoping the next guy would treat Ellen with the respect she deserved, would spoil her rotten. They both agreed Ellen was worthy of some rich dude who would whisk her off to Europe and feed her oysters on his yacht. Henry didn't exactly seem the type. To be fair, though, he also seemed pretty harmless. Rob didn't suppose he was making millions in the greenhouse business, but if the man liked sports and beer and Ellen liked him, then he was all right by Rob. He wasn't as tough a judge as his wife.

He took another sip of beer and breathed in the relaxed atmosphere. One more night and they were headed back on the ferry to the real world. It was going to be a hell of an adjustment. At least, he counseled himself, the main work was done on the art institute. Now it was just a matter of refining things here and there and overseeing the construction. That would keep them busy well into next year.

"How do you like your Summer of Lager?" the bartender asked.

"Delicious. Not too hoppy. And it's brewed right here on the island?"

"That's right. Cisco Brewers. I think they ship to a few other places, but it's mainly an island beer."

"I wonder if we could stash a case on the plane ride back?" Henry asked.

Rob laughed. "We'll have to see how much loot the girls bring back."

He knew Lanie would quiz him when they got back to their room: *What did you guys talk about? Did Henry say anything about Ellen? What are his intentions?* But every time he tried to explain to her that guys didn't "chat" like women did, she didn't believe him. "How can you just sit over beers and not talk to each other?" she'd ask. "Easy, we drink our beer and watch sports." She would think he was intentionally avoiding her grilling, but he didn't feel like asking Henry a million questions. The poor guy had been a good sport already by letting Ellen's whole "other family" come along on what he probably thought was going to be a romantic vacation. Nevertheless, Rob tried briefly.

"So, Henry, you and my sister-in-law have been dating how long now?"

Henry bit into a salsa chip and thought about it. "Guess I haven't really been keeping track. Maybe a few months? Isn't that the woman's job?"

Rob grinned. "Probably, but you should always be prepared with an answer in case she asks."

"Ah, a man who knows the ins and outs of dating."

"Well, I wouldn't say that exactly, but I do know a thing or two about the McClarety sisters."

"Now you've got me interested." Henry turned to him. "What else should I know?"

Funny how the conversation had turned into a quiz for him. "Well, don't forget to mark every anniversary—that means your first kiss, your first movie, your first shooting star—that kind of thing."

"Maybe I should be taking notes." He pulled his napkin closer and looked about for a pen. Rob thought he was serious for a second.

"And, it's good if you have a job that gets you home in a timely manner, but I think that's true for most couples." He thought back to the whole Samantha debacle of earlier this summer, grateful that Lanie seemed to have trusted his word at last. He wasn't sure what had turned the tide for her, but one day she showed up at his office all smiles with Benjamin in tow and from then on she'd been fine. She'd even gone so far as to apologize to him for jumping to conclusions. Go figure. He'd smiled to see his tie laid out for him the next morning.

"Makes sense, but we're not even living together."

"Right, but if the time should come, it's a good thing to keep in mind. Ellen—well, you probably know this by now—is a very independent woman. She can be a little intimidating, but really she's just a big softie. She raised Lanie after their mom died, more or less. And she gave me a hell of a time before I proposed to Lanie. It wasn't till afterward that she told me she'd liked me all along."

Henry grinned. "That sounds like her."

"She's a good woman, just like her sister."

Henry raised his glass. "To the McClarety sisters."

"I'll drink to that—and to our sanity." Henry chuckled. Rob liked the guy, he decided. They clinked glasses and turned back to the game. End of discussion. He had done his job, as far as he was concerned.

Still, he was sure if Lanie had been around, she would have analyzed why Henry hadn't added a few potent words to the toast himself, something like "—and to the men who *love* them."

Fall

"Kringle-making is less an art of perfection than an art
of patience. To achieve a *kringle* that is light and flaky,
one must be willing to roll out layer upon layer, wait for
the dough to rise, then spread the filling and weave the ends
together before popping in the oven—giving the artist
plenty of time to think on other matters."
—*The Book of Kringle*

Ellen was sitting on white paper, not so unlike parchment paper, a light-blue gown wrapped around her. She hated how doctors always made a person wait forever. She'd already thumbed through two issues of *People* and was eyeing the chart on the wall to see if her vision was going, too. She'd had one too many hot flashes on Nantucket, and even her antacids didn't seem to be helping her stomach pangs anymore. She was ready and willing for a little pill that would make all her symptoms fade away. Estrogen side effects or not, menopause be damned!

She was trying not to feel sorry for herself, sorry that her body was yielding to the ravages of age before she was ready. Forty-five was on the young side for menopause, she knew, but given that her periods had always been erratic, she supposed it wasn't unusual.

But how unfair! She thought back to all the times she'd sat on similar tables, waiting to get the news that the latest fertility treatment she and Max tried had failed. How many times had they tried? Too many to count. Eventually, shortly after the miscarriage, they'd given up, disheartened by their failure to achieve what seemed the most basic right of marriage.

When the doctor entered the room, Ellen quickly smoothed the paper around her.

"Ellen. Good to see you." Jean Mayer was a kind woman who had delivered plenty of bad news to Ellen over the years. She hoped, though, that she would make this appointment quick, write out the prescription, and send her on her way.

"Good to see you, Dr. Mayer."

"So tell me how you've been feeling lately."

"Not great. My stomach has been up and down, and I seem to be getting hot flashes every other day. You're going to tell me it's early menopause, aren't you?"

She smiled and took Ellen's hand. Ellen thought for a moment the news was even worse than she'd imagined. This wasn't menopause . . . she was dying!

"Actually, no." She paused, smiled again. "I have some rather surprising news, I guess you'd say." Ellen waited.

"Ellen, you're pregnant."

She laughed. "Good one. Really, what's going on?"

"I'm very serious. Your blood work shows that you're about three months along."

There were no words.

"You're kidding?" It was all she could come up with. "Pregnant? How? Immaculate conception?"

The doctor laughed. She knew Ellen and Max had parted ways. "You tell me, but you've definitely got a baby growing in there. Can you lean back for me so I can feel your belly?"

Ellen looked up at the tiles in the ceiling. Pregnant? It didn't make sense. She and Henry had been together only once, that night on Nantucket, just a stone's throw away in time. That wasn't long enough for a baby to grow to three months old, obviously.

"When was your last period?" The doctor's cool hands stretched across Ellen's belly, taking measure.

She tried to think. It had been a while. "I'm not sure. Maybe three, four months ago?"

The doctor nodded. "That sounds about right."

"But I thought I couldn't *get* pregnant . . ."

"Stranger things have happened. Sometimes the body just needs the right circumstances, less stress. We can't really say, but sometimes it just works. Chalk it up to serendipity."

"But aren't I too *old* to be having a baby? I mean, I'm practically old enough to be a grandma."

Dr. Mayer laughed. "Not these days. Plenty of women are having babies well into their forties. Haven't you heard? Forty is the new thirty."

Ellen had read some such nonsense in a magazine and dismissed it. But still. Pregnant? She thought back to three or four months ago. Whose bed had she been in? Then she realized, with a start, who had been in *her* bed. Max, of course. The evening of his unannounced visit when he'd wooed her with beef and broccoli. She felt sick to her stomach all over again.

"If you don't mind, I'd like to bring the ultrasound in here. Take a quick look and make sure everything's all right. We might even be able to see the heart beating."

"Uh, sure."

Before Ellen had time to process the news, the doctor was wheeling in a machine with a small screen attached. She squeezed cold jelly across Ellen's bare stomach and ran a small wand over her skin. All of a sudden the black screen lit up.

"Ah, there it is," she said. "Can you see the head, and the little arms and feet?" Her finger pointed to various white illuminations. It looked like a small alien.

"That's a baby?" Ellen asked in wonderment.

"It is indeed, momma. Too early to say if it's a boy or a girl, but it's definitely a baby."

"Oh my God." It was all beginning to sink in. "A baby? *My* baby?" She felt tears spring up, unbidden.

The doctor smiled as she continued to move the wand around. "And that there is your baby's heart, beating strongly." Ellen looked at the little thumping light on the screen. Her own heart quickened. How long had she waited for this moment? But now there was no Max in her life, no daddy for this child. She breathed in and the baby moved.

"Whoa. You just gave him a little squeeze."

She wiped a tear away. "Or her," she said. "A *baby*," she whispered, and the doctor squeezed her hand.

After seeing the doctor, Ellen headed straight for Lanie's office to tell her the news, then turned down another street at the last minute and drove to the bakery. She wanted to hold on to her secret for a few more hours. She needed to think it all through. Putting her hands in some dough would do her good.

It was astonishing, a miracle, really, to be pregnant after all these years. On the one hand she wanted to shout it from the rooftops, turn cartwheels down the street; on the other, she was filled with anxiety. How unfair for this child to come around now, when only Ellen was in the picture. Was one person's love enough? She hoped so.

"Sorry I'm late," she said when she walked in. Larry was manning the store in her absence.

"We're getting used to it around here," he joked. "First, she goes on vacation. Then she comes in any old time she pleases. Don't worry, the kringle's all baked to perfection."

"I can't tell you how glad *I* am that you're back," Erin said. "Someone around here is getting an awfully big head."

Ellen couldn't stop smiling. She felt like she would burst with the news. Or burst into tears. She focused on the board:

Today's Drips: *Morning Blend; Hazelnut Decaf*
Tips: *When referring to a general amount, use less.*
When referring to a specific number, use fewer. Ex: Fewer
apples picked yesterday means less kringle baked today.

"Nice." She nodded to the board. "You two will be grammar wizards in no time."

"That *is* our goal in life," Larry teased. "And, thanks to our good man Fowler, we'll reach that goal sooner rather than later."

Ellen chose to ignore the dig.

"But in bigger news, I think we've solved your kringle riddle."

"Really?" Ellen couldn't hide her surprise. She'd posted it on the board a few weeks ago to see if any of the customers could shed some light on it.

"Yeah, Erin and I were talking about it and we wondered what if "first" referred to the very first state capital of the United States? That would be New York. And lo and behold, it has seven letters!"

Ellen was impressed. "I'm with you so far, but so what? What about New York?"

"Interesting you should ask. We wondered, too, so we did a little sleuthing. Turns out the state fruit is an apple, but that's nothing new to the kringle world. So, we kept looking and discovered that the rose is New York's state flower."

"And?" Ellen wasn't following.

"And then we started thinking: Rosemary? Nah, that seemed too acrid for a kringle. But how about rose *water*? Two teaspoonsful of rose water."

Ellen's mouth dropped open. "You think that could be it?"

Larry held up a little bottle. "We ordered it online. We're going to try it in one of the kringles for tomorrow, if that's okay."

"By all means," Ellen said with a wave of her hand. "Have at it! Just think: You two may have solved the great kringle mystery!"

Larry high-fived Erin. "We'll expect a cut of all future proceeds, of course," he joked.

"Of course. Well," Ellen said after a beat, "I think I'll get started on tomorrow's dough." She excused herself and pushed through the swinging doors to the kitchen.

"Is she humming?" Larry asked loud enough for her to hear. "Looks like someone's in a better mood." True, Ellen had been cranky her first week back at the store. She'd been stuck on Nantucket, thinking about Henry and why she hadn't heard from him since, and thinking about the half moon they'd seen the night before they left. Lanie said it was a sign. *A sign of what?* Ellen asked. *Of good things to come.* At the time, Ellen thought her practical sister had gone loopy. But had Lanie suspected all along, known before even Ellen knew what her own body was home to? Now she wondered: *Should she tell Max her news?*

Larry had already lugged up the sacks of flour for today's dough, and she mixed it till it was the right gooey consistency, then dumped it onto the table and added more flour to thicken it. She sunk her hands into the cool dough. Is this what it felt like for the baby inside her? Warm skin surrounded by cozy, soft cushioning? She began the process of rolling out the layers, first dough, then chilled butter. For the past three months she'd been exposing this child to all kinds of things, unaware that he or she was even there. *My God, she'd had a wine cooler and beers on Nantucket!* She panicked. She'd have to call the doctor; make sure the baby would be okay. But then she calmed herself by thinking of her own mother, who had sunk plenty of martinis when she was pregnant with Lanie—and her sister had turned out just fine. Already this baby had been exposed to plenty of wonderful things: the sounds of Nantucket beaches; the scent of kringle. It had eavesdropped on all her conversations.

Had the baby picked up on the fact that she was dating, if that's what it was, someone other than his or her daddy?

All her life she'd wanted this, and now *here it was.* She had been happy for Lanie and Rob, truly, when they announced they were pregnant almost two years ago. But there was also a part of her that screamed *Unfair!* They'd been trying for only a couple of months, and look how easily they'd been granted a child. She and Lanie never spoke of it, this tipping of the scales in her sister's direction. Ellen counseled herself that Benjamin was just like a son to her. But now this! To have her very own son or daughter. Something that seemed unthinkable just a few hours ago.

If Max knew, would it change things between them? Not being able to have a baby wasn't the cause of their split, but still. If Max knew, would he move back? Did she want him to? Did she have an obligation to tell him or was he better off not knowing?

Somehow she just wanted to hold this secret tight to her chest, a book unopened, meant only for her.

"Haven't made much progress, have you?" Larry interrupted her thoughts as he came through the doors. She looked down and saw that she'd been rolling out the same layer over and over again.

"It seems like you've still got a case of vacation brain, boss."

"I think you're right." She set down the rolling pin and wiped her hands on her apron. "You know what? Would you mind taking over for the rest of the day? Finish up the layers and stick them in the fridge to chill overnight? My mind's off wandering somewhere else."

He looked at her curiously. "Something you want to tell me? About you and Henry? Like the two of you got engaged, eloped on Nantucket?"

She snorted. "Not even close. I've just got a lot on my plate at the moment."

"Whatever you say, boss." She could tell he was waiting for her to break some big news. If she didn't leave immediately, she'd spill the beans.

"Okay then. So you and Erin will be fine till closing?" She asked the question while she was already gathering up her purse.

"Sure."

On the way out, Lanie's name flashed on her cell. Ellen was seized with a moment of panic. Should she tell? But no, she decided as she picked up, better to tell her the good news in person. She couldn't wait to see her face.

"Hello?"

"Ellen, thank goodness you answered. Listen, I know this is incredibly short notice but I need a sitter for Benjamin tonight. Is there any chance you could do it?"

She thought for a moment. "Of course."

"Thank you, *thank you*. I owe you. I forgot that we have this benefit dinner to go to tonight. It's for the children's NICU at the hospital, so I really want to go."

"Of course," she echoed again. She felt like a five-year-old trying to keep from telling her best friend that she had a stash of candy in her lunch box.

"If you could come by the house around six thirty that would be great."

Ellen smiled to think that one day she would be asking Lanie to do the same for her. Before she headed home to change, she stopped at the drugstore and found herself at sea in the vitamin section. Where the heck did they keep prenatal vitamins? The doctor had said she should start them right away. At last she found them on the bottom shelf and was shocked to see the sticker price. When she checked out, she was thankful the cashier was a young high school girl whom she didn't know.

"For a friend," she explained nonetheless.

Back at home she showered, and pulled on shorts and a polo shirt. Her shorts felt snug. She hadn't considered that her belly was going to grow considerably before this baby came. A middle-aged woman in maternity clothes? All the things she had to do before the baby arrived! She certainly had plenty of rooms to spare in the house. Maybe she'd put him in the small corner room next to hers; it got the most sunlight. Yes, that would be an ideal bedroom for a baby. She would paint it in soft yellow hues.

Her hair still damp, she headed out the door with a pear in one hand and her mail in the other, a bundle of bills and magazines.

She hoped she'd have some time after Benjamin fell asleep to sort through it all, watch some bad TV.

On the drive over, she decided she couldn't wait any longer—she had to tell her sister. But when she arrived Lanie was rushing to find her purse, Benjamin was crying, and Rob looked like he'd rather go to a funeral than another benefit dinner. The moment didn't seem right. She took the baby and bounced him on her knee, singing, "Ride the horsey, don't fall off!" Benjamin squealed, and it gave her chills to think she'd be doing this with her own child shortly.

It was if she was seeing her godson through new eyes.

On the way out the door, Lanie looked at her. "You all right?"

Was it that obvious? "Sure, why?"

"I don't know. You look a little flushed."

"Lingering Nantucket suntan."

"Lucky you," she said and kissed Benjamin good-bye before heading down the steps. "I'm back to pale as a peach. See you later, alligator."

After his parents left, Ellen tried reading to Benjamin but he wasn't interested. He kept squirming off her lap to wobble over to something more interesting—a stray ball, a piece of fuzz, a paper clip that she snatched from his hands. She was amazed by how quickly he had gone from crawling to full-out drunken-sailor walking. His miniature cargo pants made little swishing noises as he crossed the living room floor.

He hadn't eaten much of his dinner so Lanie suggested Ellen try again later. She scooted him into his high chair now and laid out the diced chicken, rigatoni, peas, and watermelon. The baby carefully pinched the small pieces between his pointer finger and thumb and held them up, as if he were assessing rare gemstones. Eventually most of his dinner went either into his mouth or onto his shirt. Benjamin's pediatrician had likened eating to learning a foreign language, and Ellen liked the metaphor. They couldn't expect a baby to learn the language of food until he had ample exposure and practice. Ellen thought of his pasta as his pronouns, his peas as the more difficult, subjunctive case.

"*Je t'aime*," she whispered to him, and he kicked his feet and stuck a finger in his mouth.

How she loved everything about this little boy—his baby smell, his dimpled grin, his big cheeks. He was finally getting some hair, and Lanie had parted it to one side so it looked as if he'd just come from the baby salon. Would hers be a boy as well? Would Benjamin have a little cousin that was just like a brother to him? Would they grow up together, looking out for each other, sharing homework assignments, fighting over stupid things as she and Lanie had?

After dinner, he half-walked, half-ran to the table with her cross-word puzzle book and pen on top. Ellen quickly substituted a red crayon and typing paper. She watched him turn the paper, pick it up and look at it, then put it back down again. He did this almost a dozen times, each time leaning over the paper with crayon in hand, as if willing it to write. But touching crayon to paper was trickier than it might look, and try as he might, Benjamin held it suspended just above. Still, he persisted with baby stubbornness, rearranging the white sheet each time. When he tired of it at last and crawled to get a ball, she tried to reassure him.

"That's okay, baby. You'll figure it out. It's not easy, is it?"

Later she changed him into his sleeper, gave him a bottle, laid him down in his crib. He fussed only a little before rolling onto his side, eyes closed, not a worry in the world. She waited until his breathing settled into even exhales. She would need a crib, she thought suddenly. Baby bumpers and pacifiers. A changing table. She should make a list! Her world had tilted on its axis.

Downstairs she poured herself a tall glass of lemonade and collapsed on the couch. No wonder she'd been feeling tired, out of sorts. A baby was growing inside her! She wondered if it liked lemonade or if its lips would pucker in her stomach. She picked up the bundle of catalogs from the day's mail, most not worthy even of a toss. Then, there between *Hearth & Country* and a credit card bill was an envelope postmarked "Sint Maarten." Goosebumps ran across the back of her neck. Did the man no longer trust e-mail?

She undid the letter with her thumb and a thimbleful of sand fell into her lap.

Dear Ellen,

I'm sorry about surprising you at the store—and then again at your front door. I really wanted to see you, but looking back on it now, I understand that wasn't the best way to do it. I should have given you fare warning that I was in town. Still, I'd be lying if I didn't say I can't stop thinking about our night together. You made it quite clear what your future intentions are for me (none), but I'm hoping you'll reconsider.

I don't know who this new guy your involved with is, but surely he can't be treating you right if you take your ex-husband back for a night. Are you really serious about him? In love? Because despite all our troubles, I still feel like your the only person who really understands me and who loves me. As I said in the store, I'm a changed man with a peaceful soul—or as peaceful as it can be while longing for you by my side.

Please, please think about coming to Sint Maarten for a visit and seeing where things go? I promise you'll love it—and you'll never want to leave.

With love,
Max

P.S. Enclosed is a little something from the beach and a little something to ease any unexpected expenses.

From a long thin envelope, she pulled out an e-ticket, round-trip to the island, the dates open-ended, her name on top.

Talk about timing. She may not have the key to Henry Moon's whole heart yet, but getting back into a relationship with Max—and moving to Sint Maarten—was not the answer. Or was it? Was it serendipity that Max's letter had arrived just now, months after their one-night tryst? Akin to Lanie's forecasting good things to come when they'd been on Nantucket? Was this a sign that she should go back to Max?

She laughed out loud at the notion. These pregnancy hormones were making her stupid. Still, it was nice to be wanted. By her child's father no less.

She slipped the letter and ticket into her purse and turned up the volume on the television, pondering stretches of liquid aquamarine, quaint island shops, a baby playing in the sand.

What on earth were she and this child going to do?

18

"Be glad that your children have enterprise and invention. . . .
Do not say, 'You must keep still. I can't bear so much noise.
Can't you ever be quiet?' Rejoice that your children
are alive and well."
—*Talks to Mothers*

Recently he had begun to crawl into her lap with a book, pointing to the cover, waiting patiently for her to begin. It brought her such joy to see that he knew what a book was, was interested in it, if only for a few minutes. As an infant, he'd watched intently while she turned the pages, reading aloud to him from her favorite childhood stories and pointing to the colorful pictures. Now that he was full-out walking, though, those quiet, cuddly moments had grown fewer and farther between. At fifteen months, life seemed to be all about motion, putting himself and anything he could get his hands on into orbit.

Once a believer that boys were drawn to cars and trucks (and not dolls) because that's what their parents offered them, Lanie now firmly trusted that there was something inherent in the male genome, an amino acid in the DNA tagged with a little red "truck" flag that made little boys gravitate toward anything with wheels. Benjamin could have an ocean of toys before him and would grab a car every time, making *brrm, brrm* noises and pulling it across the floor.

He padded confidently these days from one room to another in their downstairs, looping big circles through the living room, sunroom, kitchen, and back to the living room. Each time he returned from a trip he grinned with pride and waved before he was off again. The first week he was fully walking he had tumbled off balance and banged his head. Lanie was sure they were headed to the emergency room, but Rob calmed her. There was no blood. Benjamin was fine, just fine.

"He's going to fall a hundred times before he's five," Rob said. "Get used to it."

She knew he meant this to be comforting, but instead it just made her want to wrap Benjamin in bubble wrap to protect him from the physical and emotional falls that surely lay ahead. Off they went the next day to the safety aisle of the baby store, where she bought an ungodly number of childproof locks, guards, and bumpers. It would be so much easier, she thought, if they just invented a bumper for the baby. She imagined girl and boy bumpers, decorated with pink flowers and blue soccer balls, and fitted with Velcro straps for their pea-sized waists.

Now she took him to places with wide-open spaces, where a baby could roam happily and fall with abandon—parks, playgrounds, the front yard. He loved the wide aisles of the children's bookstore, overflowing with beanbag chairs, bead boards, and miniature chairs. She would follow him around as he wove his way in and out of the rows, waving to customers. Walking among the stories of *The Very Hungry Caterpillar*, *Harold and the Purple Crayon*, and *Leo the Late Bloomer* made Lanie hungry to read them once more.

They had just returned from running errands, this Wednesday being the first of her half-days, in service to her new allegiance to slowing down. She had left the office a bit awkwardly, uncertain how to make an early exit. When Hannah cheerfully shooed her out, saying, "See you Monday, boss," she felt like a truant. "Call if you need anything," Lanie said hesitantly, "especially these first weeks." But

Hannah was good at putting her in her place: "Go. Don't come back till next week or I'll tell."

Once she was out the door, Lanie felt like a schoolgirl all over again, released early for teacher-conference day. She stepped down the stairs and waited. Waited for the feeling of freedom to sink in. "We did it," she whispered to herself. It was a little early to make such a pronouncement, of course; it would be a matter of months before she and Rob determined if they could really swing this part-time arrangement financially. But for the moment, she was going to seize the opportunity. Carpe diem.

She picked up the baby from day care and happily explained her new schedule to the staff. Benjamin surprised them all by insisting he walk out himself. It was the first time she hadn't carried him out the door during his year at the center. He squiggled down from her grasp and followed confidently behind her before stopping to wave good-bye to his teachers. He could have been an advertisement for the place. Her little guy, so grown up, so proud to be walking out of school. She mentally marked it as one of those turning points in a child's life. *Walks out of day care and waves good-bye. Fifteen months.* She would write it in his baby book tonight.

She packed him into the car and they headed over to Audrey's house on the other side of town. Audrey was among Lanie's small circle of friends who could understand the topsy-turvy world of a working mom. Her kids, Aiden, Gretchen, and Tom were two, three, and six respectively, and after Aiden was born, Audrey had tossed the law aside to stay home and run a cookie business out of her basement. Now that Lanie found herself with some free time, she'd vowed to reconnect with friends.

When she and Benjamin arrived, he quickly joined Audrey's kids in the sandbox in the backyard. Lanie planted herself in an Adirondack chair, accepting a welcome glass of iced tea from her friend.

"So, what's it been? Three months since I last saw you?" Audrey asked. She looked good, slightly tan and more relaxed than Lanie had seen her in years. Her short blond hair had lightened in the summer sun.

"Funny you should ask." Lanie started to fill her in on everything, on Nantucket, on Rob, on her decision to go part-time.

"Whoa. You know, you can pick up the phone every now and then."

"I know. I'm sorry—I've been a terrible friend. It's been a crazy summer."

When she got to her suspicions about Rob's having an affair and how wrong she'd been, Audrey laughed. "I think that's par for the course. The other night when I crawled into bed, Chris cuddled up next to me and said, "What's this?" He turned on the light and *voilá*! It was pasta—stuck to my nightgown. Naturally, I had to ask him what kind."

"What kind?"

"You know, like was it spaghetti, mac and cheese, rotini. I could trace it to a particular night and how long it had been there."

Lanie laughed. "I love it. And?"

"Rotini. It had been there since Monday night, three long days."

"Is this what it's come to?"

"I'm afraid so. But it's not all bad, is it?" Audrey asked. They looked out at the kids digging in the sand.

"No, it just seems there should be some way to do it all and not go to bed with pasta stuck to your pajamas."

"Let me know when you come up with it."

They sat in silence, watching the negotiations play out among the kids over who got to use the dump truck next.

"How's your sister?" Audrey interrupted the silence. "How's the kringle business holding up? Nobody's buying cookies right now with this dismal economy."

"Business is fine, I think. But more important, there's a new guy in town."

"Good for her!" Audrey exclaimed.

"Well, at least, he sort of seems to be a new guy. Ellen invited him to Nantucket."

"Wow. That's so, I don't know, *unlike* Ellen."

"Mmm." Lanie took a sip of her iced tea. "Tell me about it. The funny thing is, at first I didn't like him, then I did. I think he's a really nice guy. He'd be good for Ellen. But apparently he's made himself scarce since we got back. Ellen thinks he freaked out when things started to get serious, that he's still not completely over his dead wife. Anyway, I just wish she could find somebody she likes for longer than a month. She's tough to please."

"Yes, but in a good way," Audrey offered.

"Sometimes she acts like she's sixty-five, not forty-five."

"Well, you age faster in the Midwest," Audrey teased. "All that cheese, all that cholesterol. My father always told my brothers to marry their women young. Anyway, I'm sure Ellen will figure it out. She's a smart woman."

"Too smart for her own good sometimes." Lanie sighed. "But you're right. I'm sure they'll work things out one way or another."

Now she dumped her files and bags on the table by the door and grabbed a juice box for the baby, an apple for herself. She pulled a fleece over his head. When they stepped back outside, the day was settling into itself, the sun slipping to the west. Lanie set Benjamin down and watched while he ambled across the lawn with his arms sticking out behind his back, like a little speed skater. It was nearly twenty steps before he fell, and when he did, he was up in a second, laughing. He stopped to finger a blade of grass, pick up a pebble from the sidewalk, snag a petal from the now-tired impatiens bordering their white fence. Hidden among them was a sole red maple leaf, and he lifted it to twirl between his fingers, a sparkler shooting off bright colors.

Lanie bit into her apple, enjoying the tart flavor, while she followed her boy across the lawn. She thought of her mother, who would have been the first to point out all of the natural wonders to her grandson—the feel of rich soil between his fingers, the smooth surface of a rock, the veiny architecture of a leaf. In fact, she saw a little of Harriet McClarety in her son. His constant wonder at and concentration on all the little treasures around him. It was as if her mother had sent Benjamin to her with a sign around his neck, commanding her in big, bold letters: SLOW DOWN.

And as Benjamin came running up to hand her a new discovery—a leaf, a wrapper, a rock, who knew?—she was seized by the piercing certainty that *this* was what her life was about. This, she supposed, would be the closest she would get to finding what her mother called grace. It wasn't the hours logged at the office; the cases won; the dozens of clients she battled for, though certainly that had been important. It was a feeling that *nothing more* was demanded of her right now than being here with her son, on their front lawn, exploring each new thing. The constellation of her life might be no bigger than her family and a few friends, but it was enough, it was more than enough. She had Rob back, in spirit, body, and mind. She had Benjamin. She had Ellen. She was enormously grateful.

Benjamin stood next to her now, leaf in hand, reaching to be picked up. She lifted him and snuggled him with kisses. *How long would he let her do this?* she wondered. Till he was three? Five? Twelve? Her toddler was still just a baby. How could she ever think of him as a teenager, let alone as a grown man with a wife and children of his own?

"Up, up, up," he said now, squirming in her arms.

"You are up."

"Up," he said again, pointing to the tree this time.

She walked with him over to the maple, its lowest branches heavy with leaves.

"Tree." She said and pointed. She'd been trying to get him to say tree for more than a week now. Maybe today would be their lucky day.

"Up." She walked in farther, till the leaves touched their heads, tickled Benjamin's face while she held him. Then she watched while he reached up, leaf still in hand. What was he doing? She was amazed when she connected the dots.

"Oh, baby," she whispered. "You want to give the leaf back to the tree. What a sweet boy you are."

Benjamin waved his hand and let go of the red-tipped, five-pointed toy, only to watch it twirl to the ground. He pointed to it again. "Up."

Did she have the patience to keep picking up this leaf and pretending to reattach it to the branch?

Rob would be getting home from work soon. She needed to get the pork chops going, the vegetables steaming. There were stacks of case files awaiting review at some point before Monday.

She tugged at the zipper on her jacket, tucked Benjamin's fleece collar tightly around his neck. Did she have the patience?

The sky was fading to a dusty pink and headlights flashed by as neighbors turned down the street, traveling home for dinner around their own tables with family. She bent down, the baby suspended in her arms to grab the leaf again.

Indeed, she thought. Most certainly, *absolutely,* she did.

19

"Look back, fair reader, and reflect on what you've read,
A secret ingredient hides in its stead,
For if you like capitals first and seven, you'll quickly see
That two teaspoonsful make all the difference in your kringle *and tea."*
—The Book of Kringle

It was Wednesday, and Ellen had yet to tell anyone her secret. The longer she waited, the easier it got. When Rob and Lanie got home last night, everyone had been too tired for the kind of bombshell she was about to drop. Now another day had passed.

She was beginning to believe in those mind-body studies that claimed placebos could be just as effective as the real pill. Because ever since she'd found out she was pregnant, the hot flashes had halted and her feet began swelling. When she got home from the shop, she plopped a frozen pizza into the oven, poured herself a glass of milk, and put her feet up.

Too bad the rose water had been a bust this morning. Larry and Erin looked so pleased when they rolled out their creation, but when they all took their first bites, the pastry had been sticky, the taste of rose petals overwhelming. Erin had gone so far as to spit hers out, saying, "I'm really sorry, but that *can't* be the secret ingredient. It tastes like soap."

Larry looked hurt at first but then started laughing. "Agreed. Guess the riddle remains unsolved." She felt a little sorry for them; she'd been hoping they'd be right.

When the phone rang, Ellen debated picking up; she was that tired. But she hated it when people used voice mail as a replacement for a human voice. She picked up.

"Ellen?" His voice sounded scratchy.

"Henry? Is that you? Are you sick?" She hadn't been able to bring herself to call him. He hadn't set foot in the store since the trip. It was as if he'd vanished into thin air. How to explain it? Perhaps the romance on Nantucket had been too intense, made him realize he wasn't over Charlotte after all? Just when she'd thought their love balloon was taking flight, Henry disappeared. Reminded her of somebody else. She wasn't going to waste any more time fretting about what Henry's intentions might be. Life was short. Under different circumstances, she would have been making herself sick with worry and second-guessing. But now she had other, more important things on her mind. Like a baby.

"Ellen? I was wondering, do you think you could come over?"

"Right now?" She eyed the hot cheese melting into the tomato sauce on the pie she'd just pulled from the oven. "Is everything all right?"

"If you could just come, that would be super."

He didn't sound like himself. Had something happened at the nursery? Had a rhododendron pot capsized? Maybe a blight had wiped out his fern crop for the year? Funds embezzled by one of his employees? Something to explain his mysterious disappearance?

"Sure, Henry. I'll be right there."

She cursed herself as she slid the pizza back into the cooling oven and got her pocketbook and coat. When would she stop dropping everything to help this man? What was it that made her run to his side, wanting to comfort him? Then again, maybe it was just plain curiosity. Where *had* the man gone?

She slipped outside into the cool night. As she drove to the other side of town, she realized she'd stepped foot in Henry's house just once, after their Chinese dinner. It had been a quick stop to pick up a sweater before their nursery tour: From what she could glean in the dim light, the house was a small ranch, the kitchen set off behind the living room with a hallway to the dining room and bedrooms. School pictures of his son and daughters hung on the living room wall, frozen in time. She'd been surprised by how light the house was on greenery; she'd expected hanging plants, rubber trees in every corner. When she put the question to Henry, he said it would be like bringing work home with him.

Now when she pulled into the driveway, he was standing at the front door, the light shining on his pale face. He didn't look well; in fact, he looked somewhat like he'd just committed a terrible act, a murder maybe, and didn't know where to hide the body. She hesitated for a moment. What was she getting herself into?

But then Henry opened the screen door, and stepped out, beckoning her in. She had to go inside. She was here after all.

"Henry," she said. "What on earth is the matter?"

As she stepped into the house, he closed the door behind her and then leaned in to hug her. When she pulled back, she saw that his eyes were red, the tear ducts swollen underneath. The kitchen light shone out from the back; the living room sat in darkness.

"Ellen, you can't imagine. It's terrible. Just terrible."

"Is it your children? Is everyone okay?"

"Yes, yes, they're fine," he said hurriedly. Then he took her by the hand and led her down the hall. She noticed pretty little watercolor paintings dotting the walls. They stepped into his bedroom, where a light shone brightly.

Scattered across the navy blue bedspread was a sea of papers and books.

"*This* is what has happened." He gestured to the bed, his arm sweeping across as if to explain.

Ellen didn't understand. "Did someone rob you?" It looked as if the room had been ransacked, but then how to explain the television still sitting on the stand in the corner? She'd never set foot in Henry's bedroom, and it looked like the room of a lonely man. The taupe curtains were pulled tightly closed. A desk in the corner overflowed with junk: empty bottles, socks, unopened mail, loose change, and catalogs. A pile of unwashed clothes and a half-filled box of books sat on the other side of the bed. It all smelled musty, as if the room had been closed off for too long.

He crossed to the bed and picked up one of the papers. It was an e-mail, she could see that now from the layout of the typed print on the page. Henry handed it to her, tears in his eyes. The creases were well worn, as if the note had been folded and refolded a thousand times. She read in silence.

As she read, she blushed to see that the words gushed with feeling, excitement, with breathlessness. *"I miss you desperately . . . meet me at noon on the terrace."* It was signed, *"Love always, Me."* It was addressed to Charlotte, though the sender's address had been blacked out.

"I take it this isn't from you."

Henry shook his head and collapsed on the bed. "None of these is," he gestured to the mess.

"Oh, Henry." She knew she shouldn't be reading a dead woman's electronic missives. But she was also deeply embarrassed for Henry, devoted husband that he was and continued to be, carrying a torch for a wife who'd left him too soon and who'd left him, apparently, a cuckold at that.

"I had no idea. None whatsoever. How is that possible?" Henry whispered.

He handed her another page when she sat down beside him. She didn't particularly want to read more, but she couldn't help herself. Henry looked over her shoulder, reading it, she could only imagine, for the fiftieth time. As the e-mails piled up beside her, she struggled to make some sense of the story unfolding in her hands.

For one thing, the affair seemed to be short-lived, only a few months in length. There were eight printed e-mails all together.

The first, if it was the first, bore a date of May 2, the last August 14. "That one was written the day before she died," he whispered.

"Where did you find these?"

"You won't believe it, but I was finally packing up some of her things. Nantucket was the impetus," he paused. "So I started pulling the books off her bedside table. And with the first one I picked up, *The Grapes of Wrath,* out fell an e-mail."

"Oh, Henry," she said. "I'm so, so sorry." She paused. "I always hated that book."

He nodded absentmindedly.

"I read the e-mail and couldn't believe it, but as I continued looking, I started to realize that a few, no *several*, books had a note. This was all I found." He gestured to the papers around him. "Who knows how many more there were?"

She shook her head.

"Oh, I'm sure this is it. There couldn't be more." She took his hand and squeezed it tight. She didn't know what else to do. She thought she felt the baby turn.

"All this time I was thinking we had this great love affair for twenty years. I used to call her my sweet Iris. That was her middle name." He sniffled. "It seemed fitting that her middle name was a flower, something beautiful." He sighed. "And here she was having an affair right under my nose. I never had a clue."

Ellen stacked the papers into a neat pile, the first lying on top, as if to tidy up the mess that had fallen into their laps.

"That's the thing about affairs, Henry. They're clandestine. The other person doesn't know, until, that is, he finds out, and they always do, you know, just like in the movies—and then it's hurtful to everyone involved. I'm sure Charlotte was a lovely woman; she just lost her way. We all do in our own way."

He turned to look at her. "What are you saying? That I was an adulterer, too?"

"No, no. Of course not. Just that no one's perfect."

"Well this is pretty damn far from perfect." His cheeks were flushed, his ears red at the tips. She could feel the heat radiating off his back through his shirt. His hands opened and closed into big fists.

"Do you think," he paused, "she was in love?" How hard it must have been for him to ask such a question. And how much harder to answer.

From the tone of the e-mails, it was clear to Ellen that both lovers had been smitten. Charlotte's suitor wrote how he longed to see her, thought of her every waking moment, couldn't get enough of the smell of her shampoo, the smooth peaks and valleys of her skin. It was treacly stuff, but then what did Ellen know about love? She didn't want to break Henry's heart all over again.

"It's hard to say. Probably not. She was probably just looking for someone to love her."

"But I *did* love her. I told her every day."

"Who knows what makes us do the crazy things we do?" She was surprised to find herself defending this woman, adulteress that she appeared to be. But Ellen also recognized that if she hadn't done one particularly nutty thing in her lifetime, she wouldn't have a baby growing inside her.

Perhaps, too, she was bothered to see Henry so upset by the revelation all these months later. She could understand how the discovery of the e-mails would strike a devastating blow at first—such a large untruth knitted into a marriage he thought was nothing but a string of pearls. But had he really loved this woman so much that he now had to mourn her all over again, the woman he'd apparently not known very well? Where was his anger? Why wasn't he furious?

She read the first e-mail again, taking in the over-the-top language, and before she could stop herself, she laughed.

"What's so funny," he asked, his eyes rimmed with red and wonder.

"Oh, nothing." She brushed it off. "It's just funny, isn't it, how you'd think lovers would find original ways to express their feelings, but somehow they all sound like clichés."

"Yeah." Henry sighed. "I don't think this guy was exactly a poet. Who knows what she saw in him. What on earth did he have that I didn't have?"

He looked at her so beseechingly that Ellen wished she held the answer.

"He wasn't you, Henry," she said finally and patted his knee. "That's all. He wasn't better, or more interesting, or any of the other stuff you might be thinking. He was an escape from the life that she knew."

"He wasn't me," he repeated, softly. "I think you might be right about that."

They sat for a while longer. Then Ellen got up, took the stack of letters and stuck them in the top left-hand drawer of his desk. "Unless you want me to take them, get them out of the house completely," she offered.

"No, leave them for now, please."

"All right. But I don't think it's healthy to keep rereading them."

"Agreed."

She paused, wiped her hands on her jeans, looked around the room. He sat on the bed, looking forlorn.

"I wish I could make this better for you somehow. I really do. What would help?"

He sighed. "Just having you here. That helps. It helps a lot."

"Okay, then. Let's go into the living room, shall we? Maybe even get out of the house for a bit?"

The bedroom clock flashed eight thirty. Ellen could push her bedtime back a little.

"Yes, that's a good idea. Let's go somewhere. Anywhere, really."

He got up slowly, as if unstable on the new legs he'd been handed. She walked to him and took his hand.

"I'm taking you out for . . ." She stopped herself. She was about to say "a beer," then remembered her current state. "A late-night ice cream."

"If you think so." He sounded tentative, but willing.

"I know so. Just follow me. We'll go drown our sorrows in hot fudge and everything will be all right."

"Don't you mean my sorrows?" he asked.

"Yes, sorry," she hastened to add. "Your sorrows. Didn't mean to steal them away from you. They're all yours, Henry."

He gave her a half smile. "Thanks."

"Come on now. We want to get there before they close." She steered him into the living room, grabbed his keys off the end table, and pushed him through the door. It seemed she was destined to be people's caretaker. It was, quite literally, in her blood, she thought with some amusement.

She left the porch light on, something to point the way home for Henry later that night.

"Nothing is more divine than the sweet smell
of *kringle* baking in the oven."
—*The Book of Kringle*

On Saturday, Ellen couldn't stand the suspense any longer: she had to tell. She called Lanie and asked if she'd be up for a trip to the baby store, ostensibly to get some clothes for Benjamin. Lanie was always a sucker for baby shopping, and Rob could watch Benjamin.

Ellen pulled into her sister's driveway at eleven o'clock sharp. Lanie threw herself into the car, bundled in a blue coat, hat, and mittens. Ellen looked at her.

"What?"

"Is it really that cold?"

"For your information, it's fifty degrees out!"

"Yes, but we're going to the baby store, not the Arctic."

"Just drive!" Lanie commanded.

Ellen pulled out of the driveway.

"Remember when we used to take road trips to nowhere, just to get out of the house or so I could practice my driving?"

Ellen groaned. "Don't remind me. Those were some of the most dangerous drives of my life. We're lucky we lived."

"I'm sure mom was watching over us."

"Thank goodness." It was the first time in a long time either one of them had mentioned their mother. For years it was all they could talk about, as if they were afraid that the memory of her would slip away forever. How much their lives had changed since then. Harriet McClarety would be proud; Ellen was certain of it.

She was biting her lip, bursting to tell. If she could sit on her hands while driving, she would have. "So, I have some news to share," she began.

"Oh my God." Lanie shot her a glance. "You and Henry are getting married?"

She couldn't tell if the look on her sister's face was one of surprise, disapproval, or a combination of the two.

"No! Why does everyone keep assuming we're getting married?"

"Sorry, didn't mean to jump to conclusions. So, what is it?"

The timing was perfect. They'd just stopped at a red light at an intersection.

"Are you ready?"

"Yes. You're killing me. What's the big news?"

"I'm having . . ." she paused. "A baby."

"What?" Lanie's head swiveled. She looked as if Ellen had just told her she was buying an elephant for a pet. "A baby?"

"Yes, a baby."

"But how? I mean, are you adopting?"

"Nope. I'm pregnant. One hundred percent knocked up." She couldn't stop the grin from spreading across her face. The light turned.

Suddenly it seemed to sink in. "You're pregnant?" Her sister's voice was shrill, over the top. "Seriously? Oh my God!" She squealed, clapped her hands over her mouth. "I didn't even know you'd been trying. That's so, it's just *incredible*." She bounced in her seat, clapped her hands, then squeezed Ellen hard, so hard that the car swerved a little.

"Watch out!" she yelled to herself as much as to Lanie.

"Sorry." Her sister slammed back into her seat, took a breath. "How far along are you?"

"About three and a half months, give or take." She was back on the straight and narrow, or as much as a pregnant, single woman could be.

"It was *meant* to be. I have to call Rob—he'll be over the moon." She rolled down the window and shouted: "*Woo-hoo!!* My sister's having a baby!" Then she leaned over and honked the horn.

"Stop that!" Ellen batted her sister's hand away but she was laughing. She knew Lanie would be happy for her, but she couldn't have guessed her reaction no matter how many times she played it in her head.

"Wait, wait! You have to pull over." As if it had just dawned on her that they were still driving. "You can't just tell me you're having a baby and keep driving. Pull over—there!" Lanie pointed to an empty space near the curb. Ellen thought she might hyperventilate, so she did as she was commanded.

"But wait! Who's the daddy? Is it Henry?" It was as if the question had just dawned on her: When Ellen shook her head, Lanie's eyes widened. "Oh, I know," she began. "You went to one of those sperm banks and got some hunk's genes!"

"Actually, no." Ellen paused. "It's someone we know. He's handsome, smart . . ."

She could see Lanie searching her mind. She gasped. "Larry?"

Ellen grunted. "No. I'm not that spry." She paused and began biting her thumbnail. "Lanie, it's Max's baby."

She thought she felt her sister pull back just a touch, but maybe it was her imagination. In any case, Lanie looked at her wide-eyed now.

"Does he know?"

"Not yet." She turned off the engine. "Do you think I should tell him?"

"I'm sorry, but I'm confused here. I know Max sent you that e-mail, but when has he been around? I thought he was tucked away on that island of his."

"He was, or, he is, I should say. He was back in town a few

months ago, visiting his sister. And he surprised me at the shop, and then he showed up at my door later that night with dinner. What can I say? It had been a long time . . . one thing led to another."

"But you never told me." Ellen thought she detected hurt in her sister's voice.

"I didn't think you'd approve. Can you blame me?"

Lanie thought it over for a second. "You're probably right." She looked out the window, then back at Ellen. She shook her head. "I can't believe it. A *baby*. I'm so, so happy for you." She gave her another hug.

"How long have you known?"

"A few days. I've been dying to tell you but the moment never seemed right. The other night you and Rob were in such a rush to get to your dinner . . ."

"But, Ellen, a *baby*? We would have canceled for that!"

"Anyway, I couldn't be more surprised myself. I didn't think it was possible." She watched the cars rolling by. "Remember how I joked on Nantucket that I was 'coming down with menopause'?" Her sister giggled. "Turns out I was coming down with a baby."

"Oh, Ellen. It's just wonderful. You'll be the perfect momma." Lanie reached out to touch her stomach. "Hi, baby. Hi, my little niece or nephew. So nice to meet you."

"All right, all right, you'll have plenty of time to get to know him or her," Ellen said. "Right now, we have some shopping to do."

"For a *new* baby," Lanie gushed.

And at the touch of her sister's hand, Ellen felt a slight flutter in her growing belly.

21

"Baked into the heart of every *kringle* is one guiding impulse:
to bring people together to share in spirited conversation,
fine food, and good will."
—*The Book of Kringle*

Bright red and white balloons twirled in the wind outside the storefront, advertising the Fall Fair on the Square in Madison. It was the third Saturday in September, and today was the gala that Lanie's friend Naomi, with the help of the Boys & Girls Clubs, had been planning since spring. More than one hundred vendors would be gathered around the capitol. Ellen was wrapping up the rest of the kringles she'd agreed to donate for the event and preparing to close up the shop. She'd been up baking half the night. Henry had volunteered to help out; business was sure to be slow at the nursery today anyway.

She piled kringle after kringle in his arms. "Tell me how many is too many, okay?" But each time he nodded silently, as if he could bear the weight of her entire store, her crazy life.

"I'm not looking to make you tip over, you know," she said after she'd laid the sixth kringle onto his arms.

"You've already done that. Knocked me over with your beauty." She rolled her eyes. Lately, his affection had been front and center,

194

Charlotte's letters apparently opening a crack in his reserve. Recently Ellen felt like she was the one with all the secrets—a wayward ex-husband, a baby.

A few nights after he'd called about Charlotte's letters, Henry showed up on her front step, looking like a stray dog. Men appearing on her doorstep seemed to be a recurring theme in her life as of late. How could she not take pity on him? After a few beers, he'd turned into a mushball: He was sorry he'd been such a fool. What an idiot to have someone like Ellen fall into his life, like an errant seed about to bloom, and not realize his good fortune. It was a little corny, the whole errant seed metaphor, but it was fitting in more ways than one, she thought. Besides, she had been too busy turning cartwheels in her head. At last, Henry Moon had seen the light.

Now the question was: Did Ellen *want* him to see the light?

She hadn't yet told him about the child on its way; it seemed premature, both for the baby's sake and for the relationship's sake. But she knew that she couldn't avoid it forever. Henry would notice her expanding belly sooner or later.

Now she dusted off her apron, hung it in the back room, and grabbed the key for the store. Erin and Larry were already at the Square setting up the booth. They'd been eager to help out, and each had signed on to be big siblings, roping their own little brother and sister into helping hand out kringle today.

She locked up the store behind Henry and cranked the heater in the car to cut the fall chill. It was cool, but not down-parka cool.

"Thank goodness for small favors," she said to him. "At least it's warm enough that people can actually enjoy themselves outside today."

"How much money do you think the festival will bring in?"

"Who knows? Hard to say, but every little bit counts, right? I'm just glad to see some of the old Madison spirit returning."

"You say that like we've all lost our souls."

"Thankfully, there's still some hope for you, Henry," she teased.

They drove along the country roads, winding over to Madison.

Rolls of hay packaged in tidy white wrappers, like enormous sausages, dotted the fields. How quickly summer's bounty had come and gone.

They pulled into town and searched for a parking space in vain. Ellen pleaded with a cop to let them through the barricade to State Street (she had kringles to deliver!) but he wouldn't budge. Eventually they parked in a lot three streets down and lugged the kringles themselves.

When they arrived at the booth at last, Larry and Erin were putting on the finishing touches, including a big banner that announced in bold blue letters:

THE SINGULAR KRINGLE—THE BEST KRINGLES IN TOWN. —MAYOR FALLON.

The mayor had dropped by the store a few days ago and raved about the pastries, and Larry had encouraged Ellen to put his words to work; she hoped the mayor wouldn't mind. Since hers was the only kringle shop in town, she didn't think she'd gone too far out on a limb.

"Would you like some apple-rhubarb kringle?" A little girl, about eight and bubbling with enthusiasm, looked up expectantly at Ellen. "It's a new house favorite."

"Thank you, don't mind if I do."

"Tania, that's Miss McClarety. She owns the store. Remember I was telling you about her?"

"Oh, sorry," she said brightly. Then, "Does it taste good?"

They laughed. "I hope so!" Ellen took a bite. "Dee-licious. Nice to meet you, Tania. Thanks for helping out today."

"Erin said she'll give me ten dollars at the end of the day." Erin grinned at Ellen.

"Is that right?"

Tania nodded.

"Well, I'm glad to see your heart is all in it." She patted the girl on the arm and went over to introduce herself to Larry's little brother, Steve, who was arranging samples under cellophane wrapping. The wind was turning it into somewhat of a project.

"And you must be Steve."

He nodded. "Say hi, Steve," Larry called down from his step stool.

"Hi," he said softly. Steve looked about six years old, with big brown eyes and a wild head of hair. Clearly he was going to need Tania's exuberance to help with kringle duty today.

"Do you like kringle?" Ellen asked gently. He nodded again.

"Well, good. Whenever you're feeling hungry, you help yourself, okay?"

Another nod.

"Good. Because I like all my workers to be happy and well-fed. Deal?"

"Deal." She could barely hear him.

Larry came down beside him and draped his arm around him. "Steve's a little shy at first, but then you warm up, right buddy?" He nodded again, looked at the ground.

"That's how I am, too." Henry stood beside them now. "I like to be quiet at first and then I can be myself." Ellen felt something close to love for the man.

Steve looked up at Henry. "High five?" Henry asked. He reached out his hand and Steve slapped it hard, triumphantly.

"That's my man." Larry beamed. "I didn't know if you wanted a grammar quote on the booth, too, boss."

Ellen thought about it. "No, let's let it slide for today. I think we could all benefit from breaking the rules for one day, don't you?"

"Henry, my man, ever since you came around, Miss Ellen is getting more and more lax. You're a good influence."

That and a baby, Ellen thought to herself.

She settled into a folding chair behind their table and surveyed the street. Street vendors of all stripes lined the walkway: homemade jewelry, fresh produce, wooden children's toys, face-painting, a helium-balloon stand, even a bubble-magic magician. Naomi and her team had outdone themselves.

A young man stopped by to sample the kringle. "This is amazing stuff. I don't think I've had anything like it. It's like baklava, but better, not as sweet. What's in it?"

"Secret recipe." Ellen winked. The truth was, she *was* nervous about this batch. After poring over the riddle hidden in the book's pages, she'd finally deciphered the secret ingredient—a dash of vanilla in the batter. She'd reread the poem more times than she could count and one night it had dawned on her: "capitals first" referred not to state capitals, but rather to the first capital *letter* of every epigraph heading each chapter in the cookbook. "First and seven" meant the first capitals of the first seven epigraphs. She couldn't believe she'd been so dense, a word freak duped by a cookbook. Had her mother ever figured it out? She certainly hadn't indicated any clues in the book.

Carefully, Ellen had pieced them together, V-A-N-I-L-L-A, taking the "V" from "Very" in the *Very process of mixing, rolling.* Then the "A" from *Apple? Apricot? Pecan?* and the "N" from *Notion for the day,* the "I" from *It's important to remember.* That left two "L"s (*Lars, an old man,* and *Lemon betwixt*), and an "A" (the *Art of kringle-making*). Plain old vanilla it was, two teaspoonsful per serving!

The vanilla was subtle, but it seemed to make the delicate pastry flavor soar even more. Combined with the rhubarb and apple, it was, she thought, perhaps her most singular kringle to date. But she was sleep-deprived and maybe her palate was off.

"Can I buy three?"

"You can't buy any today—everything's free. But stop by our store in Amelia on Main Street, or enter yourself in the silent auction for ten kringles." Ellen pointed to the fishbowl that overflowed with little slips of paper. "Bid whatever you think is a reasonable amount, and if yours is the highest, you win."

"What happens to the money?"

"All the proceeds go to the Boys & Girls Clubs." Ellen pointed to the sign saying as much.

"Oh right. Good. Well, what do I have to lose?" He took a small square of paper and wrote down his bid.

"Don't forget to include your name and e-mail so we can reach you if you win."

He added a few lines, then folded the paper, and dropped it in the bowl.

"Thanks. Can I have another piece for the road?"

Tania practically launched the tray into his hands. "Here you go!" Ellen was going to have to hire her for the store.

Henry returned with six hot chocolates for the group, the steam spiraling through the cracked Styrofoam lids. Ellen had to admit it was nice having a man around who anticipated her needs before they'd even occurred to her. She helped Steve with his lid, then took a sip of hers.

"Isn't this amazing?" Lanie and Rob stood in front of their table now. Benjamin, bundled up like a little soldier, held his mom's hand. "I can't believe the turn out! We're going to raise a ton of money. Naomi is beside herself. You should see her."

"It's impressive, isn't it? I hadn't realized the amount of work she was putting into this."

"I know. Like a full-time job," Lanie said. She took some kringle from Steve, who bashfully held out a tray to her. "Thank you, young man."

"We're off to do face painting. Anyone else want to join us?"

Both Steve and Tania looked at them longingly.

"Go!" Ellen said. "Have fun. Henry and I can man the booth for a while." All four followed, looking grateful to be released from their duties.

"We'll be back soon, boss." Larry held Erin's gloved hand in his.

"Take your time," Ellen said. She turned to Henry after they'd left. "This is nice."

"What?" he asked.

"This." She gestured around her. "Everyone coming together for a good cause. All the kids running around having fun. Passing out kringle."

He reached into his coat pocket. "I was thinking the same thing. In fact, I was wondering what might come after the kringle . . ."

"Henry, don't be fresh."

"Of course not. I meant maybe a pretzel or some cotton candy . . ." Just then he squeezed her hand. She felt something hard press against her palm.

When she pulled her hand away, she saw it held a silver chain with a pendant attached. The pendant was smooth, oblong, a thin white line running across it. A friendship rock.

"Oh, Henry! . . ." Her voice trailed off. "From our trip?" she asked.

He nodded.

"And here I thought you weren't taking my friendship rock seriously. It's stunning. Thank you," she said as she closed the clasp around her neck.

He smiled. Then something occurred to her: "Wait a minute, is this your way of telling me we're just friends?"

"Well, a little more than that, I hope."

She gave him a peck on the cheek, two hearts beating beneath one exquisite stone.

22

"Buildings, too, are children of Earth and Sun."
—Frank Lloyd Wright

Rob was back from the site and was feeling a little smug. Everything had gone off without a hitch. The building permits were in place, the construction crew was ready to begin, and the designs for the institute had gotten the final sign-off from the museum's board of directors. Even the local paper showed up for the groundbreaking, shooting pictures of Walter Greenough and Frank Hobbs shaking hands with the museum director. After pressing shovels into their hands, the photographer had persuaded Greenough and Hobbs to wear clunky yellow hard hats. Greenough was probably in his eighties, and though he looked frail and small under his ungainly hat, Rob could see the conviction shining from his steely blue eyes that had gotten him to where he was today. Even Hobbs slapped Rob on the shoulder, saying, "Well done, son."

He'd take it, happily. Whatever praise Hobbs wanted to send his way was fine by him. He'd been waiting only five years.

When he got back to the office, Kate looked up from her desk and smiled. "Construction suits you. You look handsome."

Rob raised his hand, felt the cold plastic, and removed the hat. "Sorry, forgot I was wearing it. It's mandatory on the site."

"So how was it? The day you've always been dreaming of?"

"Something like that. It was pretty sweet, I have to admit. To see all that work finally come to fruition . . . it's kind of like having a baby."

"I'll bet. Though Lanie might disagree with that assessment."

He laughed. "Anyway, it was good. Hey, have you seen Samantha around? She wasn't at the ceremony."

"I think she's with Eli. They're already at work on some new project, not sure what."

"Ah." *Typical,* Rob thought. He should have known Eli wouldn't let the grass grow under his feet; it figured he'd already corralled Samantha for the next design. For a second he wondered, *was the poor guy hoping for something more with her, like a relationship?* But nah, Eli wasn't her type.

He was a little sad not to be working with Samantha again, but it was probably for the best, given the fallout with Lanie over the summer. Samantha remained upbeat, always pleasant, but something had shifted over the summer. He wasn't sure if he could pin it to the night when she'd come up to him, drunk; she'd apologized the next day for her "indiscretion" at the bar. Rob had laughed it off, tried to make it seem insignificant, which it was, of course. Or maybe it had nothing to do with that night. Maybe Samantha was simply done playing second fiddle, done with being an apprentice and wanted to take the lead on her own projects. In either case, he hoped she'd continue to move up at the firm. She deserved every little bit of praise, and he'd seen to it that a commendation was placed in her file for review time.

When his line rang, Kate picked up. Her eyebrows shot up. "Hello, Mr. Hobbs. Okay. Uh-huh. He's right here. I'll make sure he comes right down."

She hung up and turned to Rob. "Someone wants to see you."

"Uh-oh." Rob's mind flashed through the possible scenarios: They were firing him now that all the design work was finished for the museum, or maybe Hobbs wanted him to make *more* changes to the plans. He'd met with Frank Hobbs alone only once before and that was shortly after he'd been hired. He was a nice enough guy, but hard to read. A little more slick than Greenough, and younger, too. Probably in his mid-sixties.

"You're such a worry wart," Kate said. "Maybe it's something good."

"Don't start packing up my things till I'm back, okay?"

"Deal." She smiled. "And Rob? Good luck."

He headed down the hallway, feeling sweat break out on the back of his neck. Suddenly the hallway seemed particularly long, a gauntlet with Frank Hobbs waiting at its end. Hobbs was in the "interim" office, as they called it. Since he seldom set foot in the satellite Madison office, he'd set up shop in the odd corner that doubled as an intern's space and an office for traveling associates. It had a computer, a window that looked out on the lake, a trash can. *Maybe,* Rob thought absurdly, *he wants to use my office for the day, something a little nicer*. He'd understand.

He knocked with what he hoped sounded like a confident wrap of the knuckles.

"Come in."

When he opened the door, Hobbs was looking out the window and he swiveled around in his chair.

"Oh, Rob, good. Come in, come in."

His yellow hard hat was resting on the desk. He'd taken off his sports jacket, which was draped over the back of his chair. His pin-striped shirtsleeves were rolled up to the elbows. He stood up, took a step forward, and reached out to shake Rob's hand.

"Good to see you again."

"Thank you, sir." Rob noted he had a firm handshake. He tried to read from the tenor of Hobbs's voice what was coming. He couldn't decide.

"Have a seat, please." He gestured to the chair on the other side of the desk and walked back to the window.

"That was some nice work you did on the art institute."

"Thank you. I was pleased with how it all turned out."

"I understand it wasn't always the easiest row to hoe either. At least that's what Walter tells me."

"Oh, you know, we had our disagreements, Eli and I, but we always seemed to get it done. Samantha was a big help." He hoped to God that Eli hadn't ratted him out and that Walter had had to come to his defense. How humiliating. How shallow. If that was the case, he'd wring Eli's little neck.

"Do you want some water?" As if it had just occurred to him, Hobbs gestured to the bottle of Perrier sitting on his desk. Rob shook his head.

"No thanks." Why didn't the man just cut to the chase already? Was he going to fire him? Put him on probation? Move him to another state?

"Rob, we're having a few changes in-house." He paused, looked out the window again. Rob braced himself. Here it came. He'd be out on the street looking for work tomorrow. What an awesome thank-you for a job well done. Screw them! He'd find something better, a place where his superiors appreciated him.

"Eli and I, how shall I put it?" He cleared his throat. Rob waited. "We've had a parting of ways. Eli has accepted a position with Donovan, Stark, and Lyons."

"You're joking?" Rob couldn't have feigned more surprise if he wanted to. He assumed that Eli was just waiting for Greenough to kick the bucket before he'd be promoted to vice president of the company, alongside Hobbs. He and Hobbs had been buddies ever since Rob arrived at the firm. A parting of ways? It didn't make sense.

"I wish I were, but I'm not. It seems Eli has some very definite ideas about the future of architecture in this city, and they don't happen to be ones that Walter and I share."

"Oh." Rob didn't know what else to say. "I think I understand."

"I don't know. Maybe I'll be kicking myself ten years from now, but I don't think the city is quite ready for some of this newfangled design. Call me old-fashioned, but there it is."

"I couldn't agree more." Rob nodded his head eagerly now. He knew that Greenough and Hobbs were fans of "green" architecture, but maybe they'd also grown wary of Eli's insistence on catering to the "younger crowd" in all of his designs. That and his bullheadedness when it came to defending his own ideas. Rob remembered to breathe.

"Wow. Well, okay then. I appreciate your telling me."

"Of course. Eli's last day will be next Friday."

"Good to know. Thanks." Rob moved to leave.

"There's one more thing." Frank Hobbs moved to perch himself on the edge of his desk.

"I'm also looking to semiretire. I'd like to do some things with my better half—you know, cook, travel, see the world before it's too late."

Rob nodded again. "I can see why you'd—"

"Which brings me to my next point," Hobbs cut him off. Was there more? Was he shutting down the whole business? Selling out?

"I've talked it over with Walter," he paused.

Seriously, Rob didn't think he could stand the suspense any longer. *Just drop the frickin' guillotine,* he thought to himself.

"And Walter and I both agree," he continued, "that you have the vision and the expertise that have come to distinguish our firm."

Rob waited. "Thank you . . ." *I think,* he said to himself.

"I'm not done yet." Hobbs held up his hand. "Let me finish."

Rob felt his face flush. What an idiot he was. *Shut up,* he told himself.

"And since you so nicely embody all that the firm stands for, we'd like to offer you the position of vice president."

Rob couldn't speak. "Excuse me?"

"I'm sorry if I haven't conveyed to you in the past how impressed I am with your work, but you've always had the most original ideas and designs that *work* with the space and the people who will be in them. If anyone is true to the vision of Frank Lloyd Wright, it's you. Do you understand what I'm saying?"

"Yes, sir." Finally, someone had noticed!

"And that's why we'd be honored if you'd be willing to help run the firm in addition to heading up design teams. The firm will remain Hobbs & Greenough for the time being, but I suspect it will change to Hobbs, Greenough, & Taylor in a few years. Just give me a little time to fade gracefully into the distance."

"Sir, I don't know what to say. I'm beyond flattered."

"You can stop calling me sir, for one. We're colleagues. Frank works just fine."

"Okay."

Hobbs got up and held out his hand. "So, does this mean you accept?"

Rob rushed to shake it. "You bet. You bet I will. Thank you, sir, I mean Frank."

"Terrific. I know Walter will be thrilled. Let me get him on the phone and tell him the good news." He turned back to his desk. "And Rob?"

"Yes?"

"Let's wait to make this announcement public until we tell everyone that Eli is leaving. I'd like to have some good news to share as well. We'll talk money later."

"Understood."

He shut the door behind him and exhaled. He felt drunk. *A promotion! A raise!* And not just any old promotion—he was going to be vice president.

He beamed at Kate when he passed her desk.

"Good news?"

"I'd say so."

"What?"

"Can't tell yet."

"Oh, come on."

"Soon. I promise, I'll tell you as soon as I can."

He went into his office and closed the door. The stress of Lanie's not working full-time—though he hadn't told her he'd been worrying about the lack of income—suddenly melted away. They were going to be all right, more than all right. Could he ask for anything more? Well, yes, maybe one more thing. A new parking space.

He picked up his phone and tapped in Lanie's cell number. "Feel like celebrating?" he asked when she picked up.

23

*"Beware of the imposter kringle, an inferior pastry of dough
and frosting that will leave its buyer unsated."*
—*The Book of Kringle*

The beaches came into view below, wide stretches of pink sand, though she knew it only looked pink from above, one of those optical illusions that the sun played. The water, however, was truly the aquamarine of travel magazines.

When the plane landed, Ellen pulled her bag from the overhead bin and waited for the group ahead of her to move forward. A cluster of couples on a ten-year anniversary bash had been getting progressively tipsy throughout the flight, and now she wondered if a few of them would even make it off the plane. A stewardess politely led one lady by the elbow as she yelled *"Sint Maarten est fantastique!"* Ellen's French wasn't stellar but she knew slurred speech when she heard it. The woman was trashed.

And yet here she was, hardly one who could point a finger. What she was doing on the island she really couldn't say. Things had taken a definite turn for the better with Henry, so why, on a moment's notice, had she decided to head to Sint Maarten for the first weekend of October, leaving the store once again in Larry's capable hands? She hadn't shared with Henry her true reason for going and had used Lanie as her cover; they were having a girls' weekend away, she fibbed.

The thing was, she needed to see Max. And, he'd sent her the tickets with no strings attached. What was there to lose? He wanted her to hear him out before she crossed him off her list forever. And now there was the matter of the baby on the way. A little bundle of soon-to-be joy that Max had no inkling about. In the back of her mind, she wanted to tell him. He deserved to know. He would *want* to know. She wasn't sure how he would react but then that wasn't her problem. She didn't expect him to be in her child's life, unless, of course, he wanted to be. And if things really were going to get serious with Henry, she needed to make sure, no matter how silly, that her story with Max was truly a closed book. At least that's what she told herself.

The cab pulled up to a pink stucco hotel, lush palm trees shading its walkway. Brilliant orange flowers exploded around the archway framing the entrance. After she paid, she pulled her luggage into the lobby and handed the hotel manager her credit card, marveling at his wonderful accent, a mix of Dutch and English. People always sounded smarter with an accent. As far as she was concerned, a Dutchman could be the biggest idiot and yet still be charming when he spoke.

"We hope you enjoy your stay in Sint Maarten, Mrs. McClarety," he said.

"Miss," she corrected politely.

"Ah. Miss," he said and smiled. "That makes vacation more interesting, yes?"

"We'll see."

The bellhop took her luggage, pointing out the hotel pool and lounge, the restaurant and bar, the spa where she could get a massage and a foot rub. Max hadn't been that far off when he'd first described the place as Fantasy Island.

When the bellhop showed her into her room, she held her breath. There was the ocean, laid out before her window like a succulent meal. On a nearby table sat four bottles of distilled water, fresh lemon slices, and ice chilling in a metal bowl. She couldn't wait to get out of her sweaty clothes and into a cool shower. She'd wrap herself in the hotel robe, lounge on her king-size bed, and look out the window, telling her baby all that she saw. *Paradise.*

The next morning she set out to meet Max over breakfast in a little restaurant down the street from her hotel. The sun was much more intense here, and she could feel her nose burning already. When she passed a vendor selling hats, she decided to buy a wide-brimmed sunhat covered with woven flowers. *When in Rome,* she told herself.

"You look beautiful in it, yes?" The vendor held up a mirror before she handed him money. "Nothing more beautiful than pretty woman expecting baby!" He smiled at her as he handed back her change.

Ellen was stunned. It was the first time anyone had acknowledged in a public way that she was pregnant. Her hand instantly flew to her belly, and the coins dropped to the pavement. "Here, here," he said, as he bent down to pick them up.

"Thank you." She glanced down at her belly and realized he was right. She looked, well, *pregnant* in her yellow sundress. It was a slight bump, but enough of a bump that said BABY ON BOARD. What on earth would Max think? She hadn't been showing much before. It was as if the baby had pushed a foot out on the flight to announce its imminent arrival. Quickly, she grabbed one of the colorful wraps that also hung from the vendor's booth.

"How much?"

"For you? Half price." She handed the man a fistful of money. "Thank you."

She wrapped the scarf around her waist and knotted it at the side, hoping it would disguise her pregnant belly. She was starting to feel queasy. Was it the heat? The baby? The thought of seeing Max? Maybe coming here had been a mistake.

When she walked into the restaurant, she spotted him straight-away sitting at a table in the corner.

"You made it!" Max got up and walked toward her, his arms outstretched. She removed her hat and held it in front of her belly. He was more darkly tanned than when he'd visited. And was it her imagination or did his upper arms look even more muscular when he reached out to embrace her?

"Ellen, it's so good to see you. I'm so glad you're here." She felt some of the passion of that night swell up in her. She breathed in his scent.

"Good to see you, too, Max." He hugged her for what felt like a minute too long. She turned slightly sideways, bump averted, then followed him to the table. Mirrors edged in seashells and colorful artwork lined the walls.

"How *are* you?" he asked, as if he were genuinely interested. "You look super."

She took a deep breath to get her composure back. Had he noticed already? But apparently not. He leaned forward, put his chin on his hands, as if to drink her in, as if he hadn't just traced the lines of her body a few months ago.

"Well, the flight was fine, aside from some early partiers. The island is gorgeous," she quickly added. "I can see why you love it. Thank you again for the tickets." She wanted to get that out on the table as quickly as possible.

"Good, good. You're very welcome." A waiter came up to their table, and Max ordered for them both, eggs Benedict and mimosas.

"Oh, just an orange juice for me, please. Straight up." She laughed nervously. "But if you could throw in one of those cute little umbrellas?"

The waiter nodded. "Of course."

"Too early for booze," she explained.

"So, I thought we could start with a day of shopping at some of the street vendors," Max began. "I know how much you like shopping. Then, if you're feeling adventurous," he paused, "I thought maybe we could try some snorkeling. It's beautiful here. You won't believe the fish. They're out of this world. Or we could head over to St. Barts. It's just a short plane ride away . . ."

The waiter placed their drinks before them. Ellen fidgeted in her chair. She hadn't planned on grand adventures with Max; she was thinking a breakfast, maybe a dinner or two. After all, the man had given her the free tickets. But mainly, she was envisioning herself sitting on a lounge chaise, poolside, reading tabloids, resting her tired feet.

Max nudged her out of her reverie.

"Max," she began. He leaned forward, bumping his mimosa so that the orangey liquid spilled onto the table.

The anticipation on his face was almost too much to bear.

"I haven't been able to stop thinking about that night," he began.

"Max, listen."

"What?" He sat back. The poor man had no idea what she was about to hit him with. Would she? Could she?

"I flew down here because I thought it was the right thing to do—you know, to give you a chance to say whatever it is you have on your mind so we both can have closure once and for all. And to be honest, I was dying to see Sint Maarten or Saint Martin, whatever you call it. I've always heard it's beautiful and it is."

Max was biting his lower lip. She was buying time. Maybe she could get one nagging thing off her list before they got into the whole baby business.

"I want to let you say your piece. But as I sit here, I realize I also have something to ask you. It's silly, I know, and I feel almost foolish for bringing it up, but it's been bothering me for a while now."

She was stretching the truth, but it was in pursuit of a greater truth. She took a sip of orange juice. Max waited. "Okay."

"Do you remember Charlotte Moon? Henry's wife? You know, the nursery guy?"

She watched a flicker cross his face, though she couldn't tell of what.

Ellen continued. "Well, she fell in love with Henry and they had three kids. Life was blissful for them, I gather, until one day she was killed in a gruesome car accident, a missed stop sign by some drunk teenagers. I don't suppose you remember it. It happened more than a year ago."

His face blanched.

"I know, it was a terrible thing—dying that way," she said. "Well, Henry was in love with her, even after twenty years of marriage." Ellen paused and shook her head. "And so her passing turned him into a wreck. He used to come into my store looking as if it was all he could do to drag himself out of bed, and this was months later, mind you. All this time pining for her, and then one day, he opens up one of her books, and an e-mail falls out. I think it was *The Grapes of Wrath*, but that's irrelevant."

She paused to see if Max was getting any of this. He appeared not to hear her, to be looking right past her out the doorway.

"Henry hadn't been able to bring himself to touch Charlotte's things since her death. Kind of strange, right?"

Max nodded, stony-eyed. She was getting going now.

"But he does one night, packing up these books, and out falls one e-mail after another." She remembered them in her mind's eye. "*Love* notes, and *not* from Henry."

And now, as if on a downward spiral that she couldn't stop, Ellen kept talking, realizing she was going to ask Max what she'd had no intention of asking him. A nagging worry had stuck with her since the night Henry had unfurled his heart and shared his wife's slight: The e-mails had all been riddled with misspellings and typos.

Ellen knew, of course, that any Lothario could tap out an e-mail rife with mistakes, that love made a person blind, unseeing when it came to the finer points of grammar and spelling. That such blatant disregard for the English language immediately reminded her of Max seemed an unfortunate coincidence. But there was something else that had stayed with her. Something about the cadence of the sentences, the repeated misspellings of the words, like *your* for *you're* and *lead* for *led* ("You lead me to see what love could be"). The phrase "You brighten each day" was surely one that lovers exchanged often. The fact that Max had said this very thing to her during the first months of their courtship and again on their wedding day was an unlikely coincidence but a coincidence just the same. She had laughed to think where her mind could take her sometimes.

And yet now, thousands of miles from home, she found herself suddenly possessed by the urge to dispel her suspicions, to confront Max here on his own turf. To let the silly thought that he might have been involved with Charlotte Moon while they were in the final months of their marriage fly off into the thick, humid island air—and disappear.

Max, a man of big dreams, had never been able to follow through on anything. How would it be any different in matters of the heart?

He was looking at her now, his cheeks flushed.

"I was going to tell you," he began. "Not today. But eventually. It's part of my journey toward healing. Part of trying to win you back—through honesty, through full disclosure."

Ellen felt her stomach drop. Was she going to deliver the baby right there?

"What?" It was as if Max were speaking Mandarin. "You're in a twelve-step program now?" She couldn't help but joke.

"About Charlotte. I didn't mean for it to happen. Neither of us did. It's remarkable when I still think about it, that we ever met in the first place. So improbable."

"How's that?" It was all Ellen could do to get the words out. Was Max saying what she thought he was saying?

"You probably don't recall, but remember when I helped Jack out at the hardware store about a year and a half ago?"

Ellen's mind was doing flips. When had Max worked at the hardware store? Then she remembered: he had assisted when the store was getting remodeled and Jack needed someone up front to man the register.

"*Jack* knew?" She couldn't help herself.

"Oh, God, no. Nobody knew. At least I don't think anyone knew. And to be honest, there wasn't much to know till the very end."

"Oh." She laid her hands on the table, bracing herself for what might come next. Her nail beds flushed a bright pink.

"Anyway, Charlotte came in one day looking for picture frames. She had these delicate little watercolors in her bag."

Max never used words like *delicate*. Ellen untied the shawl around her waist and used it to pat her forehead. She set it down next to her plate.

"They were really something. Pastels, pretty little paintings of the lake, of the Union Terrace at sunset, of State Street early in the morning. I complimented her on them, and she told me they were hers. That she loved to paint, though she'd never done anything professionally. She was very, very talented."

Ellen thought he emphasized the second *very* unnecessarily.

"She made it sound easy. Like anyone could learn to paint. I told her she was making it up, and then I said I'd give her ten bucks if she could get me, a Neanderthal, to paint one picture as pretty as those. He paused. "It stopped her. I don't think she ever thought she was talented. I didn't mean it in a flirtatious way, I swear. I was just making small talk, you know, how people do."

Ellen nodded, her mouth open.

"Well, turns out she took me up on it. We bumped into each other again one day and she asked if I was serious about painting, and that if I were, she'd love to try her hand at teaching me.

"I know it must sound ridiculous. But I appreciated her kindness, and, well, what if there were a famous artist buried somewhere deep inside me that I hadn't yet discovered? What if I could have been making millions on my artwork?"

"Max," Ellen said with a scold in her voice. "Surely you knew better."

"You'd think, huh? Long story short, we met on the Union Terrace one afternoon when I was on break from the store, and she pulled out this tiny tin of paints, an easel, a pad of paper. I looked at it all and thought to myself, 'I'm not an artist. There's no way I can do this.'"

Ellen sighed.

"But Charlotte was patient. She was good that way. She gave me time to explore, to figure out what kind of style I'd work best in."

Ellen made a *phhff* sound. Max? A style?

"Turns out my style was more abstract than realist, but she praised me for it. Said I had an eye for the way the colors played on the water of the lake."

Ellen rolled her eyes. Then it came to her. The miniature painting of muted pinks and blues, oranges and yellows, which had hung on their foyer wall wasn't something he'd purchased. It was *Max's* painting, inspired by Charlotte's soft touch, her gentle guidance. At the time, Ellen couldn't believe he'd paid good money for those splotches of color on parchment.

"It wasn't like you think, though. It was perfectly innocent for the first few weeks." He paused. "But then we fell in lust."

"Oh, please." *If it was so innocent, why hadn't he ever mentioned their painting sessions to her?* she wondered.

"You were so busy trying to figure out what you were going to do next," he said, as if he could read her thoughts. "You'd just lost your secretarial job at the university and you were stressed about money. You wanted me to find something stable."

Ellen remembered. It was not a time she was proud of. She'd been flailing for her life's purpose, accusing Max of not doing his fair share of contributing to their financial bottom line. The unhappy reality of not being able to have children still hung over their heads.

"Being with Charlotte was my therapy. All the pressures we had at home fell away. I could talk to her. And then, well, it got so we couldn't see enough of each other. Her hair, it was so soft, and it always smelled like peppermint shampoo, and she had this cute Southern drawl and . . ."

"Please, please stop," Ellen said now. Her eyes darted around for the ladies' room; she was certain she was about to be ill.

"I'm so sorry." Max reached out for her hand, but she placed it in her lap.

"Like I said, neither of us ever meant for it to go anywhere. It just kind of happened. And then I guess you could say it turned into love."

"Just stop, please." Ellen looked away, breathed in, and clasped her hands together in front of her mouth. "Enough," she said softly.

"You never knew?"

She shook her head.

"When you filed for divorce, it was so soon after the affair, that I was sure you had an inkling."

"No. Not a clue." Henry's words echoed in her ear.

He nodded. "Just one more thing. And I'm sorry, but I have to get this off my chest."

"There's more?" She waited. "How can there possibly be more?"

"The day she died in that accident?" His voice cracked, and tears swam in his eyes. "She was coming to meet me."

Ellen sat up straight. "What?"

"August fifteenth. I'll never forget. It was a Saturday, you were out shopping with Lanie, and Charlotte and I had made plans to meet for an early dinner in Delavan. We sure didn't count on a bunch of drunk teenagers riding around like maniacs." He wiped at his eyes.

Ellen knew only the outline of the facts that shrouded Charlotte's death. Three boys, juniors in college, were out drinking beers in the late afternoon in a field outside town. They got the idea to drive into Madison and were barreling down Country Road C, going eighty miles an hour, when they missed the stop sign where she happened to be crossing at that very instant. Ironically, all the boys walked away from the crash, only a few scratches on their young bodies.

Ellen felt positively ill. "That's quite a burden to carry."

"I went to the funeral, but I could never let anyone know how crushed I was. She died because of me." Large wet tears rolled down his cheeks.

She was stunned.

"Oh, Max," she said. "How could you?" The question was all encompassing, for so many slights, so many wrongs committed.

He wiped at the tears. "I know. It's all my fault."

"I don't mean Charlotte's death. I mean us." Her words came out sharp, like little knives.

He looked at her as if the answer was obvious. "With Charlotte, I was always good enough. With you, I never measured up." He wiped his nose with his sleeve.

Their waiter hovered in the corner, looking uncertain whether to clear their untouched eggs Benedict or stay away altogether. He scurried off to hide in the kitchen.

"No matter how unkind I was, what you did, Max Nelson, was unforgivable."

"I know it was. I'm hoping, though, that you can find some way to forgive the unforgivable."

She shook her head. "Oh, Max. You've always been such a dreamer. That's one thing you're *fantastic* at." Her words carried bite.

He sat back in his chair.

"It's funny. You know I came here thinking I'd let you do all the talking, but I also must have known deep inside why I really agreed to visit.

"A part of me knew," she continued, her voice cracking. "A part of me knew, when I read those letters, that Charlotte's suitor had been none other than my ex-husband, who was, need I remind you, my husband at the time."

She felt herself building steam. "You don't miss me, Max. You don't love me any more than you did a few years ago, which is to say, not much. Those letters you wrote me? They were really meant for Charlotte. I suppose you loved me once. I know I loved you. But your heart is still aching for Charlotte."

She took a sip of orange juice. "All you really want from me is my forgiveness."

He shook his head and put his hand up, "No, you're wrong there. I've done some thinking . . ."

"Max, please. Just stop. Spare us both. I'm glad—if that's the right word—for the closure, but frankly, I think we'd both benefit if we just left it at that."

She blew her nose into her napkin, patted her hair. Then she pushed her chair back and got up, grabbing her pocketbook and flowery hat, which suddenly looked ridiculous.

"I trust you can get the check?" He looked at her, his eyes rimmed with red, and nodded.

"Good."

"Have a safe flight back?" It sounded like a question.

"Thank you. I'll do that."

She went to the ladies' room and promptly vomited. It was what she'd feared subconsciously all along. Now the truth had come out in a cheap little restaurant in the Caribbean.

When she left the ladies' room, she noticed their table was empty. She walked back to the hotel in a slight daze. Max hadn't noticed her stomach, thank goodness. The only saving mercy in all of this. She would tell him at some point; she owed him that. But not today. Today she owed him absolutely nothing. She couldn't wait to check the next flights out, couldn't wait to hear Henry's voice on the other end of the phone, couldn't wait to get her baby back home.

24

"Mothers who tell stories are the first teachers of literature.
They give their children the key to the great realm
where dwell the great and mighty of all times."
—*Talks to Mothers*

Lanie was nervous. Ellen had called from the airport, asking her to come pick her up. Evidently things hadn't gone as planned. All Saturday Lanie paced the floor, biting her nails, worrying how Max would take the news. Even with Rob's amazing promotion, she couldn't stop thinking about her sister and Max. Would he be back in their lives again, like an old, tired song that pops up on the radio? What if Max proposed? She didn't think she could take it. And what about poor Henry? Lanie was starting to feel sorry for the guy. He deserved to know Ellen's big news—not much longer and she would *have* to tell him. A woman could only hide a pregnant belly for so long.

Truth be told, Lanie was angry. How long had her sister waited for a baby, for a good man, and now she was about to turn everything upside down by bringing Max back into the fold? As far as she was concerned, Ellen was hung up on Max for all the wrong reasons, trying to live the life she thought their mother had always wanted but had missed out on. It still struck Lanie as odd that someone as smart as her sister could be so dumb, so blind about some things.

"Phew. It feels good to be back," Ellen said as she plopped herself into the car and knitted her coat tightly around her middle. Lanie detected a slight bump underneath.

"Weather wasn't good?"

"Oh, the weather was perfect. The island is beautiful. We should go sometime for a mini-vacation. Just the two of us."

"Another time maybe," Lanie said. She could already feel herself growing impatient with Ellen's small talk. *What happened?* she wanted to scream.

"You're right. I suppose it's best for us to stay out of Max territory."

"Mmm." Lanie eased out of the airport garage and fished some change from her purse to pay the parking attendant. "So how did Max take the news?"

There was quiet in the other seat.

"Not so well."

"Really?" She pulled onto the main road.

"Well, he didn't actually have any news to react to."

"Why's that?"

"I didn't tell him."

"*What?* Why?" Lanie couldn't believe it. Her sister had chickened out.

"I just couldn't. I got there. I sat across from him and looked into those lost eyes and I couldn't bring myself to tell him."

"But now what? I mean, wasn't telling Max the whole point of your trip? To let him know that he's going to be a *daddy*?" Her voice quavered. She could feel the frustration simmering beneath her words.

"Yes," Ellen said curtly. "But don't be so quick to judge. You weren't there. Things change, you know."

"I can't imagine how things can change any more than by having a baby—"

"I don't have the energy to explain," Ellen interrupted. "Let's just say that Max doesn't deserve any favors from me right now." There was a weariness in her voice, and something else. Was it sadness?

"Do you have any intention of telling him? Ever?"

"Yes, yes, of course. It's just . . . the moment wasn't right. Trust me."

Max had a right to know, Lanie felt it in her bones.

"You know, Ellen, that Max was never right for you? Never has been, never will be."

"I know." Her sister said the words softly, resignedly.

"For some reason, you seem to think that he was the be-all and end-all." Lanie could feel herself falling into lawyer mode. "Even after the divorce, I think there was a part of you that still felt that way." She paused to let her words sink in. "I think, too, that you might worry Henry doesn't compare, that he's somehow dull compared to Max. That he might be a bit like dad."

She tried to see Ellen's face from the corner of her eye, but her sister wasn't giving anything away. She knew Ellen harbored the theory that their mother had once been in love with another man, a high school sweetheart, whom their grandfather had eventually forbidden her to see because of some shady dealings with the law. Lanie had come to understand over the years that her sister had always doubted the contours of their parents' marriage, found it hard to believe that the vivacious, ebullient Harriet McClarety would choose their pensive, reserved father to be her one and only.

But Lanie never did. Perhaps it was because she only remembered their parents' relationship through the rose-colored glasses of a six-year-old, but she didn't think so. Her mother had once told them that a good husband was like a good soap: strong, reliable, sweet-smelling, cleansing. The description had stayed with her all these years. With her parents, she had sensed a love that was true, stable, secure. She aspired to have that same bond with her own husband.

"Mom loved dad, loved him deeply. It might not have been the crazy, go-by-the-seat-of-your-pants kind of love that you get from all your books, but it worked, Ellen, it stayed the course, they were *happy* together."

She waited for any reaction from her sister but only got a throat clearing. Then, after a minute, Ellen said, "I think you're probably right, Lanie. I really do."

They were quiet for the rest of the drive. When they pulled into the driveway, Ellen turned to her and asked, "Before you go, there's something I want to give you. Can you come in for a minute?"

Lanie followed her into the foyer, then the living room. It was dark and the house smelled dank, in need of air.

Ellen plopped her suitcase onto the couch and unzipped it. She reached in to produce a necklace woven from miniature ivory shells and handed it to Lanie.

"These shells are special, I'm told. They're supposed to bring their owner peace and tranquility. Thought they'd go well with your new part-time gig."

"It's beautiful," said Lanie. "Thank you." She strung the delicate chain around her neck.

She turned to leave. She should be getting back to the boys.

"There's just one more thing. Hold on a minute, I'll grab it." Ellen headed for the stairs, lugging her suitcase behind her.

Lanie sat down on the couch while she waited. *What was it that Ellen had to retrieve from upstairs?* she wondered. She cracked open a window behind her before her sister returned, an envelope in hand.

"What's this? Beach sand?"

Ellen shook her head. "Something better, I think."

Lanie turned the envelope over. Her heart stopped. Her mother's handwriting was on the front. She felt her anger toward Ellen dissipating like tiny bubbles in the air.

"I've been holding on to this much too long," Ellen explained. "Mom wanted me to give it to you when you turned forty, but I don't think she'd mind if you had it a few years early. It's the last one I've been saving for you."

Lanie felt her eyes well up.

"It dawned on me in the car that you must be sick of me always trying to be your protector. You don't need me looking out for you anymore. You've got Rob and Benjamin and you're the one giving *me* the advice these days."

"Anyway, I thought you should have mom's letter. You can decide when you want to read it."

Lanie turned the envelope over in her shaking hands a few more times. "Thank you," she said quietly before tearing it open. The faint scent of lilacs escaped from the seal.

As Ellen sat down on the couch next to her, she began reading aloud. It felt as if their mother had swept into the room and was sitting beside them.

My dearest Lanie,

It's hard to imagine you as the grown, beautiful woman that I know you must be. Do you still wear your hair down past your shoulders with bangs in the front? Somehow I doubt it! But I'll bet that you're just as striking today as you are charming and adorable at six.

I can't tell you how difficult it is to know that I will miss these intervening years with you, years that I'm sure have been filled with too many successes and joys to count . . . and probably also some hurts. That is life, I'm afraid. I wish I could have been there to wipe every tear, to hold your hand each time you were afraid, to rub your back till you grew old enough to be embarrassed by it, to slap high fives over your latest achievement.

My one consolation is that I know your father and Ellen have been watching over you, worrying over every little thing, applauding each success, just as I would, all these years. True, Ellen is not your mother, I hear you saying—and no little girl should have to do without—but I know she and your father love you just as fiercely as I do. It's a big responsibility for a big sister, though, so please, be generous with her, be patient, as I know you will.

If you're reading this, you're now well past those angst-ridden teenage years, the stress of college, and quite possibly you're now a married woman with children of your own? If I do have any grandchildren, please, please cover their faces with kisses, cradle them in hugs. You're such a sprite, spinning with energy all the time. It's hard to imagine what you'll do with it all! Whatever you decide, I know that I would be so proud. And if things don't always work out the way you intend, it's all right. Remember, sometimes it's okay to walk away.

My worry with you, sweet girl, is that you're so driven that you'll forget to stop, enjoy it all, to revel in the moment. I worry sometimes that you're so intent on the goal ahead (even at six!) that you lose sight of all the fun you're having getting there. Please, please my dearest Lanie, enjoy life to the fullest, whatever it may bring. Always remember, each day, your three good things.

Know that I'll be watching you and Ellen from above, with enormous love and pride. With wonderment at all you've become and have yet to become.

Love always,
Mom

Lanie clasped Ellen's hand, tears streaming down her face. "It's as if mom's here, isn't it?"

Ellen nodded.

"I still miss her."

"I do, too."

"A lot."

"I know."

"And I'm beginning to forget things . . ."

"Me too."

Lanie folded up the letter and slipped it back into the envelope.

"We've done okay for ourselves, though, haven't we?"

"We've done more than okay, thanks to you." Lanie sniffled. She hugged Ellen, then pulled away. "Here we are, two grown women in tears over something written thirty years ago."

Ellen wiped at her eyes. "I think I've cried more in the past forty-eight hours than I have in the past decade."

"I mean it, though." Lanie turned to her. "I don't know as though I've ever properly thanked you for all you've done. I know it can't have been easy. So much of the burden to raise me fell on you."

"Thanks," Ellen said. "Thanks for saying that." She cleared her throat. "Well, I guess we're our own goddamned Lifetime special, aren't we?" She got up and unbuttoned her coat.

"Pretty close." Lanie tucked the envelope into her purse. "I better get back to the boys before the whole house falls apart."

"What's this?" Ellen asked then. Lanie had completely forgotten about the basket of baby gifts she'd left on the dining room table the day before when she'd snuck into the house with her spare key.

"Oh, nothing. Just a little something to get you thinking about the baby's room."

She watched as her sister peeled back the layers of cellophane to reveal a sea of rattles, teething rings, pacifiers, bath towels, and blankets hiding underneath. "It's perfect. Just perfect. Thank you so much." She came over to give her a hug. Lanie squeezed back, hard. "I love it. This makes it all feel real."

"You're welcome, momma. And by the way, it's *very* real." Lanie dug her keys out of her purse and turned to go. "Call Henry, would you? I'm sure he misses you." Lanie looked at her sister with all that those words implied.

Ellen nodded. "I will."

25

"Serve *kringle* either piping hot from the oven or
freshly chilled from the refrigerator. Cut into even wedges
for an appealing display and a flavorful treat."
—*The Book of Kringle*

After she gathered herself together and threw cold water on her face,
Ellen dialed Henry, who picked up on the second ring.

"Hello?"

"Henry?"

"You're back!" She could detect the heady cheers of football in
the background. She'd called him the day before after her breakfast
with Max, told him she was going to catch the next flight back in
the morning. When he'd offered to pick her up at the airport, she
declined and said Rob was picking them up. Yet another white lie,
but somehow she felt that she needed to see Lanie first; it was Lanie
who could ground her.

"I am. I missed you."

"I missed you, too. And you've brought good luck with you.
Packers are ahead twenty-one to six."

"Mind if I come over and join you?"

"Not at all, though wouldn't it be easier if I head your way? That
way you can unpack, settle in."

"What, have to chase all the girls out of your house?" She teased. "I don't know that I have any food here, but sure, come on over."

"I'll be there at halftime. And don't worry: I'll bring my own beer and chips."

In the meantime, she called to check in on Larry. The other week she had promoted him to manager since he was doing just as much work as she was around the shop, if not more, these days, even now that he was back in school. He'd thanked her profusely, so much so that she was almost embarrassed. When she found a small CONGRATULATIONS! card for him in the back room from Erin, loopy hearts drawn all over it, she felt as if she'd finally done something right.

"Everything is great, boss," he said. "Customers are coming in demanding more apple-rhubarb kringle. I think we're going to need to make it by the caseload . . . and oh! I almost forgot to tell you. Some guy from the *New York Times* called yesterday."

Her ears perked up. "Really? What for?"

"Said he was out visiting his in-laws in Wisconsin for the weekend and got a taste of your kringle at the Fall Fair. Said he wanted to know if you shipped it out east. He also asked if you'd be interested in being interviewed for an article."

"You're kidding."

"Nope, you should call him. I've got his number right here. Jason Jackson."

She grabbed a pen and scribbled the information on the back of her *TV Guide*.

After she hung up, she called and got a voice mail for Jason Jackson, Arts & Leisure section. The very section she loved! She was thinking what a nice-sounding voice he had, when the beep came on and she was caught short.

"Um, Jason Jackson," she hesitated. "It's Ellen McClarety from Amelia returning your call. My manager told me you were looking for some information on kringles, and I'd love to talk with you. Let me give you my home phone . . ." When she hung up, she was certain he'd never call back; she'd sounded like such a bumbling idiot.

She was about to go upstairs and unpack when the doorbell rang.

"That was fast!" she said, after pulling the door open. Henry stood on her stoop, beers in one hand, a bag of chips in the other.

"I couldn't wait till halftime."

Before she could respond, he dropped the chips and grabbed her in a long kiss, the cold beers digging into her back. "Ouch, Henry!"

"What? What is it?"

"The beer cans. They're cold!"

He set the beers down and swept her up, without much difficulty she noted, and carried her into the living room, where he fell onto the couch with her.

"What's come over you?" She laughed.

"I missed you. Can't a guy miss his girl?"

"I missed you, too." She gave him a kiss after he'd retrieved the snacks and sat down next to her.

He grabbed the remote and flicked on the television. Such a grand entrance had prepared her for more, but apparently the man really was there to watch football. The Packers came up on the screen. "We've got to win this one. It's an important game, critical even."

Ellen had no more understanding of football than she did horticulture, but maybe there was hope for her yet. After all, she was opening up her life to all sorts of new things these days. Why not football? On the plane ride home, she'd debated telling Henry what she'd learned on her trip. But how to divulge that news without admitting she'd lied to him about the very reason for her getaway in the first place? And now that he was here sitting on her couch, she saw that telling him the truth about Charlotte and Max was impossible. Henry didn't need to know right now that his wife's lover had been Ellen's ex-husband. From that news at least, she could protect him—for the moment. And the baby, well, that could wait a few more hours, too. Clearly, he wasn't going to notice her bump with his favorite team playing in the background.

She had one more thing to do: She slipped upstairs for a minute and quickly checked her e-mails. Then she went to the site on which she'd been meaning to post a collector's item for the highest bidder: a rare first edition of Fowler's. She felt slightly ashamed that it had taken her this long to say good-bye to Gretchen and Anthony. Any money she got she would use to open a savings account for the baby.

Before heading downstairs, she retrieved her small gift for Henry from her suitcase, an island stone, turquoise and translucent, and smooth beneath her fingers. Back in the living room, she settled into the cushions, the stone in her pocket. Henry patted her knee. "It's nice to have you home." Then, "Come on, run the ball, you fool!" She'd wait till halftime to give him his present.

Ellen smiled to think this was what her life had come to. It certainly wasn't all bad. In fact, much of it was quite good. *The Packers on a Sunday afternoon. A good man on her couch. A baby in her belly.*

Later that night, Henry noticed the basket of baby toys lying open on the table and asked, "What's this? Something for Benjamin?" She only had the heart to say, "Something like that." But he had looked at her skeptically.

When they lay in bed, Ellen propped herself up on her elbow and turned toward him. She thought it best to speak hypothetically. "You know, Henry, all this time I've been spending with Benjamin makes me think that I might like to have one of my own."

"What's that?" He propped himself up on an elbow and faced her.

"A baby," she whispered, as if it was an ethereal thing, floating off her lips and not growing inside of her.

He was quiet for a moment. He looked down, then back up at her. He was smiling.

"Don't you have something else to tell me?" He reached out and gently stroked her stomach through her nightgown.

"You know?"

He nodded. "Well, only as much as a man can know about these things." He grinned widely. "I guessed."

"For how long?"

"I don't know. Probably a few weeks. It's not like you're getting fat anywhere else."

"Henry!" She swatted him. "That's not funny."

"Wouldn't you be more worried if I *hadn't* noticed? I mean, what kind of guy doesn't notice his girlfriend's expanding belly?"

"Is that what I am now? Your girlfriend?"

"I certainly hope so. I'm glad you finally told me." He paused for a beat, cleared his throat. "I'm guessing the baby's not mine, though. Am I right?"

How to tell him? How to tell this dear, sweet man that she was pregnant by her ex-husband but that she really hoped it wouldn't discourage him from loving her?

"I wish it was yours." She paused. "Ours. I'm sorry, Henry. It was one night, before you and I were serious. It meant nothing. I didn't think in a million years that I could *get* pregnant."

He was quiet.

"But Henry?"

"Yes?"

"I'm not sorry about this baby. I *want* this baby. I've been waiting pretty much my whole life for this child."

He gave a small smile. "I know."

"You're not mad?"

He shook his head slowly. "Nah. Well, maybe a little at first, when I figured it out. But then I realized it must have happened before we got together. I think I was more hurt that you didn't tell me. But, now, to be honest, I'm excited at the thought. When Charlotte died, I was sure everything good in my life was over. Then you came along. And now a baby? It's tough to stay mad about a baby, you know?"

She hadn't thought of it that way.

"Come here." Henry wrapped her in his arms. "I'm happy for you, I truly am." He snuggled her more tightly. "My dear, sweet, beautiful Ellen. You will make the most amazing mother. In fact, you already are." He kissed the top of her head. "Whoever this child's daddy is—serendipity or destiny—that's one lucky kid. I hope I'm around to meet him."

"Or her," she added quickly. Just then she felt a slight flutter. Ellen imagined her babe bundled in layers and layers of buttery, rich love, the chest rising and falling, the coils of the heart shaped like a sweet, scrumptious kringle.

And at that moment, she knew. She knew that they'd all be fine, *just fine*. Lanie, Rob, Benjamin, Henry, her, this new baby, who would be arriving in just a short while.

She could hardly wait.

A Recipe for Danish Kringle
(Makes 2 Kringles)

Ingredients:

Dough:
  ¾ cup butter
  ¼ cup sifted all-purpose flour
  1 package active dry yeast
  1 beaten egg
  ¾ cup milk
  3 tablespoons sugar
  1 teaspoon salt
  3 to 3½ cups sifted all-purpose flour
Apple filling:
  1½ cups chopped and peeled apples
  ½ cup brown sugar
Icing:
  1 cup powdered sugar
  1 tablespoon milk
  ½ cup sliced almonds toasted in saucepan

Instructions:

1. Cream butter with ¼ cup sifted flour.
2. Roll between sheets of waxed paper to a 10 x 4 inch rectangle. Chill.
3. Soften yeast in ¼ cup warm water.
4. Mix egg, milk, sugar, salt, yeast; stir in flour for soft dough.
5. On floured surface, roll dough to 12-inch square; place chilled butter in center.
6. Overlap sides of dough atop butter.
7. Turn dough ¼ way around; roll to 12-inch square.
8. Repeat folding and rolling twice more.
9. Wrap in waxed paper.

10. Chill 30 minutes.
11. Roll to 24 x 12 inch rectangle. (If dough begins to soften, chill again.)
12. Cut lengthwise into two strips.
13. Mix apples and brown sugar for filling. Spread each strip with filling and roll as for jelly roll, starting with long side.
14. Moisten edges; seal.
15. Stretch each to approximately 30-inch length without breaking.
16. Place seam sides down on greased baking sheet and shape into an oval.
17. Flatten to ½ inch with rolling pin.
18. Brush kringles with beaten egg.
19. Cover with plastic wrap and let rise until it doubles, about 25 minutes to 1 hour.
20. Bake at 375 degrees for 25 to 30 minutes, or until golden.
21. Cool on wire rack.
22. Drizzle with icing (mix powdered sugar and milk till of even consistency) and sprinkle toasted almonds on top.

*Inspired by a "Danish Kringle" recipe originally published in the 1963 issue of *Better Homes & Gardens® Meals with a Foreign Flair.*

**Please note: *The Book of Kringle* is a fictitious cookbook.

Acknowledgments

Thank you to my wonderful agent, Meg Ruley, who immediately understood the confluence of kringles and grammar; to the amazing Trish Todd, whose edits were always on the mark and whose enthusiasm kept me going during the revision process; to the entire team at Simon & Schuster, most especially Jessica Abell and Kate Gales, for taking me under their wing; to Cindy of Bendtsen's Bakery for generously explaining the finer points of kringle-making; and to my Uncle Terry for introducing the delights of the Danish pastry to me as a child.

Of course, I owe an enormous debt to my friends and family, the entire Francis and Holt clans, for all their support and encouragement over the past year. Most especially, thanks to my parents who taught me early on that having a book by your side is as natural as drinking water. To my mom, thanks for being the best "big sister" a girl could ever have. I know if my dad were still here to read *Three Good Things*, he'd demand, "But where are the car chases?" It makes me smile to think of it and to know that he always had "just a few more ideas" for the next book. Thanks to my brother, Peter, who has kept me humble throughout the process. To the roomies—Barb, Katherine, Lisa, and Lora—a thousand thank-yous for all the laughs and stories over the years. To Mike, my love, my mpc, you have my eternal gratitude for always believing—and for making sure the baseball lore was correct! And last but not least, my thanks and love to Nicholas, Michael, and Katherine, who remind me of my three good things each and every day.

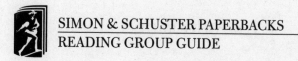

three
good
things

Introduction

Ellen McClarety, a recent divorcée who has opened a kringle shop as a creative outlet after the departure of her ex-husband, and her sister, Lanie Taylor, who juggles motherhood and a demanding career as a lawyer, are the heart and soul of *Three Good Things*. Ellen feels a connection with a customer from her store, but who will she choose when her past shows up unexpectedly? Meanwhile Lanie sees her perfect life falling apart under the demands of motherhood. Both women long for the guidance of their mother, who died years ago, but left them with a wonderful piece of advice: "At the end of every day, you can always think of three good things that happened."

Questions for Discussion

1. Serendipity is important to Ellen. What events are caused by serendipity in the book? Is serendipity always good, or does it sometimes have negative consequences?

2. How do you think the novel would be different if it had not been set in Wisconsin? How does the setting influence how the characters act?

3. Describe Lanie's and Ellen's different reactions to their mother's death. Why do you think they react the way they do? How does their mother's early death influence them as adults?

4. "The secret to a perfect kringle, she knew, was balance . . . But Ellen understood that no one element should overwhelm or supersede another" (p. 9). What does Francis mean by comparing kringles to life? How is Ellen's life like her kringles?

5. What is the meaning of the riddle in the *Book of Kringle*?

6. What do the epigraphs from the *Book of Kringle* add to your understanding of the book?

7. Ellen is very invested in proper grammar, and in *Fowler's Modern Usage*. What do you think is the appeal of a rules-based system for her?

8. Was Lanie right to be jealous of Samantha? How do you think you would have reacted in her position?

9. What is the attraction of Max to Ellen? What about Henry? Henry and Max are obviously different in many ways, but can you see similarities in them, too?

10. Rob compares seeing his project completed to having a baby (p. 202). How do work and parenthood compare in the novel?

11. Rob, Lanie, and Ellen are all invested in their respective careers. What do they get out of work that they can't get elsewhere in their lives?

12. Lanie and Ellen are different in many ways: their careers, their outlook on men, on life. How do they balance each other? Examine in your own family: Are there similar pairs?

13. Discuss the mothers in the book. What are the different types of motherhood that you see? What kind of mother do you think Ellen will be?

14. Lanie worries, "When on earth was she going to give herself free license to be herself? The thing was, she wasn't sure if she knew who that self was" (p. 108). What does she discover at the end of the novel?

Enhance Your Book Club

1. Make kringles using the recipe on p. 233 to share with your book club.

2. Kringles are a regional specialty for Ellen. Come prepared to discuss the regional foods from where you were raised. (Or prepare them for a buffet?)

3. A large part of the narrative is about how Ellen and Lanie's mother has influenced them as adults. Think about how your mother has influenced your life, and share it with the group.

An Interview with Wendy Francis

Some of the strongest relationships in this book are between sisters and mothers. Did your mother or sisters inspire the writing?
While I don't have a sister, I do have a close-knit group of girlfriends who, in my mind, are like an extended family of sisters. I also have one brother, younger by ten years, who I feel protective of in much the same way that Ellen is protective of Lanie. Perhaps most influential in my writing of this book, however, was my mom. She was in her early twenties when she became a mom, and she always says that the two of us grew up together. For me, though, it was a charmed childhood. My mom was, in my eyes, just like a big sister—kind, wise, cool, fun, and loving. She was the inspiration for both the mother and the relationship between Lanie and Ellen in the book.

Lanie struggles with how to be a working mother. How do you manage it?
I don't think it's easy for any mom, whether she works in an office or at home with the kids. There never seem to be enough hours in the day. But somehow, moms across the country, indeed the world, manage it all. I think many of us wish we could be great at every aspect of what we do each and every day. As a mom, I've had to learn to let go of my perfectionist tendencies and roll with the punches more. Some days are better than others; other days I have to remind myself that it's okay if only one thing got crossed off my to-do list or that I wasn't as patient as I could have been with my four-year-old.

It's always comforting for me to talk with friends; almost all of us seem to be confronted with similar pressures. I think the answer to "how do you manage the struggles of a working mother" has a lot to do with balancing acts (some more successful than others); pulling from enormous reserves of energy, patience, and compassion; having a lot of help (whether from spouses, family, babysitters, or friends); and being sure to carve out some alone time in the day, even if it just means sitting in the tub, reading a book, going for a walk, or writing in your journal.

Where did the inspiration to use kringles as a metaphor come from? Are you a baker?

My uncle Terry, raised in Racine, Wisconsin (home of the kringle), introduced me to the delightful confection when I was a child. It was love at first taste. I'd never had a pastry so light and flaky and yet rich and satisfying, too. Whenever my uncle came to visit, he'd be carrying a wrapped kringle in his hands. Almond was my favorite flavor, but apple came in a close second. For me, kringle was inevitably tied to warm memories of family and spirited conversation, often political in nature and usually inspired by my incredibly well-read dad, around the table. The metaphor of not letting one element overwhelm another actually came from an interview with a baker at a kringle shop— it seemed to fit the book's message of finding balance perfectly.

Am I a baker? I can hear my husband laughing in the background as I read this question. Alas, I have few culinary skills to speak of. While I've been known to bake kringles and a few pies on holidays, I'm much better at *buying* kringle than baking it. I wish it were otherwise!

Why did you choose to set the novel in the Midwest?

I've always wanted to write a novel about the Midwest. Wisconsin is where I was born and raised. It's where my heart is. My family still lives there, in the Madison and Appleton areas. Though I've now spent more time on the East Coast than in the Midwest, I'll always feel like a Midwestern girl. I love the pace of life there, the kindness of the people, the undulating, wide-open stretches of land, the ways in which life is tied to the seasons. As much as this book is a valentine to my four-year-old son, it is also a valentine to the Midwest.

Ellen, Lanie, and Rob are all such strong characters. Is there one you identified with more than the others?
It's funny. The first character I had in mind when I began writing the novel was Ellen. I knew that I wanted to write about a baker at a certain place in her life. I also knew that she had a sister, but it wasn't clear to me what Lanie's occupation (and preoccupations) would be. I think it's fair to say I identified with both Ellen and Lanie. I share Ellen's fondness for good grammar and (I hope) her sense of humor; as for Lanie, she was probably an easier character to write in the end simply because I'd lived those early years with a baby fairly recently. The sleep deprivation, the wonderful firsts, the fat cheeks and baby smell were still fresh in my mind. I enjoyed writing Rob's character because I can only imagine what it must feel like to be on the other side of a relationship with a new, slightly obsessed mom.

You go into great detail about the professions of Ellen, Lanie, and Rob. What kind of research did you do in writing this book?
I traveled to a kringle shop in Racine, Wisconsin, to make sure I had the details right about the baking process for such a large number of kringles. The folks at Bendtsen's Bakery were tremendously helpful and generous with their time (they also happen to make the world's most divine kringle, which is available online). As for Lanie's job, I had some experience with the law as a paralegal and then a short stint as a law student. I've always admired the power of the law to help people in dire situations. I hoped to convey that through Lanie's work. Rob's profession was more of a stretch, but I wanted something that would stand in contrast to Lanie's profession—a job that was more precise with fewer gray areas.

Do you think about your future readers as you write? What do you hope they'll take away from the novel?

Writing a novel was a bit of a foreign process to me, as I used to be a book editor, sitting on the other side of the desk. Whenever I stopped to think about who the book's audience might actually be, it was like putting on literary handcuffs. Too many censors! I tried to write what was true to me. I suppose the reader I was most concerned about was my mom since she knows the Midwest like the back of her hand. A few things that I do hope readers will take away from this novel: a sense of the rhythms of a Midwestern life; a story that will remind them of someone in their own lives—whether a parent, a sibling, or friend—who helped shape them; a reminder that no matter what life throws at you, you can always find three good things; and, last but not least, a new (or rekindled) love for the wonderful Danish pastry that is kringle.

What other authors do you admire? Were there any other books that you looked to as you wrote *Three Good Things*?

Boy, there are so many authors I love to read, this might be the toughest question of all. Elizabeth Strout, Charles Baxter, John Updike, Pat Conroy, Anita Shreve, Garrison Keillor are all at the top of the list. But I also love good summer reads, often with a funny bent, for which I can thank Elin Hilderbrand, Nancy Thayer, Jennifer Weiner, Claire Cook, Emily Giffin, Barbara O'Neal, and Elinor Lipman, to name just a few. While I didn't look to any particular books while writing, I was inspired by plenty of good grammar guides.

This is your first novel. How did you start writing?

My son was nearly a year and a half old. Life was beginning to return somewhat to normal, meaning I wasn't constantly exhausted. I started writing at nights after he went to bed and then I'd catch some time when he'd take a rare nap. I had the character of Ellen, the notion of a book about sisters set in the Midwest, and the kringle theme kicking about in my brain for about a year before I actually began writing.

What is your writing process like? Where do your ideas come from?

I wrote the first draft fairly quickly (in about a year), but then there were many revisions after that. I need to get the words down or a scene written first; then I can go back and revise and tweak language. I won't say that I always have the plot figured out because that would be a lie; to the contrary, the characters in this book often surprised me with the arcs that their narratives ultimately took. But I usually start with an idea of who the main characters will be and what the setting will be. Setting is very important to me, even as a reader. I like to know where I am, feel the air, see the land. It's essentially another character in my mind. As for ideas, they come from any and all parts of a day. My family is very worried that they'll one day see themselves in my pages. I'm also a good eavesdropper!

About the Author

Wendy Francis is a former senior editor in book publishing. Her writing has appeared in local magazines, such as *The Improper Bostonian*. She is currently a freelance editor and writer living outside of Boston.